**MERCURY
INK**

**SIMON
PULSE**

MICHAEL VEY

THE FINAL SPARK

BOOK SEVEN OF SEVEN

MICHAEL VEY

THE FINAL SPARK

BOOK SEVEN OF SEVEN

RICHARD PAUL EVANS

MERCURY INK

SIMON PULSE

NEW YORK   LONDON   TORONTO   SYDNEY   NEW DELHI

SIMON PULSE / MERCURY INK

An imprint of Simon & Schuster Children's Publishing Division

1230 Avenue of the Americas, New York, NY 10020

First Simon Pulse/Mercury Ink paperback edition May 2018

Text copyright © 2017 by Richard Paul Evans

Cover illustration copyright © 2017 by Owen Richardson

For information about special discounts for bulk purchases, please contact Simon & Schuster Special Sales at 1-866-506-1949 or business@simonandschuster.com.

The Simon & Schuster Speakers Bureau can bring authors to your live event. For more information or to book an event contact the Simon & Schuster Speakers Bureau at 1-866-248-3049 or visit our website at www.simonspeakers.com.

Cover designed by Jessica Handelman

Interior designed by Mike Rosamilia

The text of this book was set in Berling LT Std.

Manufactured in the United States of America

2 4 6 8 10 9 7 5 3 1

Library of Congress Control Number 2017945620

ISBN 978-1-4814-9703-9 (hc)

ISBN 978-1-4814-9704-6 (pbk)

ISBN 978-1-4814-9705-3 (eBook)

To my talented daughter, Jenna Evans Welch
(the author of Love & Gelato*), who, for seven years,*
helped bring Michael Vey to life

Nichelle

Power: Nichelle acts as an electrical ground and can both detect and drain the powers of the other electric children. She can also, on a weaker level than Tessa, enhance the other children's powers.

Nichelle was Hatch's enforcer over the rest of the electric children until he abandoned her during the battle at the Elgen Academy. Although everyone was nervous about it, the Electroclan recruited her to join them on their mission to save Jade Dragon. She has become a loyal Electroclan member.

Quentin

Power: Ability to create isolated electromagnetic pulses, which lets him take out all electrical devices within twenty yards.

Quentin is smart and, before his defection, was regarded by the Elgen as second-in-command, just below Hatch. He is now a member of the Electroclan.

Tanner

Power: Ability to interfere with the electrical navigation systems of aircraft and cause them to malfunction and crash. His powers are so advanced that he can do this from the ground.

After years of mistreatment by the Elgen, Tanner was rescued by the Electroclan from the Peruvian Starxource plant. He then stayed with the resistance so he had a chance to recover. He was killed in the battle of Hades.

Tara

Power: Tara's abilities are similar to her twin sister, Taylor's, in that she can disrupt normal electronic brain functions. Through years of training and refining her powers, Tara has learned to focus on specific parts of the brain in order to create emotions such as fear or joy.

Working with the Elgen scientists, she has learned how to create mental illusions, which, among other things, allows her to make people appear as someone or something else.

Tara is one of Hatch's former Glows. She and Taylor were adopted by different families after they were born, and Tara lived with Hatch and the Elgen from the time she was six years old until she was rescued by the Electroclan.

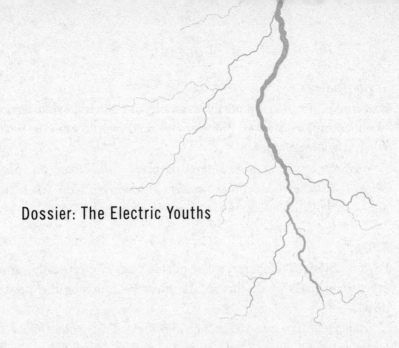

Dossier: The Electric Youths

Michael Vey
Power: Ability to shock people through direct contact or conduction. Can also absorb other electric children's powers.

Michael is the most powerful of all the electric children and leader of the Electroclan. He is steadily increasing in power. He also has Tourette's syndrome, a neurological disorder that causes tics or other involuntary movements. Elgen scientists believe his Tourette's is somehow connected to his electricity.

Ostin Liss
Power: A Nonel—not electric.

Ostin is very intelligent, with an IQ of 155, which puts him at the same level as the average Nobel Prize winner. He is one of the original three members of the Electroclan and Michael's best friend.

Taylor Ridley

Power: Ability to temporarily scramble the electric synapses in the brain, causing confusion. She can also read people's minds, but only when touching them.

Taylor is one of the original three members of the Electroclan. She and Michael discovered each other's powers at Meridian High School, which they were both attending. She is Michael's girlfriend.

Abigail

Power: Ability to temporarily ease or stop pain by electrically stimulating certain parts of the brain. She must be touching the person to do so.

Along with Ian and McKenna, Abigail was held captive by the Elgen for many years because she refused to follow Hatch. She joined the Electroclan after escaping from the Elgen Academy's prison, known as Purgatory.

Bryan

Power: The ability to create highly focused electricity that allows him to cut through objects, especially metal.

Bryan is one of Hatch's Glows. He spends most of his time playing video games and annoying Kylee.

Cassy

Power: Ability to electrically contract or "freeze" muscles from remarkable distances.

One of the most powerful of the electric children, Cassy is also the only one to be found by the resistance before the Elgen. She has lived with the voice since she was four years old. Her job, in addition to special missions and acting as the voice's bodyguard, is to keep track of the electric children. She is well versed on each of their powers and on the backgrounds of both the Glows and the Electroclan. She is a big fan of Michael Vey.

Grace

Power: Grace acts as a "human flash drive" and is able to transfer and store large amounts of electronic data.

Grace was living with the Elgen but joined the Electroclan when they defeated Hatch at the Elgen Academy. She has been working and living with the resistance but has not been on any missions with the Electroclan.

Ian

Power: Ability to see using electrolocation, which is the same way sharks and eels see through muddy or murky water.

Along with McKenna and Abigail, Ian was held captive by the Elgen for many years because he refused to follow Hatch. He joined the Electroclan after escaping from the Elgen Academy's prison, known as Purgatory.

Jack

Power: A Nonel—not electric.

Jack spends a lot of time in the gym and is very strong. He is also excellent with cars. Originally one of Michael's bullies, he joined the Electroclan after Michael bribed him to help Michael rescue his mother from Dr. Hatch.

Kylee

Power: Born with the ability to create electromagnetic power, she is basically a human magnet.

One of Hatch's Glows, she spends most of her time shopping, along with her best (and only) friend, Tara.

McKenna

Power: Ability to create light and heat. She can heat herself to more than three thousand kelvins.

Along with Ian and Abigail, McKenna was held captive by the Elgen for many years because she refused to follow Hatch. She joined the Electroclan after escaping from the Elgen Academy's prison, known as Purgatory.

Tessa

Power: Tessa's abilities are the opposite of Nichelle's—she is able to enhance the powers of the other electric children.

Tessa escaped from the Elgen at the Starxource plant in Peru and lived in the Amazon jungle for six months with an indigenous tribe called the Amacarra. She joined the Electroclan after the tribe rescued Michael from the Elgen and brought them together.

Torstyn

Power: One of the more ruthless and lethal of the electric children, Torstyn can create microwaves.

Torstyn is one of Hatch's former Glows and was instrumental to the Elgen in building the original Starxource plants. Although they were initially enemies, Torstyn is loyal to Quentin and acts as his bodyguard. He defied Hatch and joined the Electroclan.

Wade

Power: A Nonel—not electric.

Wade was Jack's best friend and joined the Electroclan at the same time he did. Wade died in Peru when the Electroclan was surprised by an Elgen guard.

Zeus

Power: Ability to "throw" electricity from his body.

Zeus was kidnapped by the Elgen as a young child and lived for many years as one of Hatch's Glows. He joined the Electroclan when they escaped from the Elgen Academy. His real name is Leonard Frank Smith.

PART ONE

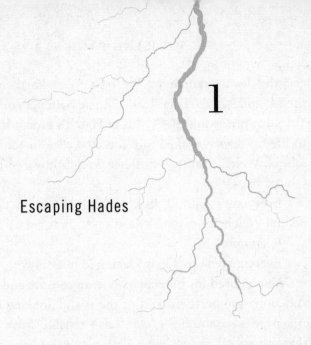

1

Escaping Hades

Former EGG David Welch stood alone on the *Joule*'s deck as he panned his binoculars over the smoldering prison island of Hades. At least what was left of it. Everywhere he looked was death. What few trees and foliage the Elgen had left on the island were still burning or glowing in heaps of red and orange embers. Around them scorched human skeletons and bones lay strewn across the landscape like straw after a windstorm. The island's sand, now mostly melted to glass, glistened where streams of morning sunlight broke through the retreating storm clouds, reflecting the vibrant prisms of the color spectrum. Had it not been so terrible, it almost would have been beautiful.

On one side of the crystalline beach were the only signs of life—the scurrying Tuvaluan natives who, along with the Electroclan, had survived the Elgen attack and taken shelter in the underground bunker before the explosion. Welch had left the natives water, food, and the *Joule*'s remaining life rafts to make their journey back to their home islands. Their leader, Enele Saluni, grandson of the former Tuvaluan prime minister (who, at Hatch's orders, had been sentenced to life on display, naked in a monkey cage in the Tuvaluan capital), saluted Welch from the distance. Welch lowered his binoculars and saluted back.

"Everyone's below," Jack said, climbing up the conning tower behind Welch. "Everyone's here."

"Everyone?"

"Everyone who made it," Jack said hoarsely.

Welch raised his binoculars one more time and scanned the horizon along the northern end of the island, looking for signs of Elgen. Again he saw nothing of the once terrible force—at least nothing that was still alive. "All right. Let's get out of here."

Welch followed Jack down the inside of the *Joule*'s conning tower, pausing on the ladder near the top as hydraulic pistons pulled the hatch closed. Pneumatic clamps hissed and clicked around him as the steel hatch was locked airtight. Then Welch climbed down to join the others in the Conn, the *Joule*'s control center.

"Take us down," Welch said to the boat's COB—the chief of the boat—as he stepped from the ladder onto the metal floor.

Even though the *Joule* could travel as much as fifteen knots faster above surface, Welch didn't want to take the chance of being seen. Outside of the *Joule*'s crew members who Welch had set adrift, he didn't know who had survived. He didn't even know if Hatch had survived. Perhaps no one had. But still, there was no sense in taking chances.

"Yes, sir," the Elgen COB replied, speaking into his microphone. "Down twenty meters."

Including the COB, there were five Elgen still on the *Joule* and one Fijian servant. Twelve hours earlier, when Welch and his Glows— Quentin, Tara, Torstyn, and Cassy—had hijacked the *Joule*, they'd disarmed the seventeen-man crew and then sent everyone off the boat, except for the *Joule*'s COB and the four crew members needed to operate the ship.

Welch had also sent J.D., the boat captain who had betrayed the Electroclan by sailing them into a trap, and his crew with the Elgen.

"Man, don't leave me here," J.D. had said, clinging to the one life raft Welch had left them. "I helped you take this boat."

"You're lucky I'm leaving you alive," Welch said. "But don't get used to it. When Hatch finds out that you helped us hijack the *Joule*, he'll feed you to his rats."

"You will all die," J.D. said. "Like *rats*."

Welch looked at him stoically. "Everyone dies. Some just sooner than others. And some, one bite at a time."

J.D. looked at Welch hatefully. "I will die as I choose. No one takes my life but me." Then, letting go of the raft, he sunk down in the black water beneath the heaving waves. He never came up again.

"So ends the traitor," Welch said to himself.

Quentin had disabled the raft's outboard motor and radio with an EMP so the Elgen would not be able to alert anyone for hours, giving Welch and the Glows the time they needed to get back to Hades to rescue their friends. That was, if their friends were still alive. Even thirty miles from Hades, they saw and heard the massive explosion. Welch's first thought was that Hatch had detonated some kind of nuclear device to destroy the island. But there was no mushroom cloud or, outside of the flash, evidence of a nuclear weapon. They weren't going to leave the islands until they knew for certain if any of their friends had survived.

Hours later, when Welch and company surfaced the *Joule* off the coast of Hades, they couldn't believe what they saw. All the Elgen boats were sunk or burning on the surface. They were relieved to find the Electroclan huddled on the beach.

Welch and Quentin sailed to shore to pick up their friends, leaving Cassy, Torstyn, and Tara on board to secure the ship.

Ten minutes after Welch and Quentin left, one of the Elgen crewmen approached Cassy. "Hey, baby. We've been cooped up a long, long time."

"I'm not your baby," she said. "And don't take another step."

He kept walking. "What's a little girl like you going to do to stop a big man like me?"

Cassy pursed her lips. "You had to ask." She froze the man's entire body, including his lungs. He fell over, dropping to the floor with a loud thud.

When she let him go, he gasped for breath, then said, "Please don't do that again."

"When I tell you to stop walking, you stop walking. Next time you won't breathe again. Ever. Do you understand?"

"Yes, ma'am."

She smiled sardonically. "'Ma'am'? What happened to 'baby'?"

Jack was the last to board, gathering the teens in one corner of the Conn. The room echoed with the sounds of grief—sobbing and crying. Especially from Taylor, who was inconsolable. "Michael," she said over and over. "My Michael."

McKenna's arms were around Taylor, the two of them slightly rocking.

"I can't believe he's gone," Taylor said.

McKenna wiped her eyes. "I can't believe any of this."

Ostin watched them silently, too emotional to speak. His eyes were red and swollen.

"I knew he had a hero's heart," Jack said. "I knew it the moment he came to my door to ask me to take him to California."

Just then Cassy walked into the Conn. She glanced around the room, then asked, "Where's Michael?"

From everyone's silence she knew something bad had happened. She raised her hand to her mouth. "Oh no."

"He didn't make it," Quentin said.

Cassy started crying. She looked over at Taylor. "I'm so sorry."

Cassy walked over, and the two of them hugged.

"I know you cared about him too," Taylor said.

"I . . ."

"It's okay that you loved him too," she said softly. "He was easy to love."

"Michael's not the only one we lost," Ian said. "We lost Gervaso and Tanner, too."

Jack swallowed in pain, fighting back tears. Gervaso had been more of a father to him than his real father. Abigail put her arms around him and comforted him with her powers.

"Please don't," Jack said. "I want to feel the pain."

Abigail stopped pulsing. "I understand."

Jack furtively wiped his eyes, then looked out at the others. "Gervaso told me that when he was in ranger training, his drill sergeant told them that they were all going to hell. The only consolation was that they'd already been there, so it wouldn't matter." He rubbed his eyes. "If there's a heaven, I think there's a special pass for heroes."

"I think so too," Zeus said. "There's far too few of them as it is."

"Someday we'll return," Welch said. "When the world has changed. We'll build a memorial to the three of them. Then the whole world will know what they've sacrificed."

There was something hopeful in what Welch had said. After a few more minutes Welch said, "You must all be exhausted. Get some rest." He turned to Tara. "Take them to their bunks."

"Yes, sir," Tara said. "Everyone, follow me."

"Except Cassy," Welch said. "You stay with me. I need some backup."

"Yes, sir."

The rest of the teens followed Tara, single file, out of the Conn. None of them had ever seen anything like the *Joule* before, which wasn't surprising, since the *Joule* was the only ship of its kind ever built—a hybrid vault, ship, and submarine. It was tight and narrow with no portholes. Air, mostly recycled, was continually pumped throughout the vessel, and filled the echoing chambers with a continual hissing. The walls were all riveted metal, as was the floor, which had been coated with thick rubberized flooring that softened and dulled the sound of their footsteps as they walked.

Tara led them down a narrow corridor past the commander's quarters to the first of two bunk rooms. The compartment was designed solely for sleeping. It was only twelve feet wide, with pipe-framed cots on both sides of the room with trampoline-like mattresses. The cots were connected, by brackets, on one side to the wall, while the other side was supported from the ceiling by chains. The beds were stacked four high, with only a few feet of headroom; the bottom bunks were suspended only three inches above the floor.

"This is where we sleep," Tara said. "It's tight, but the *Joule* is basically a submarine. Everything's tight. Welch wants us all to stay in the same room so we can lock the Elgen crew members in the other."

"I don't care where I sleep," Jack said. "As long as I'm horizontal. I feel like I'm sleepwalking." He took off his shoes and then, using the edges of the lower bunks as steps, climbed up onto the top bunk. Everyone else claimed bunks, except Taylor, who just stood in the middle of the room looking lost.

"C'mon, honey," Abigail said. "You need some rest. You'll feel a little better after you get some rest."

"Sleep won't take this away," Taylor said. "Unless I never wake up."

"I can't take it away, but I can help. Just lie down right here, sweetie," Abigail said, pulling down the covers on a bottom bunk.

Taylor took off her shoes and crawled out across the cot, lying on her back.

"Now just relax," Abigail said. She put her hands on Taylor's head and lightly pulsed. At first, Taylor shuddered; then her body calmed and she breathed out deeply. Within moments she was asleep.

"You have a beautiful gift," Tara said softly.

"Thank you," Abigail said.

For a moment everyone was quiet and the only sounds were the constant hissing of the *Joule*'s air system, Jack's snoring, and the strained, eerie groaning of the vessel. Every now and then the boat creaked like a heavy door on a rusty hinge.

"Does that sound ever stop?" McKenna asked.

"Probably not," Ostin said, speaking for the first time since they'd boarded. His voice was raw and strained.

The pain in his voice hurt her. "Hey, tell me some facts about submarines."

"Sorry," Ostin said. "I'm not in the mood."

McKenna frowned. "How deep do you think we are?"

Ostin breathed out slowly. "The *Joule* can dive to six hundred feet."

"What makes that sound?"

Ostin sniffed, then said softly, "At six hundred feet the water pressure is 282.6 pounds per square inch. That's a lot of pressure on a pressurized can."

"I heard that the Elgen carry all their wealth in this boat."

"Not all of it," Ostin said. "Just enough for a rainy day."

"That would be a lot of rain," Ian said, suddenly joining the conversation. "There are stacks of gold bullion running two feet high across the length of the boat."

"They'd have to use that much weight as ballast," Ostin said.

"There's also diamonds and boxes of paper currency. I could open the safes that hold them," Ian said. "Just for fun."

"That would be fun to see," McKenna answered. "Maybe someday we'll share in all that loot."

"Maybe," Ostin said, sounding not at all interested.

Abigail glanced back at McKenna with a sad smile, then climbed onto the bunk above Taylor.

An hour later Cassy walked into the bunk room. "Lunch is ready," she said softly. No one moved. Everyone was asleep. After a few minutes, Cassy went back to the Conn to keep Welch company.

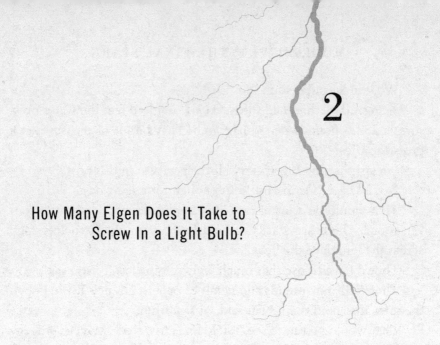

2

How Many Elgen Does It Take to Screw In a Light Bulb?

After all the physical and emotional stress they'd been through over the last week, their exhaustion finally took over and they slept more than eighteen hours. Jack was the first to wake. He looked around the dark room lit only by the glows of his electric friends. With no portholes there was no way of knowing if it was day or night.

He climbed down from his bunk as quietly as possible, then walked back up to the Conn. Welch looked up at him as he entered. Jack had bed hair, the bulk of it pressed to the right side of his head.

"Looks like you got some rest," Welch said.

"Yeah."

"Anyone else up?"

"Not yet."

"We probably should wake them in the next hour or so or they'll be up all night."

"There is no night and day down here," Jack said. "What does it matter?"

"We need a schedule," Welch said. "Cassy and I are going to need sleep."

Just then Tessa, Zeus, and Ian walked into the Conn. "We can watch the Conn," Zeus said.

"My men need sleep too," the COB said.

"We can't stop sailing," Welch said.

"We don't need to. The *Joule*'s completely automated. We can program our course, and she can run on autopilot. If there's a problem, she alerts our room."

Ostin, McKenna, Abigail, and Tara walked in.

"Everyone's up except Taylor," Tara said.

"Let her sleep," Welch said. "Cassy, you can go rest."

"No problem," she said, yawning as she stood.

"Tara, would you mind showing them to the dining room?" Welch asked.

"I can," Cassy said. "I think I'll get something." She turned to the others. "Let's go." Cassy led them down a ladder and then in the opposite direction of the bunks to the *Joule*'s dining area. Like the rest of the boat, every inch was used as efficiently as possible. Against one wall were bins of dried fruit and grains. Jack opened a canister that read: DRIED MANGO. He grabbed a handful of the dried fruit and tossed it into his mouth. The others followed his example, opening other bins of fruit: pineapple, guava, and apple. They were hungrily devouring the fruit when a young Fijian girl walked into the room. She stopped near the door, looking at all the people. "Cassy?"

"Hey," Cassy said. She turned to the others. "Guys, this is Kiki. She's the ship's cook. We didn't think she would be safe with the Elgen, so we kept her with us."

"Welcome to the *Joule*," Kiki said with a slight British accent. "The new captain Welch asked me to prepare something for you to eat. I'm making spaghetti for tonight. For now, I have baked rolls and meats for sandwiches."

"What kind of sandwiches do you have?" Jack asked.

"We have fish, pork, Vegemite, and Nutella."

Jack squinted. "What's Nutella?"

"It's chocolate spread," Tara said. "It's good."

"A chocolate sandwich," McKenna said. "It's about time someone invented that."

"I think you all must be very hungry," Kiki said.

"Starving," Ostin said. "We haven't eaten anything for more than a day."

"I will fix that." Kiki opened a cupboard and brought out a basket filled with scones. "The Elgen liked my scones with papaya jam and cream." She set the container on the table. "I also have fruit salad." She took out another bowl and set it on the table. Then she brought out a stack of bowls and several handfuls of utensils. "Please, help yourself. Eat."

Taylor walked into the room. She hesitated near the doorway. McKenna thought she looked a little better. Not good, but better.

"How are you?" McKenna asked.

Taylor shrugged.

As she walked over and sat down next to McKenna, Kiki began boiling water for tea while Cassy cut the homemade bread into slices and then brought out plates and what they needed for sandwiches: grilled pork steak, salted mackerel and tuna, lettuce and tomatoes grown on the islands, mayonnaise, mustard, Vegemite, and a large plastic container of Nutella. Everyone ate ravenously except for Taylor.

McKenna said to her, "You need to eat."

"I'm not hungry."

"That's why you need to eat. We don't know what's ahead, and we all need to keep our strength. If you won't eat for yourself, eat for the rest of us."

Taylor looked at her. "If I slow you down, you can leave me."

"You know we would never do that." McKenna gave her a slice of bread with Nutella. "Please. Eat something."

Taylor just looked down at the sandwich.

"What would Michael say?"

Taylor erupted. "Nothing! He'd say nothing! He's gone!"

Everyone stopped eating and looked at Taylor. Taylor looked around, then said, "I'm sorry."

McKenna touched her chest over her heart. "He's not gone. He's here." She touched Taylor's chest. "And there. He will always be there."

Taylor dabbed at her eyes with a napkin. "I'm sorry. I'm so sorry."

McKenna hugged her, and Taylor put her head on the other girl's shoulder.

"You don't need to apologize," McKenna said softly. "We understand. Everyone understands."

After a few minutes Taylor stopped crying and sat back. Then she lifted the bread and took a bite.

"Thank you," McKenna said.

"Thank you," Taylor said. "You care more about me than I do about myself."

A few minutes later Cassy said, "The tea's ready. Help yourself. I'm going to bed."

"Wait," Kiki said. "I have a surprise." She opened a cupboard and brought out a cake topped with baked pineapple. "The Elgen were celebrating a birthday and made me bake a cake for them. They never got a chance to eat it."

"That makes me happy on two accounts," Jack said. "You, Kiki, are the best thing that's happened to us for days."

"With the days you've had," Kiki said, "I don't think that would be very hard to do."

PART TWO

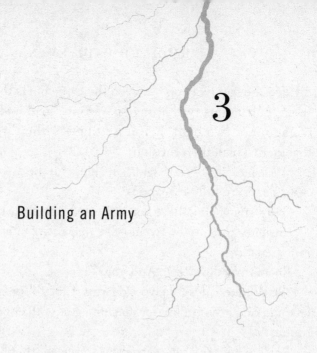

3

Building an Army

Almost two hours after the
Joule set sail, Enele Saluni and the rest of the Tuvaluan prisoners
completed their walk-through of Hades island, gathering the Elgen
weapons and ammunition that had survived the battle. Many of
the rifles were pried from the charred, skeletal hands of dead Elgen
soldiers. The bones crumbled as the Tuvaluans pulled the weapons
loose. With the magnitude of the Elgen's assault, Enele's men easily gathered more weapons and ammunition than they could use.
Still, at Enele's insistence, they took all they could, filling the bottom of their small boats with as many rifles and as much ammunition as they could carry. They planned to provide weapons for the
Tuvaluans they recruited into their army, and they didn't know if
weapons would be available on the other islands.

Tragically, of the hundreds of Tuvaluan natives that the Elgen
had sent to their prison on Hades, only a few dozen remained. Enele

divided the survivors up between the three boats that Welch had left them, putting his two strongest warriors, Zeel and Nazil, in charge of the other two craft. Before setting sail the three men gathered together to plan their mission.

"We're ready," Nazil said, speaking for both himself and Zeel. "Our boats are full of weapons."

"How many arms have you collected?" Enele asked.

"Seventy-three rifles, twenty-five magazines of ammo, and twenty-four grenades."

Enele turned to Zeel. "And you?"

"Sixty-nine rifles, twelve sidearms, thirty-four magazines of bullets, and one fifty-millimeter machine gun with about three thousand rounds."

Enele wiped the sweat from his forehead, then said, "That will do for now. It's time to go."

"Where are we going now?" Nazil asked.

"We sail to Nanumaga."

"Nanumaga?" Nazil said with surprise.

"Yes. Then Vaitupu."

Nazil and Zeel glanced at each other in surprise.

"Not to Funafuti?" Nazil asked.

"If Hatch is still alive," Zeel said, "he will be in his Starxource plant in Funafuti. We should sail to Funafuti first."

Enele looked at them angrily. "You don't think I have more reason than anyone to sail to Funafuti?! My grandfather is being held there in a monkey cage. Yes, I know Hatch will be in Funafuti. And for good reason. It's his stronghold. The man, Welch, told me that Hatch has enough weapons in his Starxource plant to destroy our nation many times over. What are you thinking? To attack him with the thirty-two of us? Any fool can attack an army and die. A wise man doesn't plan an attack; he plans a victory. I will act the part of the wise man. We will build an army, then, when we are strong enough, attack. Do you disagree with me?"

Both men sheepishly shook their heads.

"Then we sail to Nanumaga. The Elgen brought many of our

people there to work the fields and run cattle. There we'll find food, soldiers, and large produce boats to transport them. If we are lucky, we can gather more than five hundred soldiers. After we have taken what we can, we'll sail to Vaitupu, where the Elgen train their soldiers. There we'll find more weapons. There may even be warships.

"Then, after we have sufficiently armed our soldiers, then, and *only* then, will we attack Funafuti. Then we *will* be victorious."

"Our apologies," Nazil said. "You are wiser than us. You let your intelligence not your anger rule you."

Enele looked at his comrades sympathetically. "You both have great reason to be angry. You are loyal Tuvaluans, as well as courageous warriors. You've seen Hatch's cruelty to our people. You've suffered that cruelty. I too am filled with anger so deep, I fear it might consume me. There's no doubt that the time will come when anger will rule us all. But for now, we must remain in control. We've an army to build."

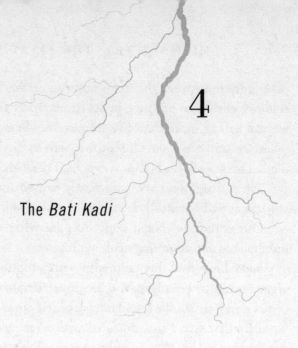

4

The *Bati Kadi*

It was shortly before noon when Enele's three boats sailed nearly due west for Nanumaga—the diamond-shaped Tuvaluan island that Hatch had renamed Demeter, for the Greek god of agriculture.

Demeter island was nearly the same size as Hades, but the similarities stopped there. Hades had been a vast, ugly wasteland even before the battle. At Hatch's command, the Elgen had slashed and burned their way through the once beautiful island, stripping it of its foliage, making it more difficult for prisoners to escape or hide. The uglifying of the island had another effect that worked well with the Elgen's plans. It made the island look like death. The Tuvaluans said of Hades, "No one ever comes back."

Demeter was the opposite of Hades—it was a lush, tropical paradise abundant with vegetation and farming. Originally, the Tuvaluans grew only a few crops on the island: copra, coconuts, and breadfruit, all largely for export. But the Elgen had interest only in their own self-sufficiency, so they now grew only what they needed and consumed: tomatoes, potatoes, sweet potatoes, onions, cabbage, eggplant, arugula, strawberries, taro, and, at Hatch's request, jalapeños.

Demeter was sixty-two nautical miles from Hades, which took the small boats almost three hours to traverse. With Enele in the lead boat, the small Tuvaluan force landed on the island's northern shore beneath the inland cover of a partially submerged mangrove forest. They hid their boats among the trees, taking only the weapons they could use, and then made their way, on foot, to the labor camps where the Elgen had forced their families and friends into slavery.

The Elgen had realized that one of the advantages of operating on a small island was that there was no need to build fences to keep the workers in. Without boats, there was no escaping, and the only fences were those around the Elgen compound, for protection in case of a slave uprising, and the fences around the Tuvaluan sleeping quarters, to keep the slaves under control at night.

In addition, the workers had all been injected with RFIDs, radio-frequency identification, technology that the Elgen had mastered when their headquarters were still located in California. By tagging each of the slaves, the Elgen could not only track their movements, but even monitor how much work each person accomplished or not, and punish them accordingly.

The force stopped when they reached the edge of the forest. Before them lay acres of crops tended by hundreds of Tuvaluans. It made Enele angry to see the condition his fellow Tuvaluans were in. Their clothes were dirty and torn, some barely covering the emaciated bodies that wore them. The Elgen fed them little, making the threat of withholding food a severe punishment if not a death sentence.

"Look at them," Zeel said. "I will kill the first Elgen I see."

"I don't see any Elgen," Enele said. He turned back. "Nazil?"

"None."

"They may be watching their slaves from cameras," Enele said. "They love cameras." He turned to the men. "I will take just two with me, Adam and Raphe. Divide the rest of our people into two groups. Nazil, take your group to the south side of the field and work your way through, gathering soldiers as you go. Zeel, you keep your group hidden here. If the Elgen attack, they will not suspect a hidden force, and you can attack them from behind. Understood?"

"Yes," Nazil said. "But what will you and the two young men do?"

"We will be the *Bati Kadi*."

Zeel and Nazil both nodded. *Bati Kadi*, meaning "the pinchers of the black ant," were the ninjas of the South Pacific, stealthy warriors who infiltrated the enemy line to slay their unsuspecting foes.

"We'll sneak into the Elgen's headquarters and take them by surprise."

"Why don't you take more men against the compound?" Zeel asked. "It is their most fortified place."

"That is why, Zeel. It is their most fortified place and far too powerful to attack with as few men as we have. But a mouse may enter where a lion cannot." Enele leaned over and strapped a holster around his leg, instructing his two new companions to do the same.

The two men Enele had selected were brothers, Adam and Raphe Sopoaga. Enele had met the brothers in prison on Hades, where they had been sent for beating up an Elgen guard who had tased an elderly Tuvaluan woman for the amusement of it. Enele had gotten especially close to Adam, who was the younger of the two brothers, but more outspoken in his passion for liberty. They were young and nimble, traits more important than size when playing the role of *Bati Kadi*. But even more important, both of them had spent time working as slaves on the island before being sent to Hades. Adam had even been inside the compound before being transferred off the island.

"If we do not return," Enele said, "you will lead your new soldiers back to our boats and arm all you can. Then you will attack the Elgen compound. After you have defeated them, take their weapons, reclaim the rest of the weapons from the boats, and then take their boats and sail to Vaitupu for weapons. Free our country."

"Yes, Enele," Nazil said. "But let us hope that you return."

"That is my hope as well." Enele saluted them. "Go with strength."

"Go with strength," they echoed.

The soldiers separated. Enele and the brothers moved quickly north through thick foliage toward the Elgen's compound. Enele hoped that Hatch had depleted his Demeter forces in his attack on Hades, but he didn't count on it. When they reached the edge of the compound, Enele crawled beneath a bush to get a better look at what they were facing. He didn't like what he saw. Getting into the compound undetected seemed nearly impossible. The compound was completely fenced in, and the Elgen had motion detectors and cameras mounted almost every twenty yards. Still, surprisingly, they could see no guards in the watchtowers or patrolling the grounds.

"There are more secluded places near the back," Adam said. "Follow me."

As they circled back around the compound, Raphe spotted what looked to be a weakness in the compound's security. At the far back side of the building, dark in shade, a giant dakua tree limb partially extended over the barbed fence. The windows facing out toward the tree were frosted or covered with blinds as well as metal bars.

The guard compound hadn't been built by the Elgen. It had originally been the island's sole school building, but the Elgen had added the fence and security, along with other adaptations. The fact that the tree limb was still there seemed to be a huge oversight, a sign of Elgen arrogance, or a trap. Raphe inspected the tree to see if there were any wires attached but found nothing out of the ordinary.

"Maybe there are land mines in the yard," Adam said.

"Perhaps," Enele replied. "Just a moment." He walked a little way into the forest and came back with his arms full of large green coconuts.

"Keep back."

One at a time he lobbed the coconuts over the fence, and each landed on the leaf-strewn ground beneath the limb. Nothing happened.

After tossing the last one, Enele said, "I think we're good." He checked once more to make sure no one was watching. Then one by one they shimmied up the tree and across the bridging tree limb, dropping about eight feet to the ground below. They ran up against the side of the building then, crouched down, and drew their handguns, before cautiously making their way to the first door they could see. It was a heavy iron door with a vertical, mesh-reinforced Plexiglas window not three inches wide. Not surprisingly, the door was locked.

"We need to go in through the front," Adam said. "I'll go first."

"We'll go together," Enele said.

Using the surrounding foliage for cover, the three stole quietly around the side of the building to the front door. There was a long row of windows covered with bars, and video cameras panning along the front walkway into the building. But there was still no sign of Elgen anywhere.

Enele crawled up to the first window and peeked inside through the partially drawn blinds. He could see several desks, but none of them were occupied. He pulled his gun into his chest and turned back to the others and waved them on. They crawled under the windows to the front door, then stood, hidden behind a brick frame.

Enele pointed at the door, counted down from three with his fingers, and then threw the door open. Adam and Raphe stormed inside, their arms outstretched with their guns, prepared for battle.

Nothing.

Enele stepped inside, looking around with caution. They walked across the open lobby to an office, looked inside, then went in, crouching behind the door.

"Where is everyone?" Raphe asked.

Adam shook his head. "I don't like this."

"I like it more than a building full of Elgen," Enele said. He slowly opened the door, then turned back. "Can you smell that?"

Raphe nodded. "Coffee."

"Someone's here."

"Maybe they're in a meeting," Adam said.

"I wish I had a grenade," Raphe said. "Finish them all at once."

"I'm sure they have grenades," Enele said, "if we can find their armory. Do you know where it is?"

"I never got that far," Adam said.

"Let's keep looking."

The three of them felt as if they were walking through an abandoned building. But it clearly wasn't. In addition to the smell of coffee, they could faintly hear rock music playing from some distant room.

"Music," whispered Adam, pointing toward a long corridor. Just then an electric camera panned toward them.

"Hide!" Enele said, pushing Adam back through a doorway into another empty office.

"I think we were too late," Adam said. "If anyone's watching the control panels, we were just seen."

They waited a moment for a reaction—any reaction—an alarm or a siren, a PA announcement, the crash of Elgen boots. Nothing came.

"This is weird," Raphe said.

"Very," Enele replied.

"Maybe they're all out in the fields," Adam said.

As they crept farther down the hall, the music grew louder. Then Enele looked down a darkened stairwell and pointed his gun. The music was coming from downstairs. He turned back to Adam, who nodded. All three of them slowly walked down the stairs, their guns extended, with Raphe covering their backs.

When they got to the bottom of the stairs, Enele looked both ways, then walked toward the music, which seemed to be coming from a room nearly halfway down the corridor.

As they got closer, they could hear low voices coming from behind the door. Enele looked at the other two, making a gesture toward the room. They both lifted their guns. Enele slowly turned the doorknob, looked back at the other two, who nodded, and then threw open the door, stepping inside with his gun ready to fire. "Hands in the air!"

In front of him were three Elgen guards sitting at a table playing poker. They looked over at him in surprise, but no one raised their hands or made a move toward their guns or weapons. In fact, there weren't any weapons visible. None of the men were dressed in regulation uniforms, rather they were in various stages of undress. Only one of them had shoes, two wore only wrinkled pants and T-shirts, and the third's shirt was unbuttoned and he wore exercise shorts with black Elgen socks.

The table they sat at was littered with cans of beer, and there was a nearly empty bottle of vodka.

"Put your hands in the air," Enele repeated.

One of the guards threw down his cards angrily, then raised his hands. His voice was slightly slurred. "Just when I finally get a winning hand. Look at that, a straight flush."

Adam and Raphe moved in on opposite sides of the table.

"One move, and we open fire," Enele said.

"Calm down. No one's goin' anywhere," the largest of the guards said in a thick Australian accent. He turned to one of the others. "I told you to lock the front door. That could have been a Zone Cap'n comin' 'stead o' this brown skin."

"I did lock the door," the other returned.

"No, he didn't," Raphe said.

"Where are the others?" Enele asked.

"They all went off to war and never came back."

"Who's watching the workers?"

"They don't need watchin', mate. Once you get it into someone's mind they're a slave, they act the part. Like sheep herd'n'. One man can drive a thousan'."

"You," Enele said. "Stand up, hands on your head."

The man stood.

"Raphe, check him for weapons."

"I got none."

Raphe patted him down. "Nothing."

Oddly, the man in the gym shorts still had his utility belt.

"Take that," Enele said to Raphe. "And handcuff him."

Raphe took the man's utility belt, then handcuffed him and pulled him aside.

"Now you two, on your stomachs. Hands behind your back."

The other two men got on their knees, then stomachs. Adam handcuffed them. Then he cut a nylon cord from the blinds and tied their feet together. He took the extra cord, hooked it around their feet, and lifted them up, tying one's legs to a sink faucet, the other to a refrigerator handle, raising them on an incline so their weight was mostly pressing on their chest and face.

"This ain't the most comfortable," the smaller of the guards said.

"Would you like a pillow?" Raphe asked.

"Be mighty decent of you," he replied.

Raphe slapped the guard on the back of his head. "You're as stupid as you are ugly."

Enele approached the man still standing. "Who's in charge here?"

"I am."

"What's your position?"

"Commandant."

"That's your new name, Elgen. Commandant. Take us to the main control room, where you keep the surveillance."

"No problem, mate."

"I'm not your mate. Where's the rest of your men?"

"You just tied them up."

"The rest of them."

"That is them."

"How many are outside?"

"None, I told you. It's only us."

"I don't believe you."

"I'm tellin' the truth, mate. Do you think we'd be dressed like this if there were others around to report us? Hatch picked the bone clean for his last escapade. We expected them back by now."

Enele put the barrel of his gun to the back of the commandant's head. "If you're lying, if I see one other Elgen, I pull the trigger. No explanations, just lead through your head. Care to change your story?"

"No. You won't find another guard outside this building. Not unless they just landed."

"You should hope they didn't," Enele said.

They walked behind the commandant out of the room, and Adam shut the door behind them. With his last stretch of nylon cord, he tied a grenade to the door handle, then looped the end around a fire alarm, then brought it back, tying it to the grenade's pin.

"What are you doing?" Enele asked.

"They open the door, it blows up."

"Where'd you learn to do that?" Raphe asked.

"The telly," Adam said. "*MacGyver*."

"You totally MacGyvered it," Raphe replied. "Love that show."

In spite of the commandant's assurance, or partially because of it, Enele expected more guards. They walked back up the stairs using the commandant as a shield, but still encountered no one else. The commandant led them down the hall to the surveillance room. The room was fairly small but had more than three dozen video monitors. The surveillance room was empty.

They could pretty much see everything on the island, including Nazil leading several hundred natives to the compound. They could also see the compound's entire circumference. Had anyone been paying attention to the monitors, Enele and the boys would have been captured or killed long before they'd made it to the building.

"How did the battle of Hades go?" the commandant asked.

Without looking back, Enele said, "You lost."

"Crikey," he said. "Four thousand men against a dozen of them electric kids?"

"And us," Enele said. "But yes." Enele could see Nazil creeping through the fields, rounding up the Tuvaluan workers. Although he looked as if an Elgen attack were imminent, there were no Elgen visible on any monitor.

"Is there a PA system?" Enele asked.

"It's those buttons right there next to the microphone. Push them all down, that will get you to the whole island."

Enele sat down in front of the microphone and pushed down the row of buttons. They all lit.

"Fellow Tuvaluans, this is Enele Saluni, grandson of Prime Minister Saluni. We have taken this island. It is time for us to fight for our freedom. Do not be afraid. Nazil, Zeel, there appear to be no guards outside the compound. Bring everyone to the Elgen compound."

Enele turned to the commandant. "Where are your weapons?"

"What are you going to do with me?"

"I haven't decided yet."

"If you're going to kill me anyway, I've no reason to cooperate. Just get on with it."

"I'm not going to kill you."

The commandant looked at Enele skeptically. "You promise on your ancestors' souls?"

Enele thought it an odd thing for him to say but went along with it. "I promise."

"All right, then. One thing I know about you people, when it comes to your ancestors, you Toovoos keep your promises. The weapons locker is down at the end of this hallway, and there's a full armory downstairs at the end of the corridor where you found us. You'll need my fingerprint to open it."

They first went down to the weapons locker. It held about twenty rifles, utility belts with radios, and grenades and ammunition. Enele, Adam, and Raphe put on utility belts, then upgraded their handguns to automatic weapons. "Nazil and Zeel are likely close by now," Enele said. He turned to the commandant. "How do we open the front gate?"

"There's a switch in the guard booth. Says 'open.' Can't miss it."

"Raphe," Enele said, handing him two radios. "Go open the compound gate. Give Nazil one of the radios and tell him to gather everyone together so we can arm them. Adam and I are going down to check the armory. Keep your radio on. I'll meet you out front."

"Yes, sir," Raphe said, running off down the hall.

As Enele, Adam, and the commandant started back downstairs, there was a sudden grenade explosion. "I guess they got themselves untied," Adam said. "Should have done as they were told."

The commandant led them past the still-smoking room to the other end of the corridor. The armory was a large, broad room almost identical to the armory on Hades, with all walls lined with weapons.

"We can use all that," Enele said.

"Like candy," Adam said.

Just then Enele's radio chirped. "Enele, this is Nazil. Can you hear me?"

Enele lifted his radio. "I'm here."

"I'm coming inside; we've got a problem."

"I'll be right up." He turned back. "Come on, Commandant. Let's get back up."

By the time they returned upstairs, Nazil had already entered the building with five of his original men. The grounds outside the building were crowded with more than six hundred native Tuvaluans, men and women, who had worked the fields.

"What's the problem?" Enele asked.

"They won't fight."

"What do you mean they won't fight?"

Nazil's face tightened. "They are cowards. They refuse to fight the Elgen."

"I'll talk to them," Enele said.

"Just a minute," Adam said. He ran back downstairs, returning with a bullhorn. "You'll need this."

Enele took the bullhorn, then walked outside, followed by the others. He lifted the bullhorn to his mouth. "Fellow Tuvaluans. The time has come for us to fight for our freedom and reclaim our country from the Elgen enemy. Now may be our only chance. What say you?"

No one answered. Then a young woman stepped to the front of the group. "You do not order us. We will not fight. Tuvaluan people are peaceful. We do not murder. We do not shed blood."

"What do you know of the shedding of blood?" Enele said. He looked at her carefully. Enele knew many of the people in front of him but not this woman. "Who are you?"

The woman looked at him proudly, her chin up, her arms crossed at her chest. "I am Tabisha. And these people listen to me."

"Where are you from, Tabisha?"

"I am a Tuvaluan citizen, if that's what you're getting at. I was born in Niulakita. But I was educated in Melbourne. I had just returned a year earlier when the Elgen came."

Enele looked at her suspiciously. "Tabisha, why do you seem . . . better fed than the others?"

Her eyes narrowed. "We will not follow you."

Enele again lifted the bullhorn. "Tabisha is right. Tuvaluan people are peaceful people. We do not provoke war. But neither do we accept the peace of slavery."

"We don't carry guns!" Tabisha shouted to the people, shaking her fists above her head. "If we act in violence, we are no better than them. We are only lowering ourselves to *their* level."

"Lowering ourselves?" Enele said. "How much lower can you fall than slaves?" Enele looked at them with disgust. "What has become of you? Fools. You won't carry arms? Then you'll carry chains, and so will your children and grandchildren. That is the future and legacy you leave them. As for me, I will fight for my freedom and my future children's freedom. And, though you don't deserve it, I will fight for yours as well. Even if I must fight alone. But make no mistake. If you get in my way, I will treat you as the enemy." He turned to walk away.

Then someone shouted, "I'll fight with you!" A young man standing near the front of the group turned and looked back at the others. "Do you not remember what the Elgen did to us? To our elders? Our families? I'm not a coward. I'd rather lie in a grave than bend as a slave. Enele Saluni is right. You used to be men. You used to defend your women; now you hide behind their skirts. Go back to working your fields and to your hunger and fear, you cowards! You, with the hearts of slaves, you belong in the fields. Go back to kissing the Elgen feet." He walked toward Enele. "I will fight with Enele. And, if need be, I will die with Enele."

"As will I," another man shouted.

Then two other women came forward. "We're with Enele."

Then an older woman shouted, "Tabisha is with the Elgen! Last week I saw her with one of the guards behind the compound. They were drinking wine. . . ."

"She's lying!" Tabisha said. "That's not true. I've made life easier for all of us."

"Our life is easier?" the woman said. "Easier than what? You've made it easier for yourself."

An elderly woman next to her crossed her arms. "Where were you the night before last, Tabisha? I waited for you. You know we are not allowed to leave our cages after dark. And yet, somehow you always do and somehow you are never punished. Where do you go?"

Tabisha looked around fearfully. "Who are you going to believe? I have attended the University of Melbourne. I have two degrees. I am educated; these common people are not."

"Common!" a man shouted. "A college education does not make one wise; it just fills your head with others' voices." His voice lowered. "I have often wondered why it is the Elgen don't whip you when you stand around while we sweat."

"She's an educated *fool*," shouted a man.

"She's a traitor," someone else shouted. "She's with the Elgen!"

"She *is* an Elgen!"

Tabisha looked at the angry crowd gathering around, then suddenly ran off.

"Let her go," Enele said. "She can't do us any harm." He looked at the young man who had started the small revolution. "What is your name?"

"Niko. I am the grandson of Malakani and Tevita, who have passed."

Enele nodded. "I knew your grandparents. They would be proud of you."

"Thank you, but I am not seeking honor, just freedom."

"Which is why you deserve honor. Thank you for bringing these people to their senses."

"How may I help?"

"I will need your help organizing these people. Do you know how many boats we have?"

"Right now there are four large shipping vessels docked."

"How many people will they fit?"

"They are all different, but more than a hundred each. One will hold more than two hundred."

"Are any of them military ships?"

"No. They are used for shipping food to the other islands."

"That's okay," Enele said. "If there is still an army of Elgen on Vaitupu, it's best they only see the arrival of a shipping boat. That will not cause suspicion. Who do we have who can pilot the boat?"

"We have many skilled boat captains. The best are Pita, Daniel, Jimi, Noa, and Pio."

"Zeel, go with those five and whomever they choose to prepare the boats. Nazil, arrange the people who are willing to fight so we can arm them. Take as many soldiers as you need and retrieve our weapons from the boats."

"Yes, sir."

"Adam, gather fifty to help us distribute the compound weapons."

Adam shouted, "I need fifty strong men and women to come with me to get weapons."

More than fifty hurried up to the front of the building.

"Single file," Enele said to Adam. "Give us a minute to prepare." Then Enele and Raphe went back downstairs to the arms closet. A moment later the first of the fifty appeared. They loaded each worker with as much as he or she could carry, moving through a steady line until the entire arms room was emptied.

When Enele went back upstairs, Adam had all the weaponry, ammunition, and clothing, piled by type, on the ground in front of the building. As far as Enele could tell, nearly all the Tuvaluans had volunteered to fight.

"Who of you have experience in using a gun? Please come forward."

Only two dozen from the group stepped forward.

"Okay. You are the patrol leaders. Each of you will select twenty-five soldiers to lead. As soon as Nazil returns with the others, we will begin arming you."

Fifteen minutes later Nazil and his people came out from the trees, each carrying multiple weapons.

"If you can use your weapon, keep it," Enele said. "Bring the rest up here."

Within ten minutes the rest of the weapons were arranged and the squad leaders began arming their squads.

"This is good," Enele said. "We are still few, but we know our islands. It's time to sail for Vaitupu."

PART THREE

5

Auxiliary Fuel

After the *Joule* had sailed more than sixty nautical miles from Hades, the COB said to Welch, "If I'm putting her on autopilot, I need to know where we're going. Besides 'south.'"

Jack and Zeus were sitting on either side of Welch, and they both turned to him.

"Panama," Welch said.

The COB looked up from the controls. "We don't have enough fuel to make it to Panama."

"You're lying," Welch said. "This craft can carry enough diesel to cross the Pacific."

"It can if it's full. But we haven't been refueled since we crossed over from Peru with the rest of the fleet. We were one day from refueling."

"Show me."

"The fuel gauge is here," the COB said, tapping a small screen. Welch looked at the monitor. It had a blinking warning light that read: AUXILIARY FUEL.

"What about auxiliary reserve?" Welch said.

"We're *on* auxiliary reserve. That's why the light is blinking."

"How far will our fuel get us?"

"About eight hundred nautical miles."

"Can we make Fiji?"

"Yes. Fiji is about six hundred nautical miles."

"What about New Zealand. Or Australia?"

"New Zealand is two thousand nautical miles, and Australia is about eight hundred nautical miles farther. We can make Fiji and refuel there."

"There are still Elgen on Fiji. What other options do we have?"

"Samoa."

"How far is that?"

"Almost the same distance as Fiji, but it won't be any safer. There are almost as many Elgen, and we'd be more noticeable. I suggest we make Fiji, refuel, and then sail immediately to Australia, where we'll have more opportunities to hide, which is to both of our benefit."

Welch thought for a moment, then said to Zeus, "Get Taylor."

"I think she went back to sleep."

"Wake her. It will only take a few minutes."

Zeus ran out of the room. A few minutes later he returned with Taylor behind him, her eyes puffy.

"I'm sorry I had to wake you," Welch said. "But I need your help."

"It's okay. How can I help?"

"I need you to tell me if the captain here is telling the truth or not." Welch looked at him. "We have a game here. I ask you a question. If you give me the wrong answer, you get shocked."

"That would make a good TV show," Zeus said. "Truth or . . . Electrocution."

One of the Elgen sailors nodded in agreement.

"What do you mean?" the COB asked.

"This young lady can read your mind. So, unless you want Zeus to shock the truth out of you, I suggest you tell the truth the first time."

The COB looked at her warily. "I *was* telling the truth."

"We'll see," Welch said. "Taylor?"

She stepped up to the COB, put her hands on his temples, and then turned to Welch. "I'm ready."

Welch looked the COB in the eyes. "Do we have enough fuel to make Fiji?"

"Yes, sir."

"Do we have enough fuel to make New Zealand?"

"No, sir."

Taylor nodded. "It's true."

"Set autocourse to Fiji," Welch said.

The COB turned to his navigator. "Set course for Fiji."

"Cruising depth?"

"Maintain."

A moment later the man said, "Course is set."

The COB turned back. "Our course is set."

"Are the Elgen able to track us?"

"Yes," the COB said.

"He's telling the truth," Taylor said.

"Is there any way to turn off tracking?"

"No."

"He's not telling the whole truth," Taylor said.

"Zeus."

"Wait," the COB said, holding up his hands as if surrendering. Zeus had already shocked him twice in the taking of the boat, and the COB wasn't eager to get shocked again. "I wasn't trying to deceive you. What I meant was, you cannot turn it off from the control. You would have to manually destroy the GPS broadcaster. But it's built into the circuitry. It would be nearly impossible to get to."

Welch turned to Taylor.

"He's telling the truth," she said.

"*Nearly* impossible is still possible," Welch said.

"It wasn't meant to be deactivated, so there's no way to get to it."

"Could it be deactivated by an EMP?"

"If you wanted to put our entire computerized control system out of order." He looked at Welch intensely. "Trust me, you don't."

Just then there was a crisp burst of static from the radio.

"What was that?" Welch asked.

The COB shook his head. "I don't know. Some kind of interference."

"A broadcast?"

"I hope not. The only broadcast we'd receive would be from EHQ. They're the only ones who know these frequencies."

After a moment Welch said to Taylor, "All right. Thank you. Go get some rest."

Taylor walked out of the room.

Welch stood. "I'm going to my quarters. Zeus, take these men to bunk room two and lock them inside. Have Ian keep an eye on them."

"Yes, sir." Zeus turned to the men. "Let's go."

"Gladly," the COB said.

After they were gone, Welch said, "Jack, I'm going to my cabin to sleep. You have the Conn."

"Got it."

"No Elgen are allowed in the Conn."

"Yes, sir," Jack said. "How long will you be out?"

"Just until I wake up. Or unless there's a problem. Wake me if there's anything irregular."

"Yes, sir," Jack said.

Welch started out of the Conn, then turned back. "I suggest you don't touch anything."

"I wasn't planning on it."

"Good. I'd hate to end up back at Hades by mistake." He turned and walked out of the room.

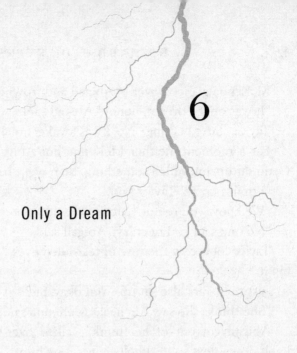

6

Only a Dream

Several hours after Taylor had gone back to sleep, she bolted up in bed, as if someone had woken her. Suddenly, in the dark room, there was a bright light floating above her, flickering like a projection. The light was in the shape of a person. The image was hazy but grew in intensity and clarity until she thought she recognized who it was.

"Michael!" she screamed.

The image flickered, then disappeared.

"Tay?" McKenna said hoarsely, dimly illuminating her index finger to light the room. "Taylor?"

Abigail also woke. "What's wrong?"

"Did you have a bad dream?" McKenna asked.

Taylor was shaking. McKenna got up, standing to the side of Taylor's bunk. "What's wrong?"

When Taylor could speak, she said, "I just saw Michael."

McKenna glanced over at Abigail and frowned.

"It was only a dream, honey," Abigail said.

Taylor started crying. "No. I was awake. I really saw him. I did."

For a moment, neither McKenna nor Abigail knew what to say. Ostin sat up, mumbled something, then went back to sleep.

"I'm not crazy," Taylor said.

"We know you're not," McKenna said.

"No one said you're crazy," Abigail said.

Taylor looked at them with tear-filled eyes. ". . . But you're thinking it."

Just then Tara also sat up. "You okay, Sis?"

"She thinks she saw Michael," McKenna said.

Abigail got out of her bunk, walked over to Taylor's bed, and knelt down next to it. "I believe you saw him."

Taylor wiped her eyes. "You do?"

Abigail nodded. "Jack told me that after Wade died, he kept hearing Wade's voice. Once he said he was sure he saw him. Grief does strange things to the mind. It happens."

"I didn't make it up," Taylor said. "I saw him!" She began to cry again. "I *think* I saw him. I don't think I made it up."

"Taylor, you and I both know how the mind can fool itself," Tara said.

Taylor wiped her eyes again, then looked at her sister. "Can you give me Michael?"

"What?"

"Just for a minute."

"Tay . . . please don't ask me to do that."

"I know you can do it."

"It's not . . . right. It's not healthy."

"Please."

Abigail and McKenna both glanced back and forth between them, and McKenna lightly shook her head.

Tara finally said, "All right." She got out of her bunk and stood a few feet in front of her twin. Suddenly she looked exactly like Michael, though she looked at her sister with sad eyes.

Taylor began sobbing. "Stop. Okay, stop. You were right."

Tara took Taylor in her arms. "I'm so sorry. It's not fair. It's just not fair."

"That was really wrong," McKenna said.

Abigail nodded. "Yeah. But I probably would have asked too if it had been Jack."

PART FOUR

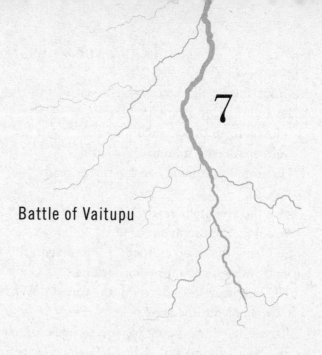

7

Battle of Vaitupu

The rising early morning sea was calmer than Enele's heart as the northwestern Vaitupu harbor came into view. He led the four-boat armada aboard the ES *Regulator*, the largest of the Elgen shipping boats, along with two hundred and fifty Tuvaluans, only sixty of whom were armed. They were followed at a short distance by the three other ships they'd commandeered from Demeter: the ES *Pulse*, the ES *Proton*, and the ES *Neutron*.

Unlike Hades and Demeter, Vaitupu—renamed Ares by Admiral-General Hatch, after the Greek god of war—was technically not an island, but rather was an atoll, a ring-shaped coral reef consisting of nine isles. It was the largest of the six Tuvaluan atolls and had the second-largest population in Tuvalu, only smaller than the Tuvaluan capital of Funafuti.

Seagulls circled the ship, and to the east the sun was rising like fire from the Pacific Ocean. Enele sat in the control deck next to Adam and the ship's captain, Noa.

"How long until we reach the dock?"

"Fifteen, twenty minutes," Noa said.

He turned to Adam. "Are the troops ready?"

"Yes, sir."

"Are they mentally ready?"

"We'll find out soon enough."

Suddenly the radio chirped. "ES *Regulator*, this is Ares Dock. We have no authorization for your docking."

The radioman looked over at the captain. "What should I do?"

Captain Noa turned to Enele. "Sir?"

"Ignore it," Enele said. "Prepare to dock." Enele grabbed the mic for the boat's PA system. "This is Enele, your commander. We have reached Vaitupu and are about to dock. First-wave soldiers on deck, armed and prepared to attack. Second- and third-wave soldiers remain inside on level two and wait for further instruction. Everyone keep low, especially those soldiers on deck. Do not be seen until I give the signal. Do not fire unless commanded. Expect hostility."

As the *Regulator* sidled up to the Vaitupu dock, they were met by an armed Elgen officer and six other dockworkers. The officer was wearing the Elgen insignia beneath two stripes, the markings of an Elgen naval lieutenant. He walked up to the starboard side of the ship and lifted a bullhorn to his mouth. "You're not scheduled to dock here, *Regulator*. Pull away now or face consequences."

"We just lost a war," Enele shouted over the side of the boat. "No one is scheduled anywhere. You haven't heard?"

The officer looked at him suspiciously, then, lifting a radio, said, "I'm going to have to check with EHQ for authorization."

"Drop that," Enele said, pointing a gun at the officer and simultaneously giving his soldiers the signal. Two dozen Tuvaluan soldiers rose up over the side of the boat, their rifles aimed on the dockworkers. "You just got your authorization. Pull us in now, or we'll blow you apart and do it ourselves."

The officer hesitated, then said, "Pull them in."

The Elgen dockworkers pulled the boat in, lashing her to the dock's cleats.

"Shoot anyone who tries to leave the dock," Enele shouted to his men, loud enough for the Elgen to hear. "Adam, tell the captain to open the starboard port door and signal the other boats to dock. I want you to lead the first wave out. Take the dock, commandeer all communications, and establish a hundred-yard perimeter."

"Yes, sir."

A large metal door opened on the starboard side of the ship, and the *Regulator* crew lowered a gangplank from the boat. Twenty Tuvaluan soldiers dressed in Elgen uniforms were the first to storm out of the ship. Behind them came the rest of the *Regulator*'s soldiers.

As the other boats moved up behind the *Regulator*, Enele went belowdecks and disembarked. He walked up to the dock's main building. The Elgen officer he'd been talking to had already been cuffed and bound and was sitting on the ground with three other Elgen. Two armed Tuvaluans in uniform stood to either side of them.

"How many Elgen on the island?" Enele asked.

The Elgen officer looked at the other Elgen, then said, "I'm not talking."

Enele looked him in the eye. "What's your name?"

The officer scowled. "Earl."

"Earl," Enele repeated. "That's an American Southern name, isn't it?"

"Yes."

"Where are you from in America?"

"Jackson, Louisiana."

"I only know that name because of that country song. 'Earl had to die.' Clever song." Enele said to one of the Tuvaluan soldiers, "Take these men inside. Leave Earl with me."

"Get going," the soldiers said, one of them pushing the closest Elgen with his foot. The Elgen struggled to their feet, then walked off.

"So does Earl have to die?" Enele said, taking an Elgen Taser prod from his utility belt. He knelt down and put the Taser on Earl's neck. "How many Elgen are on the island?"

Earl just swallowed. Enele didn't wait two seconds to push the Taser's button. The sound of arcing electricity filled the air, and the officer's frozen body fell to the side. He groaned out in pain.

"I know that hurts," Enele said. "Do you want to guess how I know? Because your Elgen buddies used to do that to us every day in Hades. In fact, they especially liked to do it to us when we were in the shower. Yeah, that was hilarious." Enele pushed the Taser button again, and the man stiffened and groaned.

"You can't make me talk," he said.

"Earl, you're so brave," Enele said. "Stupid, but just so . . . brave. So let me tell you what I'm going to do." He moved the electric prod to Earl's face. "After I'm done shocking you a few hundred times, and if your heart holds out, I'm going to tie a rope to your feet and hang you from one of those cleats, just a few feet above the waterline, then let the tide slowly drown you. And, while all that fun's going on, I'm going to bring out one of your other men, show them you, and then make them the exact same offer. I'm pretty sure that one of them will tell us everything. So, you can tell me what I need to know, or you can die a slow, painful, and very worthless death, since it will accomplish nothing." At that, Enele again pushed the electric prod's button. This time Earl screamed out.

"I wonder what it would feel like to have your eye at the center of all that voltage," he said. He moved the prod to Earl's right eye.

"I'll talk," he said.

Enele moved the prod away from Earl's face. "I thought you might come to your senses. Just so we're clear now, if you so much as stutter, we'll test the eye thing, and then you're shark bait. You understand?"

"Yes."

"Say 'yes, sir.'"

"Yes, sir."

"How many Elgen are on the island?"

"Just a handful. Sir. Hatch called almost everyone off to the battle."

"Why?"

"Who knows why? He called it real-world training."

"How many is 'a handful'?"

"Maybe thirty, including us. But they're mostly the office workers."

"Where are the office workers now?"

"They're in the main headquarters."

"Where's the headquarters?"

"It's about two hundred yards from here. There's a map of the island inside the office."

"What weapons do they have?"

"They have thousands of weapons. It's the Elgen's armory."

"Where do they keep the weapons?"

"The main armory is in the south wing of the HQ."

"How many armories are there?"

"There's one in almost every main building. The explosives have their own building behind the HQ. The office workers didn't want to store them where they worked."

"Of course," Enele said, nodding. "How do we get into the headquarters?"

"They'll see you. There are cameras everywhere."

"You're Elgen. There are always cameras everywhere."

"They haven't been as vigilant watching. With everyone gone, things have been a bit lax. I think there's been a lot of drinking going on."

"We've noticed that." Enele stood. "Adam, take Earl on board with the other Elgen prisoners. Then get back here. Tell your men we're going to attack in fifteen minutes."

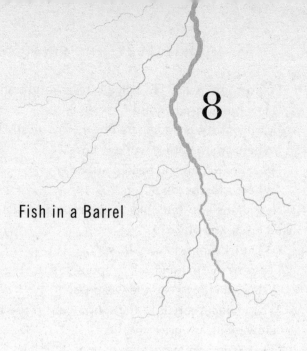

8

Fish in a Barrel

When Adam returned, he was directed inside the dock house by the soldier guarding the door. Enele had already gathered the other leaders around the map of the island and was writing on it.

"Back, sir," Adam said.

"Good. I'll start again from the beginning. Surprise and speed are vital to our success. The last thing we want is a handful of men hunkered down for a week in the building. Zeel, I want you to march the men from your boat and position here, east of the HQ." Enele moved his pencil down the side of the map. "Split your group; have half the men take the explosives armory behind the main building." He looked up at Nazil. "How many of your men are armed?"

"About sixty."

"I want you to take your soldiers and position them here, at the west side. I want you in behind me. We'll send word.

"Me, Raphe, Adam, and all our men in Elgen uniforms will drive up through the front gate. If we're lucky, they'll think we're just soldiers returning from the battle. We'll leave fifty of my men here to hold the dock.

"Do not fire until you've been fired upon or you hear gunfire. This is a surprise attack. If we can do this without firing a shot, we're better off. Our pigeon said that the Elgen they left behind are mostly paper pushers, not fighters. They might not fight unless they think they have to. But don't count on them going peacefully. They are still Elgen.

"After we've taken the building, we'll pull the trucks up and load them with every weapon they've got. We'll put all the explosives on one boat."

"Which boat?" Nazil asked.

"The one farthest from mine," Enele said. Everyone looked at him, and a sudden, unexpected smile crossed his face. "I was kidding. What's our smallest boat?"

"Mine," said Pio, one of the four boat captains. "The *Neutron*."

"How many passengers are you carrying?"

"Forty-six. Six crew."

"We can take your soldiers on the *Regulator*. We'll fill the *Neutron* with the heavy explosives and your crew. Grenades and mortar shells we'll divide between the rest." Enele looked around. "Any questions?"

No one said anything.

"Let's do this. Have your men ready to move in five minutes. My team won't make our entrance until everyone's in place."

Zeel held up a handheld radio. "We got these. Should we use them?"

"No. From here, those are powerful enough to reach Funafuti, and we don't know who's listening. We go in radio silence."

Enele and his men waited ten minutes for the other squads to take their positions before driving the dock trucks up to the Elgen's main building. The front gate was attended by only one guard. As they approached, the man stood at attention.

"You made it back, sir," he said.

"Barely," Enele said.

The guard looked at him, then at his badge. "You aren't Collins."

"No, I'm not," Enele said, lifting his pistol at the man. Three of his soldiers pointed their guns at the man as well. "Hands on your head," Enele said. "Speak into that radio, and we blow your mouth off."

"Yes, sir. I mean, no, sir."

"On your knees."

"Yes, sir."

Two men, Adam and one other, jumped down from the truck and went inside the guard booth. They cuffed the guard's hands behind his back, then took his radio. Then they went through the booth, confiscating all the weapons inside.

"Sir," Adam said. "We can see inside the building from here."

Enele climbed down from the truck and walked around it to the guard booth. There were four different monitors on the wall, all of them switching camera views every few seconds.

"Right there," Adam said. "They're in those two offices."

"And the break room," Enele said. "They're playing Ping-Pong."

After a moment Adam said, "They're not very good."

Enele laughed. "Earl wasn't kidding, was he? It looks like a bunch of accountants."

"What kind of uniform is that?" Adam said, pointing at one of the monitors. "It looks . . . wimpy."

"So far I haven't seen a single weapon."

"That guy has one," Adam said, pointing at the screen. He leaned forward to read the small type across the bottom of the image. "That must be the explosives armory." He turned back. "Should we warn Zeel?"

"Not for one guy. They'll handle him." Enele started back to the Jeep. "Let's go catch us some Elgen."

"Like fish in a barrel," Adam said.

"Elgen fish," Enele said. "They stink more."

Only one Elgen even noticed Enele and his men as they entered the building. He wore thick glasses and was carrying a stack of papers.

"It's about time you got back," he said. "It's gone to pot around here. Literally."

Enele pointed his gun at him. "On your stomach, hands behind your back."

"What?"

"Do it. Now."

The man dropped to his stomach. Two soldiers ran to him, cuffed him, and dragged him out of the hall.

"Raphe, find Nazil. Tell him we're in the building."

Raphe nodded.

". . . And don't surprise them. You might get shot."

"Check." He turned and ran out the front door.

Enele split up his men, and they went separately down opposite corridors.

"This should be the room on the monitor," Adam whispered.

Enele put his ear up against the door, looked back, and nodded.

Adam signaled for his men to line up behind the door, then turned back to Enele. Before Enele could open the door, the knob turned and began to open. They let the door open enough to expose a sloppily dressed, middle-aged man holding a porcelain coffee cup. His eyes were dull and his face was remarkably calm as he stared at the Tuvaluans in Elgen uniforms. He looked more confused than worried.

"Now!" Enele shouted, kicking open the door and knocking the man onto his butt. Coffee flew everywhere. Adam and his men ran into the room, brandishing their rifles. "Everyone, hands up. Now."

The men inside the room watched the intrusion as casually as if they were watching a TV show.

"Up!" Adam shouted.

The men slowly raised their hands.

"What's the meaning of this?" one of the men asked, his voice soft and slightly slurred.

"Hands on your head! Mouth shut!" Enele said.

The man looked back and forth between the Tuvaluans, lifted a drink to his mouth, and then said, "Thank God, you're just Tuvaluan.

For a moment I thought Admiral-General Hatch had sent you."

Their behavior was so peculiar that Enele walked over to see what they were drinking. He held up a cup. "Kava Kava."

The Tuvaluans nodded knowingly.

"Kava," Adam said. "That explains everything."

Enele's soldiers lined the men up, checked them for weapons (the only thing anyone had resembling a weapon was a letter opener), cuffed them, and then put them all into a closet and locked it.

"You're going to let us out eventually?" the last man into the closet said.

"Eventually," Enele said.

"I rather need to use the water closet. That's where I was going when you barged in."

Enele left one man to guard the closet, then went back out into the hallway. One of their soldiers was bringing a man back from the bathroom. "Found this guy in there."

"Put him in the closet with the others."

"Enele," someone shouted.

Enele looked down the hallway. Raphe had returned with Nazil. The two men came down the hallway after him.

"What's going on?" Nazil asked.

"Only thirty on the island. We just locked up a roomful of krunked accountants."

"Krunked? You mean drunk on kava?"

Enele nodded. "They were more afraid I was Elgen than Tuvaluan."

"Not surprising," Raphe said. "Hatch would have them fed to rats."

"When the cat's away, the mice play," Nazil said. "What do you want us to do?"

"Check the rest of the rooms throughout the building," Enele said, stopping outside a door. "Adam and I will take this one."

Nazil's forehead furrowed. "What's that sound?"

Enele grinned. "Ping-Pong."

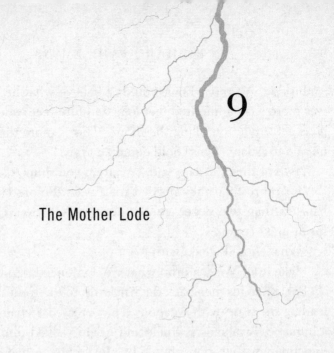

9

The Mother Lode

Hatch had wildly underestimated the Electroclan and had never considered the battle of Hades as anything more than an easy victory and practice for his soldiers. War games. In this he had left himself wide open. Had Enele and his Tuvaluans arrived before the battle, they would have met the fiercest, best-trained squads of Elgen in the world. They wouldn't have even made it off the dock. They wouldn't have made it off the boat. But that was before the battle. Now the most opposition the Elgen put up was when one of the soldiers was hit in the face with a Ping-Pong paddle.

It took Enele less than an hour to secure the whole of the Elgen's war headquarters, with only one shot fired. They forced the guard stationed inside the armory to open the room, which wasn't hard once Enele threatened to blow up the room with the man still inside.

Inside the armory Enele couldn't believe what he saw. The room was more than a hundred feet long and fifty feet wide, with racks of guns and munition filling the room. "This is more than we can use," he said to Adam. "This could equip an army."

"Two of them," Adam said. "What do you think it's all for?"

"It's more than they needed for Tuvalu. Before Hatch came, we had less than two dozen guns in the whole nation. He's arming up for his next conquest."

"What should we do with it?"

"Take it all. We can drop what we don't need into the sea."

Enele had his men back the trucks up to the front door and began loading them up with weapons. They created a chain of more than a hundred Tuvaluans as Enele and Adam walked through the room, directing what weapons should be moved first. A half hour later Zeel walked into the armory. "We've secured the explosives armory."

"Any trouble? I heard a gunshot."

"No trouble," Zeel said, looking slightly embarrassed. "That was one of my men dropping his rifle. He was inexperienced. What do you want me to do with the explosives?"

"What did you find?"

"Half the room was filled with grenades, mortar shells, land mines, and munitions. The other half was filled with heavy stuff. C4. Blasting caps. Slurry. Even some dynamite. There's enough in there to make a very big hole in the world."

"Take your men and one of the trucks and start transporting the heavy explosives to the *Neutron*. Leave the land mines but take all the ammo, grenades, and shells and leave them on the dock with the other weapons. Do you have anyone who knows anything about explosives?"

"Just the Elgen guy who was working there."

"Will he cooperate?"

"I think so. He says he has a secret Tuvaluan girlfriend on Nui."

"Have him help you, but have two guards on him at all times. Let him know that you'll shoot him if he tries anything."

"Yes, sir."

Only a few minutes after Zeel walked out of the armory, Raphe walked back in. "We've already filled the first truck."

"We haven't even made a dent in this," Enele said. "Take everything to the dock and unload it in organized piles, then come back for more. Don't put anything on the boats yet. We'll do that after we know where we want everything."

"Yes, sir."

"Pass the word on to Nazil and the others."

"Yes, sir."

Adam frowned. "This is going to take us all day."

"That sounded like a complaint," Enele said. "That's like complaining because you got too much for Christmas."

"Sorry," Adam said.

Enele put his hand on Adam's shoulder. "We were wondering if we'd find any weapons. I'd say we hit the mother lode."

It took three hundred men nearly five hours to clear out the armories. When Enele drove back to the dock, he was surprised to see just how much they had confiscated. Stretched out in the open, it looked like a military flea market.

Zeel walked up to him. "We've filled the *Neutron* with the heavy explosives. The rest we've piled over there."

"Good," Enele said.

"Not for the crew," Zeel said. "That's one nervous group of men. Sterling told them there were enough explosives on board to blow up a third of Funafuti."

"Sterling?"

"He's the Elgen."

"That's good to know," Enele said.

"Again, not good for the crew."

Enele grinned. "Just tell them that if the C4 explodes, they'll never even know. But if they suddenly find themselves on a beautiful island with perfect weather and fine hula dancers—just relax. They're already dead."

Zeel grinned back. "I'll let them know."

"How's your Elgen? Sterling."

"He's swapping stories with the men."

"Just keep your eye on him. Nazil!"

Nazil had just arrived at the dock and was climbing out of a truck. He walked up to Enele. "Yes, sir."

"We need to get the boats loaded before dark. Have each soldier arm himself with the best weapons he can find. Have them take a utility belt, grenades, and ammunition as well. I want them armed and prepared to fight."

"Yes, sir."

"After they've armed themselves, have them secure their weapons and then start transporting the rest of the weaponry and ammo to the ships. Adam and Raphe will oversee the distribution."

"Yes, sir." He looked puzzled. "We leave for Funafuti tonight?"

"No. Our men need rest. And food. When they're done, send your men back to the headquarters to eat. I'll order their chefs to cook for us."

"We can trust the Elgen chefs?"

"I should hope so. They're Tuvaluan."

The sun was setting in the western Pacific as Enele watched the men close up the last doors on the ships.

"It's done, sir," Adam said. "The ships are full."

"Well done. Let's get us something to eat."

"Thank you."

They drove the last truck over to headquarters. Most of the men had already eaten, and some were out in the yard, shouting and laughing.

"What's going on over there?" Enele asked.

"Looks like sport," Adam said.

They pulled up outside a wide circle of men. In the clearing were two Elgen stripped down to their underwear, fist fighting.

"What's going on?" Enele asked.

"Just having a little fun," one of the men said. "We put wagers down on who's the better fighter. The loser gets fed to the rats."

Enele flashed with anger. "Stop this." He pointed at the two men, who were both bloodied. One of them had a broken nose. "Elgen, stop this right now."

The men gladly obeyed.

Enele turned back to face his own men. "What are you, Elgen? This is not us. We are here to liberate our islands from the Elgen, not to become them. Do you wish to offend the gods? Go to your boats. Now!"

The group quickly dissipated, all except one, whom Enele ordered to stay and gather up the men's clothes. Enele walked up to the two Elgen men. He threw them their clothes. "Get dressed." The men looked at him with surprise. "We are not uncivilized," Enele said. "We leave that to you." He turned to the soldier he'd kept back. "Take them back inside where you got them."

"Yes, sir."

Adam looked at him. "They were just releasing tension, sir. They may be killing Elgen soon enough. Or being killed."

"I know." He started to the building. "There are worse things that could happen."

"Sir?"

Enele stopped, then said, "After slavery was abolished in America, many Africans were returned to their own country. Instead of returning to their way of life, they imitated the cruel world they had left and began capturing and enslaving other Africans."

"Why are you telling me this?"

"I'm worried that we might not get the Elgen out of our islands. But I am far more worried that, after the cruelty our people have suffered, we might not get the Elgen out of our people."

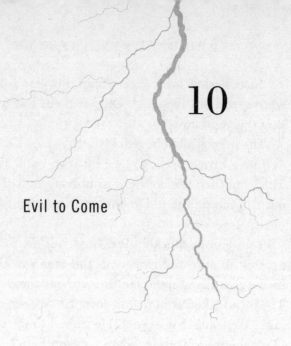

10

Evil to Come

The compound's mess hall was designed to seat a thousand Elgen soldiers and was easily large enough to accommodate the small Tuvaluan force. The room was dull and gray, but the emotion was bright and festive. The Tuvaluan cooks were happy to be with their own people again, and they joyfully cooked the traditional foods they were not usually allowed to make: cassava, boiled tapioca, curry, and stew with fish and beef. They made special Tuvaluan bread and cakes and dipped into the Elgen's best butter, wine, and cream. They also cooked large, meaty steaks imported from New Zealand that had been reserved for the Elgen officers. They made enough food to provide the soldiers with as much as they could eat and some to take away.

Enele walked among his soldiers, observing them and shouting, "Eat up. The next feast you have will be on free Tuvaluan soil."

After the small army had eaten, Enele told the cooks to eat their fill and then to prepare as much bread and food as they could for the coming days of battle. All the cooks volunteered to follow Enele into battle. They took about seventy-five soldiers and ransacked the Elgen's food supplies, filling the trucks with the Elgen's food and bottled water.

After Enele had eaten, he gathered his leaders together. The men were in high spirits—a few of them high on spirits.

"We are an unstoppable force," Nazil said, lifting a glass of wine. "We have put down the Elgen."

"We put down thirty drunk accountants," Enele said grimly, angry to see his men so quickly off guard. "Drink no more."

Nazil set his glass down. "Sorry, sir."

"When do we sail to Funafuti?" Adam asked.

Enele paused a moment, then said, "We're not sailing to Funafuti."

The men looked at him in disbelief.

"You're joking with us, Enele," Raphe said.

"I don't joke about serious matters. We're not sailing to Funafuti. We're sailing to Nui."

The men looked back and forth at one another. "Nui?" Zeel said, not hiding his disapproval. "Why would we sail to Nui? That is the opposite direction. It's time we attacked. We have soldiers. We have found more weapons and ammunition than we hoped for. Our people need us. It is *time*."

"I will tell you when it is *time*," Enele said. "Yes, our people need us. Our country needs us. But this is not our way. We are sailing to Nui."

The men glanced furtively at one another with concern.

"Excuse me, sir," Adam said. "But what is not our way?"

Enele took a deep breath. "I have just learned that the great Elder Malakai is still alive and residing on the island of Nui. We will not go to battle until we have counseled with him."

"Enele," Zeel said. "I beg you to please reconsider. This change of course could delay us three or four days. Any delay gives the Elgen more time to build up strength. Just a few minutes ago the cooks told us that new Elgen soldiers are arriving on Funafuti every day. They are growing in strength. Soon our window of advantage will be gone."

Enele looked disturbed. "I know the risk," he said. "This was originally not my plan. But my heart has guided me correctly so far. I feel that this is something we must do."

"But, Enele," Nazil said. "We—"

Enele abruptly stood. "This is not a matter open to discussion. We will set sail at four a.m. Have your soldiers ready." He turned and walked out of the room, leaving the men sitting in stunned silence.

"Adam," Zeel said. "Go after him. He listens to you. You must talk sense to him."

"I'll do what I can," Adam said. He got up and ran out the door after him.

When he reached Enele's side, Enele said, "You wish to discuss the matter more?"

"You said this is not a matter open to discussion," Adam said.

"But you would if I allowed," Enele said. "Or perhaps the group sent you to reason with me. Why else would you run to catch up with me?"

"Yes, they asked me to speak to you. But that is not why I ran after you. I ran to you because it is not wise that the leader of our nation walk alone, in the dark, on enemy ground."

Enele stopped and looked at him. "Thank you. But this is not enemy ground. This is our home."

"It *was* our home," Adam said.

"Exactly. And it will be again." Enele's voice softened. "I do value your advice. What would you like to say about my change in plans?"

Adam looked down uncomfortably, then back up into Enele's eyes. "I have such respect for you. Always. So please, if what I say is foolishness, just tell me and I will own it."

"Speak," Enele said.

"I would like to say that I would never disagree with you in front of the others, but it seems to me that Zeel was right. Every day brings added danger. Every day the Elgen grow stronger. The gods have blessed us with great weapons and people willing to fight. So between us, as friends, as my leader, are you sure this change of course is right?"

Enele was silent for a moment, then said, "No. In this crazy new world, I am sure about few things. But I am sure about the wisdom of our elders." Enele looked Adam in the eyes. "I have always considered you wise for your age. But still, you are young in years, so there is much you don't know about this world, even in our small corner of it.

"Many years ago, at the inauguration ceremony of my grandfather, there was, as is our custom, a great celebration. For six days we ate our traditional foods and laughed and danced. There was much wine and yaqona. After nearly a week everyone was . . ."

"Happy?" Adam said.

A slight smile bent Enele's lips. ". . . wasted."

Adam laughed.

"Not me, of course. I was only eight years old. But during those days I noticed that the Elder Malakai was not celebrating with everyone else. He alone was solemn and grim. I don't know why it bothered me so, but it did. I took him a glass of wine to drink, but he said, 'I will not partake.' I said, 'You do not drink to my grandfather?' He replied, 'I do not celebrate.' His words angered me. 'Then you do not accept my grandfather as our new leader?' 'That is not why I do not celebrate,' he said. 'Your grandfather is a great man. And I mourn for him.' 'Mourn?' I said. 'Why would you mourn?' He looked at me and said, 'There is evil to come in this world. Evil without a name. Evil that will, in time, reach even our small islands. It is that I mourn. For what begins with a crown will end with a cage.'"

Adam's jaw dropped. "He really said that?"

"It's not something I would ever forget. After that, for the longest time I didn't like Elder Malakai. But my grandfather respected him, so my grandfather often invited him to our home for the annual festivities. I, having wise parentage, showed the elder due respect, but I avoided talking to him or being with him.

"Many years later, on the night of the Tuvalu Independence Day, Elder Malakai said, 'Enele, come to me. We must talk.' I obeyed uncomfortably. He looked at me for what seemed a long time. Then he said, 'You do not like me.'

"I started to make some excuse about why I never talked to him, when he raised his hand. 'Do not add deceit to your troubled heart. You do not like me because many years ago I shared with you unhappy news. Listen carefully to me now. It does not matter to me whether you like me or not. I like you, and that is enough. So I wish to give you this wisdom. If you love only those who give you happy news, you will never love those worthy of your trust. For those who love you will speak truth, and truth is not always happy, but it is always a blessing.' He then smiled and patted me on the back. 'You are a good boy, Enele. A strong boy. You will bless your people some-day. In your hands you hold the future of our nation.'" Enele took a deep breath, then looked into Adam's eyes. "So, my friend, what do you think I should do?"

"I think we should sail to Nui as soon as possible."

Enele smiled and put his arm around the young man. "I thought you might agree. Now let's get some sleep. Tomorrow comes far too soon."

PART FIVE

11

Hatch Arrives

The life pod that Hatch and twelve crewmen had taken when escaping from the sinking *Faraday* was no speedboat. On smooth seas she could only reach speeds of twelve knots. But with stormy seas and a fair headwind that blew them off course, they were slowed considerably and it took nearly twenty-six hours for the boat and its occupants to reach the island of Nike.

When they reached the island, everyone on board the pod was ill and the floor was wet and sticky with seawater and vomit. Hatch was apoplectic. All but Hatch and three of his guards had been blinded by the flash, and the helplessness and moaning of his men only added to his rage.

As the pod approached Nike, the men working the dock were surprised to see them. They had expected large boats returning, not a single escape pod. They pulled the vessel in tight, securing it to the dock's cleats. They were even more surprised when they discovered that Admiral-General Hatch was one of the pod's occupants.

Hatch practically burst from the pod, closely followed by the three guards who still had their eyesight. "Get me out of this puke," he growled. He had ample reasons to be furious. In addition to losing his ship and armies and having to endure the long, uncomfortable journey to Nike, he was also afraid. He was afraid because he was vulnerable. If the Tuvaluan natives decided to reclaim their islands right then, he could be overrun before help arrived.

"Get us to the plant," he shouted to the first dockworker he saw. "Now."

"What about the others on board?" the dockworker asked.

Hatch ignored the question.

"You're going to have to come back for them," one of the guards answered. "They're blind."

The men looked back and forth at one another. "Where should we take them?"

"Take them to the plant," Hatch said. "We'll find something to do with them."

"Rat food," one of the dock men mumbled.

Within minutes an olive-green Hummer pulled up to the dock. Hatch and his three guards climbed in, then sped off to the Starxource plant. The gates opened as they approached, and the Hummer didn't stop until it had pulled past a raised metal door of the plant, which shut immediately behind them. Hatch climbed out of the car. As he walked inside the plant, he was greeted by EGG Amon and EGG Grant.

"Welcome back, sir. It's good to see you."

"Come with me," Hatch said.

As he followed Hatch down the corridor, Amon said, "We lost all radio contact. What is the status of the siege?"

Hatch turned and scowled. "The *status* is that our forces were decimated."

The EGG looked at him blankly. "How did that come about?"

"Somehow Vey went supernova and exploded himself like a

nuclear bomb. He wiped out everything." Then he said in a softer tone, as if to himself, "At least Vey is gone."

"How many men did we lose?"

"Everyone. As far as I know, we're the only survivors. Which means we're vulnerable. We need to rally our guards to the plant. Immediately. I want our forces brought in immediately from Fiji, New Zealand, the Philippines, and Taiwan. Leave only enough men to guard the plants. I want the Lung Li here. Contact the Philippine Navy. I want the *Joule* refueled and out to sea immediately."

The EGG swallowed. "I have news regarding the *Joule*, sir."

Hatch's eyes narrowed, as if daring the EGG to give more bad news. "What?"

"The *Joule* has been hijacked. We picked up the crew two hours ago."

Hatch erupted. "Hijacked?! By whom?"

"The traitor Welch and the Glows."

Hatch's face turned so red, the EGG feared his general might suffer an aneurism.

"How many guards do we have on this island?"

"Twenty-eight, sir. That includes the *Joule*'s crew and those in the center guarding the cages."

"We'll deal with the *Joule*'s crew later. How many nonmilitary personnel do we have on the island?"

"Including scientists?"

"Every last man and woman."

"Thirty-six, sir."

"That leaves us sixty-four plus the five of us. Secure the compound. Electrify all fences to lethal levels. I don't care whether they've ever touched a gun or not, I want everyone armed and loaded in case the natives revolt. There will be complete radio silence. There is to be no mention on air of what has happened; we can't afford to let this information slip out. Do you understand?"

"Yes, sir."

"The natives probably don't know we're exposed. Let's keep it that way."

"Yes, sir."

"Where are Bryan and Kylee?"

"In their quarters, sir."

"Send them to me."

"Yes, sir."

Hatch turned to leave.

"Where are you going now, sir?"

"To get back my boat."

PART SIX

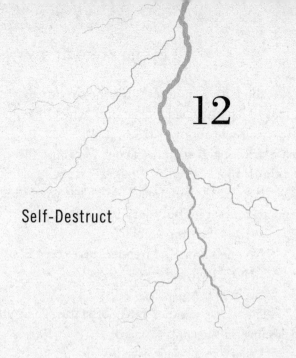

12

Self-Destruct

There were three quick bursts of static on the *Joule*'s radio, followed by a sustained voiceless transmission.

"Is that normal?" Jack asked Zeus. It had been seven hours since Welch had gone to bed, and Jack and Zeus were still sitting at the *Joule*'s controls. Everyone else except Kiki had come up to the Conn as well.

"How would I know?" Zeus said. He turned to Ostin.

"No idea," Ostin said. "Proprietary."

"Whatever that means," Jack said. "I don't want to wake Welch."

"We could call the radio guy," Zeus said.

"Welch said no Elgen allowed in the Conn."

"So, we keep him outside the door. He steps inside, I'll drop him."

Jack thought a moment. "All right. You and Ian go get him."

"Okay," Zeus said.

About two minutes later they returned with the radioman. He looked like they had woken him, which they had.

"You sent for me, sir?"

Jack looked at him. "There were just three loud blasts from the radio. Is that normal?"

"No, sir," the radioman said. "That would mean someone was trying to contact us. But that's impossible."

"Why is that impossible?"

"No one knows the frequencies except EHQ."

"EHQ?" Jack said.

"Elgen Headquarters."

There was another burst of static. Then an amber light started flashing on the control board.

"What's that?" Jack asked.

The man looked afraid. "That's a problem."

"Why?"

"We're being hailed by Elgen command."

Jack pushed a button on the panel next to him. "Welch, it's Jack. We've got a problem."

"I'll be right there," Welch said.

A minute later Welch walked into the room. Jack stood, and Welch took the captain's seat. "What's going on?"

"The Elgen HQ is trying to contact us," the radioman said.

"Get the COB."

"He's on his way," Jack said.

"I'm here," the COB said, walking into the Conn. "What's going on?"

"EHQ transmission," the radioman said. "Emergency frequency."

The COB turned to Welch. "Someone at Elgen Headquarters wants to talk to us."

"All right," Welch said. "Let's find out who. Open communications."

Hatch's voice suddenly burst over the *Joule*'s radio. "This is Admiral-General Hatch. To those who have hijacked the *Joule*, you cannot escape. We are tracking your movements. You have ten minutes to turn my boat around, or I will detonate the self-destruct." His voice changed to somewhat less official. "What were you thinking, Welch? You fool."

"Good try, Jimmy," Welch said, knowing how much Hatch hated it when people didn't call him by one of his self-appointed titles. "First, may I tell you how genuinely disappointing it is to learn that you're still alive. Second, I don't take orders from you anymore. And third, I don't believe you have a self-destruct mechanism. What sane man would put a self-destruct mechanism on a boat? Especially one that's carrying all your money. Not that the word 'sane' has ever applied to you."

"There is a self-destruct," the COB frantically mouthed to Welch. Welch glanced at him but didn't say a word.

"A *brilliant* man," Hatch said. "Especially on one carrying all my money. There are pirates in this world, and I, having foresight, *as well as sanity*, have prepared for fools like you. The *Joule* is carrying more than two billion dollars in jewels, currency, and bullion. I can sink it and salvage the treasure later. It's just like changing accounts."

"Then why didn't you just sink it already?"

"I have crew on board."

"What? You suddenly grew a heart? It's a medical miracle," Welch said. "Come on, James. I know you better than that. Hostages mean nothing to you."

"Yes, you do know me. But there are people on board who have information I desire about the resistance. That and the fact that the *Joule* took three years and three hundred million dollars to build. She's a treasure herself. All things considered, I would rather not destroy it."

"You're going to have to," Welch said. "If you can. Because we're not turning back."

The captain again mouthed emphatically, "There *is* a self-destruct."

Again Welch ignored him. "Go ahead, Jimmy. Show me your self-destruct."

"You have no idea how tempted I am," Hatch said. "But enough of your insolence. I presume you have Ian on board. Tell him to look above the sonar panel, about six feet into the component. There he will find a GSX explosive device with an electronic detonator. It's not hard to find, as it is marked as such. There is enough slurry to blow an eight-foot hole in the wall of the boat and puncture both ballast tanks."

Welch turned to Ian, who was looking at him. "Can you see it?"

"Just a minute . . ." Ian walked over to the panel and began examining it. After a moment he looked back at Welch and nodded.

"Well?" Hatch said.

"He sees it," Welch said.

"You should know I'm a man of my word."

"Except when you're not," Welch muttered. "Why would we come back just so you could torture and kill us?"

"If you bring back my *Joule*, I give you my word none of you will die."

"Or be tortured."

"Or receive torture," Hatch said.

Welch hesitated a moment, then said to the COB, "Turn the ship around."

"Smartest thing you've done this year," Hatch said.

"Cut off all communications."

The radio went dead.

Everyone in the Conn was quiet. After a moment Jack said, "You know he's lying."

Welch looked at him stoically. "Of course I do."

"I'm not okay with this. I'd rather die instantly in an explosion than return to Hatch to be tortured, then killed."

"He's right," Zeus said. "I'm not going back."

"I have no intention of going back," Welch said, turning back to the captain. "Maintain course. I guessed there was a self-destruct on this boat. I just wanted Hatch to reveal where it was so Quentin could neutralize it."

"That was brilliant," Ostin said. "Freaking brilliant."

"Can you do it, Quentin?" Welch asked.

"Help me, Ian," Quentin said.

Ian touched a part of the console. "It's directly through here. It's wrapped around with wires and stuff. Looks like a bowl of spaghetti."

"If it's as surrounded by electronic junk as the captain says, I may take out something else with it," Quentin said.

"You know the circuitry," Welch said to the captain. "What components surround the detonator?"

"The sonar."

"We can sail without sonar. Anything else?"

"Nothing we can't sail without. But if it doesn't work, you know he'll detonate."

"You prefer to take your chances with Hatch?" Welch asked.

"At least it's a chance. It's better than certain death."

Welch laughed. "Don't fool yourself. It's still certain death. Your only choice is how you want to take it. Personally, I'm with Jack. I'd take a fast death to a prolonged, torturous death any day. And if you believe Hatch has a speck of mercy in his black, rotten heart, you're a bigger fool than you know. When you were made an officer, you took an oath to resist capture or die trying. The second you took control of this ship for us, you broke that oath. Hatch will feed you to the rats just out of principle. He'll make an example of you for the rest of his officers."

The COB knew Welch was right.

"Destroy it," he said to Quentin. "Before Hatch realizes we lied to him."

"All right," Quentin said to Ian. He pressed his hand against the metal wall. "Right here?"

"About a hand to the right."

Quentin slid his hand. "Here?"

"Good."

"How far in?"

Ian held up his hand to help him calculate the distance. "About four and a half feet to center."

"You're sure?"

"Sure enough."

Quentin turned to Welch. "Go?"

"Do it."

Quentin pressed his fingers harder against the stainless-steel panel, then surged. A light across the room flickered and then went out, along with a row of lights on the console.

"There goes our sonar," the captain said. "And the cooling in the bow mechanical room."

"How will we know if what Quentin did worked?" Cassy asked.

"If it didn't, we'll never know," Welch said. "We'll all be sleeping with Davy Jones."

"Who's Davy Jones?" Tessa asked.

"He was lead singer of a rock group called the Monkees in the midsixties," Ostin said. "But Welch was more likely referring to Davy Jones's *locker*, a nautical idiom meaning 'the bottom of the ocean,' which is where we'll all be if Hatch detonates the *Joule*'s self-destruct."

"I just hope it happens fast," Tara said.

"The explosive device will immediately kill everyone within a seventy-five-foot radius of that console," the captain said.

"Why does that sound so comforting?" Jack said, shaking his head.

"I know, right?" Tessa said. "Our life is so jacked up."

PART SEVEN

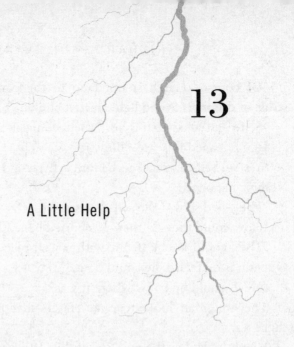

13

A Little Help

About ten minutes after the last transmission, the Elgen technician tracking the *Joule* turned back to Hatch. "They're not turning around, sir."

Hatch stepped up to the console. "You're sure?"

"Yes, sir. They're maintaining their southbound course."

"Are they still maintaining radio silence?"

"Yes, sir. Shall we initiate the self-destruct?"

"Only if we're at a salvageable depth," Hatch said. "How deep is the ocean where they are?"

"I'll check, sir." He slid his chair to a computer and punched in some numbers. "Depth, two hundred twenty-seven knots."

"Well within our capacity. Is the GPS transmitter functioning?"

"Let me verify. Yes, sir."

"Mark the ship's location and sink the *Joule* on my word."

"Yes, sir. You will need to type in the code for self-destruct."

"Of course." Hatch stepped up to the console and typed in a string of numbers. A red light started blinking on the monitor.

"Self-destruct switch is hot," the technician said.

Hatch leaned forward. "Blow it."

"Yes, sir. Self-destruct mechanism activated." He pushed the button. Nothing happened.

"They've disabled the self-destruct."

"How could they do that? It's buried beneath six feet of metal."

"They could knock it out with a well-placed EMP. If the Glow Quentin is on board, he could do it."

"How would he know where it was?"

The crewman looked up at Hatch sheepishly. "You just told them, sir."

Hatch looked at the man spitefully. "What's the fuel level on the *Joule*?"

"They're running on reserve."

"How far will that get them?"

"Auxiliary reserve will get them about eight hundred nautical miles."

"He's got to refuel. What's his options?"

"Fiji and Samoa."

"Which is closer?"

"Fiji."

"He'll go to Fiji. I want you to send out a message and find who of our allies are closest to Fiji. I want to intercept the *Joule* before she refuels."

"Yes, sir."

"Now."

"Yes, sir." Just six minutes later the technician said, "The Philippine Navy is running exercises at one hundred seventy-six degrees longitude, eight hundred kilometers east of Vanuatu."

"How long would it take her to reach the north coast of Fiji?"

"At thirty-five knots, six and a half hours."

"We've got them. Amon, get me Secretary of National Defense Lorenzana."

"Yes, sir."

"Sir," EGG Bosen said, "the ship is carrying the Glows. They're too powerful for the Philippine Navy."

"Which is why we will send RESAT projectors and RESAT vests to the Philippine ships."

"What if they submerge?"

"That's what depth charges are for, EGG."

"Yes, sir."

"Admiral-General, Secretary Lorenzana is on the phone."

Hatch grabbed the mouthpiece. "Secretary Lorenzana. Thank you for taking my call. We have a small problem, one that is rather embarrassing. One of our submersibles carrying an extremely volatile cargo has been stolen. . . . No, not nuclear. But advanced technology. We've been tracking their movements toward Fiji. . . . Yes, I'm aware that you have ships in the area; that is why I thought to contact you first. We need your help to avoid an international incident. . . . Thank you, Secretary. I knew I could count on you. Let me fill you in on the details. . . ."

PART EIGHT

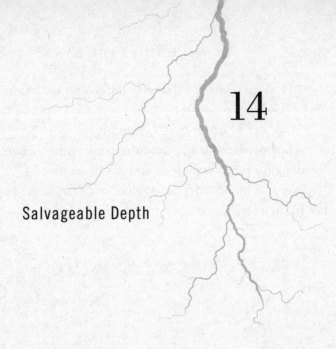

14

Salvageable Depth

About an hour after the Elgen's last transmission, the COB said, "I guess Hatch isn't going to blow us up."

"Either we're not at a salvageable depth," Welch replied, "or Quentin succeeded."

"We *are* at a salvageable depth," the COB said.

"So Quentin succeeded."

"He can still track us," the COB said.

"Yes, but what can he do about it?"

"He'll think of something," Quentin said. "Hatch always has a card up his sleeve."

Welch slowly nodded. "You've got to give it to him. He's a genius of chaos."

"What do you think he'll do now?" Quentin asked.

"If I were Hatch, I'd try to intercept us before we refueled," Welch said.

"How would he do that?" Quentin asked.

"The only boat of his we didn't sink is the *Edison*, and we're too far along for him to catch us," the COB said.

"No. But he has friends," Welch said. "Let's just hope that they're not in the area."

PART NINE

PART NINE

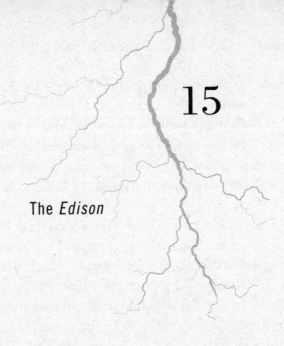

15

The *Edison*

It had been more than thirty hours since Hatch had slept, and after he hung up with Secretary Lorenzana, he went to his quarters, leaving strict instruction to be disturbed only in the case of a dire emergency. That call came almost twelve hours later from EGG Amon.

"Admiral-General, we have a crisis developing."

"What kind of crisis?"

"The natives are restless," Amon said. "They are preparing to attack."

"Our island?"

"Not yet. It's best I show you. I'm in the war room."

"I'll be right there," Hatch said. He climbed out of bed, poured a glass of Scotch, and then walked down the corridor to where EGG Amon was waiting outside the door. "What is going on?"

"We have footage, sir," Amon said. He walked with Hatch to the side of the room covered with monitors. A third of the monitors were static.

"Why don't we have images on Ares or Demeter?"

"The cameras have been destroyed, sir. But we picked up this footage before they were taken out." Amon turned to the technician. "Roll Ares videos six and seven."

"Yes, sir."

One of the screens showed the Vaitupu dock with the ES *Regulator* approaching. Suddenly men appeared over the side of the ship, pointing guns at the Elgen. "Who is that?" Hatch asked.

"Tuvaluans. Keep watching." The dockworkers tied up the ship. Then one of the dockside doors opened and a host of Elgen guard ran out.

"Our men?"

"No. They're Tuvaluans wearing our uniforms."

Just then Enele walked out of the boat.

"Who is that?" Hatch asked.

"That's Enele Saluni. He's the grandson of Prime Monkey Saluni." Just then one of the soldiers pointed a gun at the camera and blew it out. The video went static. The other video was from inside the dock building. Men began walking inside. They pulled a map from the wall. Saluni pointed toward the camera, and one of the men walked over and shot it out as well.

"That's enough," Amon said. He turned to Hatch. "Saluni appears to be leading them. We've lost all contact with Vaitupu. I mean Ares."

"Where did Saluni come from?"

"He was imprisoned on Hades."

"So he survived."

"He survived and appears to be leading a revolt."

"Where are our soldiers on Vaitupu?"

"There's no open communication. It would appear that the Tuvaluans have overthrown the island."

"Where did they get the boats?"

"We've identified the boats as the *Regulator*, the *Pulse*, the *Proton*, and the *Neutron*. They're agricultural ships from Demeter."

"Have you contacted Demeter?"

"Demeter are these screens right here," Amon said, pointing at more static screens. "Same story. Cameras out, no one's home."

"How many soldiers does Saluni have?"

"We have no way of knowing how many he took from Hades, but there were a little more than five hundred workers on Demeter. There were limited arms on Demeter, so I'm guessing that he took the people, then commandeered the boats and sailed to Ares for more weapons. If he's gotten into the Ares armory, they'll be completely armed."

"Where is he now?"

"We don't know. We expect that he is preparing to sail here."

Hatch turned white. "Where are our soldiers?"

"They're coming, sir. We expect two hundred by midnight."

"Initiate a curfew. Any Funafuti resident seen outside their homes after dark will be shot on sight. Set up patrols on all landing sites. If they try to dock, we'll blow it up."

"We don't need to, Admiral-General," Amon said. "We still have the *Edison*. She's undermanned but still fully operational."

Hatch's demeanor changed from anger to delight. He laughed. "Of course, the *Edison*. EGG, this is excellent, excellent news. Here I've been worried about the natives rising up against us, and Saluni has done us the greatest possible service: he's gathered all our enemies together and put them all on indefensible, lumbering, unarmed cattle boats. He might as well have sailed his rebels here in coffins. They'll be easy targets for our battle cruiser. We'll blow them out of the water long before they reach our island. We just have to make sure they never reach our island. How are our surveillance drones?"

"Operational."

"Perfect. Send them out. Order the *Edison* to prepare to sail. Find the Tuvaluan rebels, then alert me." Hatch turned to go.

"Yes, Admiral-General. Where are you going, sir?"

"I'm going back to bed, EGG. Finally I can sleep easy. Vey's dead. We'll bury Saluni and his revolution in the sea, and soon I'll have the

Joule, Welch, and the Glows back in hand. Everything is going our way. I'll see you in the morning."

"Good night, sir. Sleep well."

Hatch smiled. "You can be certain I will, EGG. You can be certain I will."

PART TEN

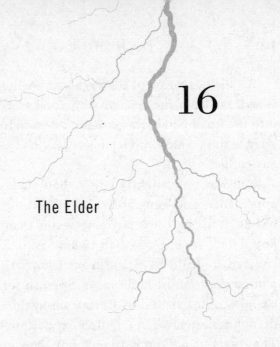

16

The Elder

Enele's boats pulled out of the Vaitupu harbor precisely as he had planned at four a.m. He had no information about the Elgen, and he wasn't taking any chances that they might have more of a force than he realized. He got less than three hours of sleep before going up to the *Regulator*'s bridge to coordinate his army's departure. The boats sailed close together except the *Neutron*, which held so much explosive capability that an accident near the rest of the fleet could possibly sink all the ships.

The distance between Nui and Vaitupu was a little more than one hundred and seventy kilometers. Because they were sailing as a convoy, they matched their speed to the slowest of the ships, the ES *Proton*, an older produce cargo vessel that sailed between seventeen and eighteen knots, so it took the armada nearly six hours to reach their destination, the southernmost isle of Fenua Tapu.

All the boats except the *Regulator* anchored a mile out from the island, far from the reef's rocky, coral wall. The *Regulator* moved into the small Nui harbor usually reserved for the *Volta*, the Elgen's science ship, which, at Hatch's orders, had sailed to Funafuti only a day earlier.

Nui was only slightly larger than Hades but very different in appearance and geography. Like Vaitupu, it was not an island but an atoll, so it was far more water than land and was sparsely populated, with more than twenty isles. The atoll was first discovered in 1568 by Spanish navigator Alvaro de Mendana. He named the island Isla de Jesús, Spanish for "Island of Jesus." The island was not visited by Europeans again until nearly three hundred years later, when a Dutch expedition came upon the island. They named it Dutch Island, but, curiously, it was also called Egg.

On Hatch's overthrow of the nation, in keeping with his renaming of the islands after Greek gods, he had renamed the island Athena, for the goddess of wisdom, craft, and war. It was dedicated to scientific research and was where the *Volta*, and her seventy-six scientists, was primarily based.

Prior to the Elgen's arrival, the Nui atoll had had a population of 521 natives. That number had since dropped significantly as, under the stress of foreign occupation, many of the older natives had died, and most of the men and half the women had been sent to other islands to work. By the time Enele arrived, there were only 172 natives—153 of whom were female.

Hatch had dedicated the island to research, and science and experiments were conducted on GPs with the MEI and new weaponry. Occasionally the Elgen guard would bring in one of the island residents if they were out of GPs, but that was rare, as the GPs were usually brought in from Hades, and the scientists were uncomfortable experimenting on natives they might know by name or might have seen in the marketplace. As one of the scientists crudely said, "You should never name a hog if you plan on slaughtering it."

* * *

"Where is the elder?" Adam asked, looking out over the waves breaking on the island's reef.

"He is on Piliaieve. It is one of the smallest of the islets. He won't be hard to find."

The *Regulator* docked around noon. Because Enele had no idea if there were any armed Elgen guards on the island, he sent out two of their women with baskets of fish, to walk around and observe. They encountered no Elgen, and when they felt bold enough to speak to one of the residents—a fisherman on the beach who was mending his nets—they were told that the only Elgen guard on Nui were assigned to the Elgen's large boat (the *Volta*) and only occasionally came to town looking for kava or women or both. But just a week before, for reasons he didn't know, the Elgen guards suddenly left the island, leaving only a few to guard the *Volta*. With the departure of the *Volta*, all traces of Elgen were gone. When the women asked the fisherman about Elder Malakai, the man turned away and refused to speak anymore.

After receiving the women's report, Enele, Adam, Nazil, Zeel, and a force of six armed men—two of them in Elgen uniform—left the *Regulator* a little after three in the afternoon. As the isles of Nui were not all connected, they took one of the ship's tenders and sailed north along the eastern side of the reef until they came to the fourth isle, Piliaieve.

They pulled their boat onto shore and stepped off onto a white sandy beach. There was no one around. While still a way from the island, Enele, using binoculars, had spotted a young boy near the isle's shoreline, but he had gotten up and run off when he'd spotted their approaching craft.

"Where is everyone?" Adam asked.

Enele looked at him. "Perhaps bringing men dressed as Elgen guards was not such a good idea."

They made their way off the beach to a line of palm trees and a dirt road.

"The good news," Adam said, "is that it's a small island. It won't take long to search all the houses and find him."

Enele stood silently with his arms crossed, a cross wind blowing back his hair. "I don't think that will be necessary."

In the distance an elderly man rode a bicycle toward them. The bicycle's line was erratic, and several times the men thought the man, who looked too old to be riding a bicycle, might fall over. Enele's men gathered around him to watch the cyclist.

"Who is that?" asked one.

"I'll wager two coins that he'll fall," said another.

"He won't fall," Enele said.

When the old man reached them, he stopped the bicycle and got off. He wiped his brow, smiled at the men with a row of yellowed teeth, and then turned to Enele.

"My dear, dear friend. How you have grown. I am very glad you made it. I have been expecting you."

17

The Lightning God

Enele dropped to one knee, then Adam and the rest of his men followed. "Elder Malakai," Enele said. "It is my honor to see you again."

"Stand. Stand," the elder said. "It is my great, great joy that you have come. I have prepared a meal for you. Come to my humble home and eat."

Enele picked up the bicycle and offered it to the elder, but he deferred. "I will walk with you, my friend. I don't often take my bicycle. I'm too old for it. But I was told you had finally landed, and I didn't want you to have to wait."

Enele smiled. "You are very kind."

"How did you know we would be here?" Adam asked.

The old man looked at him but didn't answer.

"So the Elgen are all gone," Enele said.

"For the time being," Malakai replied. He pointed to a grass hut fifty yards ahead of them. In the yard was a fire burning inside a ring of coral rocks. "That is my humble home."

Enele grimaced. "You once lived in a magnificent house," he said. "Not so many years ago."

"An Elgen officer decided that he wanted it," Malakai said.

"I am sorry," Enele replied. "It is an injustice to be corrected."

Malakai just smiled. "It is only a house, a fleeting thing. I have a roof; it matters little."

The house was of typical Tuvaluan design—small with woven walls and a thatched roof. The men sat in the yard while a young woman brought out *pi* (drinking coconuts), *lolo* (taro leaf in coconut cream), and then fish wrapped in banana leaves.

After they finished eating, they went inside the small house. There was a long mat on the floor made of woven palm leaves.

"We will sit," Malakai said. He spoke to the young woman. "My dear, bring us kaleve."

"You are very kind," Enele said.

"It is still our way to be hospitable when a guest arrives."

"But you must have prepared for days."

"I knew you and your men would be hungry when you arrived."

"Then perhaps you already know why I have come."

The elder nodded slowly. "I knew before the great flash."

"The great flash," Enele repeated.

"Tell me your story," Malakai said.

Enele wiped his mouth. "We escaped from Hades—I mean Niutao—with fifty of our people, then sailed to Nanumaga. We met little resistance from the Elgen. There we brought on five hundred more and confiscated four large Elgen ships."

"A wise plan."

"Thank you. Next we sailed to Vaitupu and again took the island. We have filled our boats with weaponry and are ready to fight. I came to seek your counsel."

"Time is of the essence," Zeel suddenly interjected. "It is time we liberated Funafuti. The Elgen are gathering from around the world as we—"

Elder Malakai raised his hand and stopped him. "They have already gathered, my eager friend."

"The Elgen have been crippled," Nazil said. "It's time that we gather and fight."

The old man looked down for a moment. When he looked up, he said, "*Kāfai e tō te vaiua kā 'siu tātou.*" He spoke in an ancient dialect unknown to any of the men except Enele.

"What did he say?" Zeel asked.

"He said, 'When it rains, we shall get wet.'"

"What does that mean?" Nazil said rudely. He looked at Malakai. "Elder, this is no time for cowardice. This is the time to fight, while our enemy is weak."

"Wisdom is not always cowardice. Boldness is not always courage. The evil man is not as weak as you think, my son. If you fight now, you will die, and then the evil man will have the land always. It is patience and wisdom that opens the blossom, not force. The time will come."

"What time?" Zeel asked.

"There will be a moment of opportunity," Malakai said. "You will know when it comes. It is when *he* comes."

"When who comes?"

"The one the ancients spoke of. *Uira te Atua.*"

Enele looked at him quizzically. *"Uira te Atua?"*

"What does that mean?" Adam asked.

Enele turned to them. "The elder speaks of the lightning god."

Zeel looked angry. "This is no time for silly tradition." He raised his fist. "It's time for revolution!"

"Yes. It is," the old man said calmly. Then he was quiet for a very long time. "But not in the foolish manner you have planned."

"Foolish!" Zeel shouted. "This is ridiculous. We're wasting valuable time. We need to go to war! Now!"

"So eager to die, are you?" The old man looked at him with dark, steady eyes. "You want war? Fear not, you will have your fill of it. But don't worry. You need not rush to it. It will come to you. All you can decide is where you shall meet it. But I warn you. If you meet it in the open sea, the water shall be your grave." He looked at the other men. "Did I not warn the people that the Elgen would come?"

"Yes, Elder," Enele answered. "You did."

"Did I not warn the people to not take the gift of electricity?"

"Yes, Elder."

"So now I tell you that someone will come to liberate us. Will you not believe me?"

"Forgive our lack of faith, Elder," Enele said.

"If you truly wish to be liberated in a means other than death, listen to me. The Elgen have already built their army from without. They have brought in soldiers from other nations to fight their war with us. They have brought in navy ships and cannons. If you meet them on the sea, then your demise is assured." He turned to Zeel. "Funafuti is not as weak as you believe. If you go to Funafuti, you will all die. Then who will liberate our home?"

"Where shall we go?" Enele asked. "Shall we wait here?"

"No. Nui cannot be defended. You will go to Nukufetau, the island the evil ones call Plutus. There you will find a fortress that will, for a time, stand against the Elgen host."

"The great vault they are building," Enele said. "For just a time?"

"Yes. It will fall. All fortresses fall in time. But there will be enough time for *Uira te Atua*. He will come. He will deliver you. Then you will know that it is time to expel the evil one and liberate Funafuti."

"The lightning god," Enele said again. "Are you sure?"

"Most assuredly," Malakai said. "I have seen him. I have spoken to him. When he is ready, he will come."

18

The Drone

"We need to leave immediately," Enele said. "We need to reach Nukufetau before the Elgen find us."

The old man stood. He suddenly looked more stooped, as if sharing the prophecy had stolen energy from him. "Have faith. He will come. *Uira te Atua* will come."

"Be safe," Enele said.

The old man said, "Safety is but an illusion. You will not see me again in this world. Now go with God."

Enele looked at the elder sadly. "Then this is good-bye."

The old man nodded. "Until we meet again in better realms."

Enele again dropped to one knee, but the elder just said, "Rise and sail," then embraced Enele.

Enele and his men got back into their tender and sailed quickly back to the *Regulator*. Enele radioed Noa and told him to contact the other ships and instruct them to leave immediately for Nukufetau. "Tell them I will explain when I return," he said.

"Roger that," Noa said.

Several hours after they had departed, Enele went out onto the deck. He was tired and anxious and wanted to feel the cool air on his face. A little more than a half hour later Zeel walked out to join him.

"I'm sorry to bother you. Do you wish to be alone?"

"No," Enele said. "We can talk."

Zeel put his arms over the rail next to Enele. After a moment he said, "I wish to apologize for my behavior of the last day. I have been . . . difficult."

"I would expect that of a warrior," Enele said. "You are following your heart." He looked over at Zeel. "Why the change of heart?"

"Adam told me about the prophecy. I can understand now why you have put so much trust in this man." He rubbed his chin. "What do you think of this lightning god the elder speaks of?"

Enele shook his head. "I don't know."

"Does he speak metaphorically?"

"I don't think so."

"The lightning god was the Greek god Zeus," Zeel said.

"And Thor, in Norse mythology. Nearly every ancient culture prophesied of a lightning god."

"There was a boy with us in Hades named Zeus. Could it be him?"

"I don't think so," Enele said.

After a moment Zeel said, "This will be something to see."

They both fell silent. The boat's hull crashed against the sea in a steady rhythm. Not far from them a school of porpoise chased along with the ship. Zeel took in a deep breath, then said, "If the elder is right and the Elgen have already rebuilt, do you think we will survive their assault?"

"All things are possible with God."

"And if there is no God?"

Enele turned back. "Then we're just dust and beasts, and what does it matter?"

They were both silent again. Suddenly Zeel pointed to something in the sky. "What is that?"

They both strained their eyes toward the rapidly dimming horizon. There was a white, airplane-like craft with a V-shaped tail and wings longer than its body. It soared about a thousand feet above them.

"I've seen one of those before," Enele said. "It's a long-range observation drone." He turned pale. "They've seen our boats. They know where we are. This is not good. I must go." Enele hurried back up to the bridge, followed closely by Zeel. Captain Noa looked back at them as they entered.

"Did you see the drone?" Adam asked.

"Yes. How much farther to Nukufetau?" Enele asked the captain.

"We have about two more hours."

"The Elgen could be there in an hour," Enele said. "How much faster can we go?"

"Maybe six knots," the captain replied.

"Do it," Enele said.

"And leave the *Proton* behind?"

"Yes. They can lag behind. If we're attacked, perhaps they can slip off and escape."

"What about the other ships?"

"Tell them what we're doing."

"I'll radio them."

Zeel looked afraid. "What did the elder say about being caught at sea?"

"Don't remind me," Enele said. "It wasn't good."

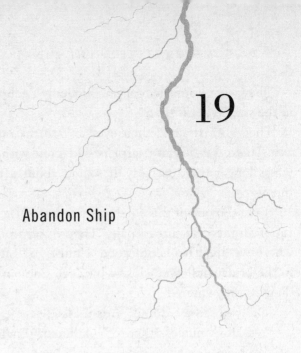

19

Abandon Ship

The *Proton* quickly fell behind as the remaining three ships, the *Regulator*, the *Neutron*, and the *Pulse*, moved ahead at speeds above twenty-three knots. Ninety minutes later, as the sun sank into the sea to the west, the jagged silhouette of the Nukufetau atoll came into view. "There she is," Enele said. "That's a beautiful sight."

"I'm happier at what I'm not seeing," Adam said. "Elgen boats."

"Where's the Elgen compound?" Enele asked Noa.

"Hatch's Fort Knox is off Motulalo," Noa said. "It's the largest islet and the only deepwater port."

"Where is that?"

"Southeastern tip of the island."

"Then why are we sailing west?"

"Have you ever sailed to Nukufetau?"

Enele shook his head. "No. I was only there as a kid."

"She's a true coral atoll. The island's pretty much a big rectangular frame filled with water. There's a deepwater port into the lagoon on the northwest side of the island. If we can enter the lagoon, we can sail south inside the reef and dock closer to the construction and the seawall our people just built. If there are Elgen ships, we'll be better concealed and better defended. If it's a big ship, the lagoon is shallow enough that she won't be able to follow after us."

"Well done," Enele said. "How far are we from the entrance?"

"We're about ten kilometers."

"Let's get there fast."

Just three kilometers from the deepwater opening in the atoll, there was suddenly a distant flash, followed by a loud explosion, echoing like thunder. A shell hit the water two thousand meters from the *Regulator*, exploding water several hundred yards into the air.

"There they are," Enele said.

"That missile was fired from a battle cruiser," Noa said. "It's the *Edison*. She's still intact."

"How far away is she?"

"She's covering the entry," Noa said. "They must have guessed our play. They know if we get in there, they can't follow."

"Can we get in there first?"

"No. They'll reach it before we do." Noa turned on his radio. There came the clamor from a foreign tongue, followed by English with a heavy Russian accent.

"Rebel ship. This is the ES *Edison* battle cruiser. Reduce your speed and surrender, or we will sink your ship."

"What are our options?" Enele asked.

"We can't outrun her," Noa said. "Only the *Neutron* can."

"We can't outgun her either," Adam said.

"It's like we brought a knife to a gunfight," Zeel said.

"A butter knife," Enele said.

"A plastic butter knife," Zeel added.

"We could try to ram her," Enele said.

Noa shook his head. "She'd sink us long before we reached her."

"We need to beach and get everyone off. Could we make it?"

"The reef will rip the bottom out of us," Noa said. "She'll definitely sink."

"At this point that's a given. We need to get the weapons off the
ship. How far up the shore can you get?"

"At twenty-four knots, I think I should be able to get at least a
quarter of the boat on land."

"I'll take a quarter," Enele said.

"Our soldiers need to be prepared for impact. It's like crashing a car."

"I'll alert them."

"And they'll need to abandon the ship fast. The *Edison* will continue to shell us. Even on land they can blow us up."

"We've still got a better chance of surviving a ground shelling
than being sunk at sea. Give me the radio," Enele said.

Noa handed the mic to Adam, who handed it to Enele.

"Attention, all ships. The Elgen Navy is about to engage our ships.
We can't fight them. We are going to force our boats up the beach.
Beach your craft on the nearest shore and abandon ship. I repeat, beach
your craft and abandon ship." He then switched the mic to the ship's PA
system. "Soldiers, this is Enele. We have come under fire from the Elgen
battleship. If we stay on the water, they'll sink us. We are going to beach
our ship. Grab your weapons and brace yourselves for frontal impact. As
soon as we hit, abandon the ship as quickly as possible. I repeat, brace
for frontal impact and abandon the ship as quickly as possible."

Enele turned back. "Zeel, I want you belowdecks. If I don't make
it, you're in charge."

"Yes, sir."

"Noa, radio the *Proton*. Tell her to stay away."

"Yes, sir."

Suddenly, to the east of them, the *Neutron* banked hard to the
port side, then picked up speed. She was the smallest and fastest of
the four ships, capable of sailing upward of forty knots.

"Where's Pio going?" Enele asked.

"Apparently not with us," Noa said.

Adam lifted binoculars. "His crew is jumping off the boat."

"What is he up to?" Enele said.

"He's smart," Noa said. "He's the only one who can outrun them. That's what he's doing. By the time they finish with us, he'll be long gone."

"Where do you think he's going?"

"Vaitupu," Noa said, suddenly swinging the rudder. The entire ship rolled to its side. "Prepare for impact."

Even in the growing twilight the brilliance of the white sand beach reflected the moon and loomed before them, growing larger with each second.

"Sixty seconds," Noa shouted.

Enele lifted the PA system. "Sixty seconds to impact."

"Forty-five."

"Forty-five," Enele repeated.

"Thirty." Noa laid his hand heavily on the ship's air horn.

"Thirty." Enele glanced over at Adam, who was gripping his chair, his feet up against the front wall.

"Fifteen."

"Fifteen seconds!" Enele shouted. "Brace yourselves!"

"Impact!" Noa shouted.

Before Enele could speak, there was a loud, tearing, grinding sound of metal and rock. To Enele it felt as if everything had turned to slow motion. Noa was thrown into the boat's controls, and Enele flew more than ten feet, crashing against the front of the bridge. Still, the ship remained remarkably stable as she cut into the beach far enough to rip out trees and foliage. When the motion had stopped, Enele jumped up and grabbed the mic.

"Abandon ship! Abandon ship! Grab your weapons and abandon ship."

Men began jumping off all sides of the boat into the water and sand, like rats fleeing a burning ship.

"Here she comes," Adam said, pointing to the north. The battleship was bearing down on the *Regulator*, now only a couple of kilometers away and moving in quickly.

"Get off the ship!" Noa shouted. "She's going to blow us up."

"Open the level doors," Enele said.

Noa pushed a switch, then turned back. "The hydraulics are gone. We don't have time to get the weapons. We've got to get everyone off. Especially you." He turned to Adam. "Get him out of here."

Adam grabbed Enele's arm. "Come. Now."

Adam's words were answered by an explosion as a shell struck the boat's stern, knocking them all to the ground.

"Go, go, go!" Noa shouted from his knees.

Adam and Enele got up and ran outside the bridge. The boat had burrowed so deeply into the sand that it was now only fifteen feet above the ground. "It's sand," Adam shouted. "Jump!"

They both jumped over the side of the boat. Just then a second shell hit near the middle of the ship, blowing it in two. Fire sprung up from the center of the boat.

"Noa's got to get off," Enele said. Almost as if in response to his words, there was a small explosion near the forward section of the boat, followed by a larger one as the flames reached the ship's fuel tank. The large explosion destroyed the whole of the bridge.

Both men gaped in shock. "He's dead," Adam said.

"We'll be dead too if we don't get out of here fast," Enele said, standing.

Just then the sound of high-caliber machine-gun fire began, leaving a path of sand flying up and down the beach.

"Get to the other side of the knoll!" Enele shouted to his men. Several had already fallen, hit by the gunfire. Enele and Adam found temporary shelter beneath a concrete seawall. Machine-gun bullets strafed the beach and struck the wall Enele and Adam had taken refuge behind, chipping the rock but not penetrating it. The battleship continued to draw closer to the *Regulator*.

"She's going to blow up our weapons," Adam said.

"She's going to blow us up first," Enele said. "Look at her guns." The ship's turret revolved toward them.

More gunfire flipped sand up off the beach and shredded the foliage around them. Enele's civilian soldiers ran in panic from the gunfire, something none of them had ever experienced. Then mortar shells started blowing up around them as well.

A kilometer to the north of them the *Pulse* beached. The older boat didn't fare as well as the *Regulator*, and the reef tore the boat fully in half. The back half of the ship rolled starboard, then burst into flames.

The battleship fixed its massive cannons on the beach, blowing large craters in the sand. Then the firing suddenly stopped.

"She's anchoring," Adam said. "They're putting boots on the ground."

"They'll run right over us," Enele said. "We need to gather everyone we can and get to the compound."

"It's nearly twenty kilometers from here."

"Or we'll die here," Enele said.

Just then Adam's eyes grew wide. He pointed toward the battleship. "Look!"

Bearing down at full speed on the battleship's stern was the *Neutron*.

"She's going to ram her," Adam said. "She's too small to do much damage."

"No, she's full of C4," Enele replied.

"Oh yeah," Adam said.

The *Edison* discovered the *Neutron* too late and tried to swing its guns to its stern. The *Neutron* plowed into the back of the battleship. It was only a few seconds before the tons of explosives in the *Neutron*'s hull detonated. The explosion decimated the *Neutron* and lifted the battleship into the air, sending fire through the entire boat and igniting the explosives and fuel it carried. The resulting explosion destroyed everything in the vicinity. When the smoke from the blasts cleared, there was nothing left of the *Neutron*, and the battleship was burning against the night sky like a funeral pyre.

"Pio," Adam said.

"That was the bravest thing I've ever seen," Enele said, standing. "Let's gather everyone. You take everyone here and start unloading weapons. I'll take some men down to the *Pulse*." He turned to walk away, then stopped and turned back. "Someday we'll build a monument to Pio right here." Then he turned and sprinted off toward the *Pulse*.

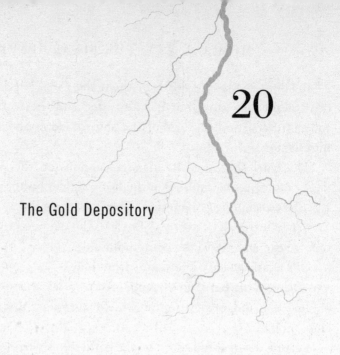

20

The Gold Depository

In spite of the violence of their landing, only a few dozen of the *Pulse*'s soldiers were injured, and the forward hull of the *Pulse* was completely intact. Enele got on the boat's radio and called in their location to the *Proton*. As the *Proton* was the slowest of the fleet, they had loaded it with the fewest soldiers, which meant there was room to carry almost half of the stranded soldiers. Enele instructed the *Proton*'s captain to load up with weapons and soldiers as Enele and a contingency of men went to check out the Elgen's Plutus facility.

Four of the *Regulator*'s life rafts were still intact. Enele and twenty of his best soldiers, including Adam and Raphe, dressed in Elgen uniforms, loaded as many arms as they could, and then sailed back to the opening in the atoll's lagoon. It took them only a half hour to reach the massive Plutus depository that Hatch was building.

"What is that?" one of the soldiers asked.

"That's the Elgen's own Fort Knox."

"What's Fort Knox?"

"It's the Americans' gold depository. The Elgen plan to fill this building up with gold."

The man shook his head. "I'm in the wrong business."

In the darkness, they ran the raft up onto the beach, then quickly moved up toward the still incomplete fortification.

The gold depository that Hatch was building was smaller than Fort Knox, only because there wasn't the land to build one larger. The building was designed to be a fortification as much as a vault. The walls were four feet of reinforced concrete, enough to withstand a direct missile strike. When it was complete, it would be six stories high and windowless, looking from a distance like a large concrete cube rising out of the ocean. There were also three levels built belowground, but they had been rendered useless, then concreted over, when seawater kept seeping in through the foundation. Around the base of the cube was a level of security and living quarters.

The structure was a little more than half-built. The bottom floor and first two levels were structurally complete and, in part, functional. Hatch had already started moving gold into the first-level vault, one of twelve independent vaults to be built.

There were three layers of chain-link fences around the building, with a guardhouse at each opening. Enele didn't expect to find the compound unguarded like on the other two islands he'd approached. If there was gold inside, Hatch would leave his troops there. Enele gathered with his men. "We'll never shoot our way into here. If they close up this place, there's no touching them. So act like Elgen."

As they approached the first checkpoint, Enele was surprised to hear the guard shout out to him in a thick Australian accent. "You're late, mate."

The greeting took Enele a little off guard. He spoke with his best Aussie accent. "We had a detour, mate. Didn't you see the explosion?"

"Sure did," the guard said. "They said over the radio some Toovoo rebels had stolen ships."

"They did. Three of them agriculture ships from Demeter. We took care of them. Now they're fried Toovoos."

The man laughed. "How many you got with you?"

"Twelve."

"Twelve? You're short six."

"Everyone's short these days. Since the battle."

The man shook his head. "Ain't that the truth. We've been pulling double shifts. Everyone has."

"We're going to be pulling doubles?" Enele asked, doing his best to look agitated.

"Oh yeah," the man said with a grin. "No one told you?"

"No, they left that out."

"Course they did."

"Maybe we should just go back."

"Nothing doing. I'm off two hours ago. Who's taking my place?"

After a brief hesitation Enele pointed at Raphe and said, "That man."

The guard looked him over. "You're new."

"We're all new," Enele said. "We're part of the New Zealand corps."

"Of course. That's why you're all brown. Well, get in here."

Raphe stepped into the room, and the guard came out. "There's an esky in the corner there; help yourself. It's full of beer. Sorry, just lite stuff." He shut the door, then turned back to Enele. "I'll show the rest of you where to check in."

"What about me?" Raphe asked.

"You stay put, mate. I'll check in for you."

"Anyone ever come here?"

"What do you mean? We're here every day."

"I mean try to get in?"

"Nah. Before everyone went to battle, I'd get some lookie-loo guards on R & R, wanting to see the gold. Like that's going to happen. I've only seen it once myself, and I've been here four months."

"None of the . . . brown skins?"

"Toovoos? There hasn't been one of them on the island since the tradies arrived and we started construction. It's the one place we don't use the slaves. The general don't want them to know a thing about this place. Word is, it's open season on Toovoos, mate. There's a twenty-five redback on Toovoo hide."

"That's a lot of money," Enele said, wanting to club the man. "Anyone ever collect?"

"One bloke tried. Turned out the guy he shot was a lost Samoan. Doesn't count."

"What about all the Toovoos we just fried?"

"Were they on island?"

"Almost."

"Almost don't count," he said. The guard stopped at the next checkpoint. It was unmanned.

"Why is no one here?" Enele asked. "This should be guarded."

"No drama, mate. We're only guarding from ourselves. Foreigners don't get anywhere near here before they're sunk. Besides, like you said, we're short. There's only sixteen of us. And one of them's in the brig." He opened the second gate, and they walked through.

Enele processed the information. Sixteen guards, one in jail, one other with them. "Why is that?"

"Why is what?"

"Why is he in the brig?"

"He's waiting transport." He looked at Enele. "Oh, you want the skinny. He was caught where he shouldn't be. Restricted area. Like I said, we're only guarding from ourselves. I tell you, gold fever is a real thing. I've seen people here go crackers."

They walked on past the third checkpoint. It was also unmanned, even though the lights were on and there was music playing. They walked another sixty feet to the main door. Enele looked at it in wonder. It was solid steel with heavy bolts surrounding it.

"That's some security."

"Bloody oath. That door can take a direct hit from a tank; it won't even scratch it."

Enele understood why the elder had directed them to this place. The guard held his key up to a pad, then pushed his fingerprint onto a screen.

"Where do we get our keys?"

"I'm taking you there, mate. Then I'm going to grab a Scotch and go to bed."

"Drinking's allowed?"

"Was it allowed where you came from?"

"No."

"Did you still drink?"

Enele pretended to be embarrassed. "Sometimes."

The man shook his head and laughed. "Sometimes."

The door opened, revealing the hydraulics employed to operate it. "Like I said, ain't no one coming in through that door."

The inside was marble tile and virtually without decoration of any kind. Not even furniture. Their footsteps echoed down the long corridor.

"Place could use a rug," Enele said. "Or two."

"You'll get used to it."

"Where is everyone?"

"It's night. They're in bed. Half of us should be on, but with everyone gone, we're covering for each other. I expect the same from you. We don't like troublemakers. Don't make us look bad, or you might find yourself accidentally locked in a vault for life."

"I wouldn't dream of causing trouble," Enele said. "So how many of us are on?"

"After I go to bed, just you and your man Louis."

"Who's Louis?"

"You're about to meet him." The guard led them to a small, darkened room filled with monitors. "Louis, here's our replacements."

The man turned around. He was bald with Maori tattoos across his face. "Replacements? The replacements were canceled," Louis said. His accent was American. "Who are you?"

Enele pulled his gun, and the other Tuvaluans followed suit. "Like the man said, we're your replacement. Get away from the console. Now."

Louis stood. He was shorter than he appeared when sitting down, barely five feet tall. "What have you done, Oliver?"

"Your name is Oliver?" Enele said.

"Oh, buggers," Oliver said. "I'm in the dunny now. This is gonna get me fed to the rats."

"Only if the Elgen win," Enele said.

They handcuffed the two men and made them lie facedown on the floor of the room. Enele put the gun to Oliver's head. "Everyone else is in the bedroom?"

"Yeah, mate."

"Where is that?"

"Just straight down the hall, mate."

"Where's the brig?"

"Opposite end. Door at the end, down the stairs."

"Peter," Enele said to one of his soldiers, "check out the brig. The rest of you come with me."

The men walked out of the room, leaving just one soldier behind with Oliver and Louis. Enele and his men could have found the sleeping quarters from the snoring. It was seismic. As they positioned themselves outside the door, Peter returned. "I found the brig," he said. "The keys to the cells are in the control room."

"How many cells are there?"

"Three."

"Good. That's where we'll put them. Go get the keys. I'm sure that Louis will know where they are."

"Got it."

"Ready?" Enele asked his men. He opened the door, then turned on the lights.

Someone immediately groaned. "Put out the light, you wanker."

Enele fired one round into the ceiling. The bullet ricocheted, striking the metal frames of one of the beds and ringing like a bell. Everyone woke.

"To your feet! Now! We don't have time to waste. Any erratic movement, and we shoot!"

The men, still groggy, stood.

"Take it easy, mate," one of them said. "Just getting a little shut-eye."

"We're not your mates," Enele said. "We're Toovoos."

The men were suddenly afraid.

"Get in line, hands on head. We're taking you down the hall."

As they lined up, Enele counted the men. "There's only twelve. We're missing someone." He pointed his gun at the men in line. "Where's the missing man?"

"He's in the dunny," one of the men said.

"The toilet," one of the soldiers translated.

"Go get him," Enele said to the soldier closest to him.

A minute later the soldier came back with a handcuffed man. The man looked terrified.

"Let's move out," Enele said.

Peter met Enele as he came out into the hall. "I've got the keys."

"Let's lock them up."

They marched the men down to the brig, locking four or five in each cell. A few minutes later Oliver and Louis were brought down as well.

"Oliver was on guard," one of the Elgen said. "You the one who let these blokes in?"

"He's the man," Louis said. "Waltzed them right in here and offered them dinner."

"Shut up," Oliver said.

"Shut yourself up," Louis said. "You done us in."

Oliver turned to Enele. "You can't put me in with them, mate. They'll bloody kill me. You're right in what you said. The only chance I got is if you win. So let me help you win. I know this place inside and out. I know all the codes and tricks. There are things you won't know without me."

"Listen to the snivelin' traitor," one of the guards said. "Let us 'ave him, mate. We'll take good care of him."

Enele looked at Oliver for a moment, then said, "You give us any reason to doubt you, you die. If we're overrun by the Elgen, you're the first to go. You join us, you're burning the boat . . . mate."

"My boat's already burned, mate," Oliver said back. "I'm thrown in with you."

Enele thought a minute more, then said, "All right. Lock Louis up with the rest. You, Vete, have the brig. If anyone tries anything, don't wait; shoot. If they try to mess with the door or give you any trouble, shoot them, then shoot everyone else in the cell with them. Everyone. We'll see if they can police themselves."

Enele walked back upstairs with the rest of the men. He turned to his fifth-in-command, a short, muscular man named Satini. "Go tell Raphe to radio Nazil and tell him we're in. Start transporting the weapons and supplies. I want this place locked down before the sun comes up. Then relieve Raphe up front, lock the gates, and have him report to me immediately."

"Yes, sir."

Enele turned to Oliver. "As soon as my men get here, I'm going to have you give us a look around."

Oliver took Enele, Raphe, Adam, and three other soldiers around the building, first to the vaults, then up the stairs to the third floor. The third floor was complete, though without tile flooring or windows, and the plumbing and wiring were still visible.

"This is where they stopped work when the battle started," Oliver said. "This room is secure."

"What's above us?"

"The fourth floor. It's still open."

"What do you mean, *open*?"

"It's not finished. I'll show you." They walked up a flight of stairs to the next floor. Oliver unlocked then opened a door, and a rush of moist air enveloped them. The walls and beams of the building were mostly up but there was no roof; the sky visible above them. "Like I said, it's still open."

Enele went to one side and looked out a ten-inch opening. He could see all around the island for miles as the moon rippled off the dark waters below them. Then he went up to the north wall and looked out. He could see the *Proton* flanked by several rafts, making its way toward the compound. He turned back to Adam. "We'll put our machine guns up here." Then he added, "Too bad we didn't have a place like this in Hades. We might still be fighting." He turned back to Oliver. "Where is our electric power coming from?"

"There's a mini Starxource plant in the basement. The power is self-contained."

"Where do we stand on water and food?"

"This place was designed to withstand a siege. There's no natural springs in the Hatch islands, so our water comes from rainwater. We have a five-thousand-gallon tank and rainwater catchment on the roof. Also, a three-thousand-gallon storage tank on the second floor. How many men do you have?"

"A little more than five hundred."

"Even if they take out the water tank on top, we'll still have enough water for a month. Maybe more."

"What about food?"

"There's a café and a huge pantry on the main floor. It's practically a supermarket. There's additional food storage in the basement. Nothing you'll grow fat on, mostly dry foods and rations."

"We can hunker down," Enele said. He stifled a yawn.

"You need to get some sleep," Adam said.

"We all need sleep, but not until we're locked up," Enele replied. "Raphe, I want you to pick twenty-five soldiers and have them sleep for the next four hours."

"Four hours?"

"That's about how long it's going to take us to unload the boats."

"Yes, sir." Raphe hurried off. Enele turned to Oliver. "Where do you bring in shipments?"

"Around the east side."

"Are there any trucks or vehicles we can use to transport things inside?"

"Around the side are cargo doors. There are two flatbed trucks."

"Keys?"

"We usually just leave them in the ignition."

"Take us there." He turned to Adam. "The *Proton* just arrived. Let's help them unload."

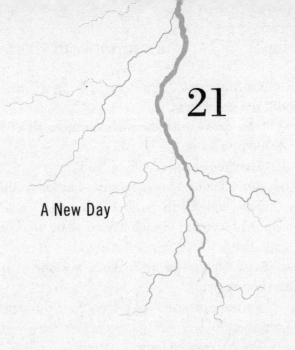

21

A New Day

Oliver led Enele and his men back down to the main floor, then down a side corridor to the east of the compound, where the loading gates were located. As he'd said, there were two trucks.

"Let's drive them around front," Enele said to Adam. "Oliver, Temo, and I will take this truck. You guys take the other."

"You'll have to go around the side," Oliver said. "There are puncture spikes all through that section."

Enele leaned out the window. "Follow me."

They took a circuitous route that led them out near the second checkpoint. Ahead of them the *Proton* had just docked, and men were walking up to the front gate. Enele and Adam drove the trucks forward to the first checkpoint. "Satini," Enele said.

"Hey, boss."

"Open the gate."

"You got it, boss."

They drove past the walking men, all of whom were carrying weapons or food.

"They're exhausted," Temo said.

"But still alive," Enele replied. "Let's keep them that way."

Enele and Adam backed the trucks up to the boat, and men climbed up on top of each flatbed while others started handing things up to them.

A soldier walked up to Enele's window. "Is everything going to the same place?"

"For now, yes. We'll take everything through the side doors. Is this everything?"

"No. We've got another boatload."

"Then have them take everything off the boat before carrying them to the trucks."

"Aye, sir." He walked away. A moment later Jimi Laafai, the *Proton*'s captain, climbed down to talk to Enele. One of the soldiers pointed the way to Enele, and Jimi walked up to him. "Enele." He leaned up against the truck.

Enele shook his hand. "What's the situation on the *Pulse* and *Regulator*?"

"Bad and good. The *Pulse* lost half her munitions in the water. She had already broken in half when she hit shore. When the battleship exploded, the waves pulled the back section into the sea and we lost her. We salvaged everything we could out of her. That's what the men are unloading now, along with our payload."

"And the *Regulator*?"

"She's a tough old ship. I think we can salvage just about everything, some water damage, but minimal. We have about a hundred and fifty men with her right now carrying everything out. After I finish unloading, I'll sail back and pick up the rest of the supplies, then bring everyone back with me. We'll have twice the men unloading, so we'll make quick work of it."

"You can carry everyone back?"

"Yes. I mean, we'll look like a train in India with people riding on the roofs, but she'll sail."

"How many did we lose?"

"Twelve. Twenty-six injured. I brought them with me. The injured ones."

"Who's taking care of them?"

"We've got a doctor from Vaitupu."

"How about the dead?"

"We've put them aside for now. You want me to bring them?"

Enele thought. "Yes. I don't like the message it sends to our soldiers by leaving them."

"You got it."

"Do you have any blankets?"

"A few dozen."

"Wrap them up and bring them back. We'll leave them on the boat." Enele looked back at the *Proton*. "Looks like they're about done clearing her out."

"All right," Jimi said. "Back to work. See you in a couple."

Jimi ran back to his boat while the men began filling the trucks.

"It's going to take a couple of loads," Temo said.

"Tell them to fill the trucks, then jump on. We need men to unload."

Temo nodded and climbed out.

"Where'd you get all your men?" Oliver asked.

"Some from Vaitupu. Some from Demeter. Some from Hades."

"No one leaves Hades," he said.

Enele looked at him. "I did."

"You came from Hades?"

"Sure did, mate."

"Crikey," he said. "No wonder you're so tough."

Adam's truck started and pulled out ahead of them, the headlights illuminating the way. The truck was piled high with munitions, and men were balanced on top of the cargo and the truck's cab itself. Temo jumped back into Enele's truck. "We're loaded."

Enele started up the truck and followed Adam.

* * *

The trucks made two more trips before they had transported everything inside.

"You need to get some sleep," Adam said to Enele as they walked back into the building. "The *Proton* will be another hour. We can handle this."

"I'm not going to sleep while my men work," Enele said sternly. "And we won't sleep until we have fortified ourselves."

Just then Nazil ran in the front door of the compound. "Enele! Enele!"

"What is it, Nazil?"

Nazil had a large smile on his face. "Look who has come!"

In through the door walked a soaked Captain Pio.

"Pio!" Enele shouted. He ran to him, and they embraced. Everyone turned and looked. They spontaneously broke out in applause. "How are you here?"

"Once I knew my path was set, I jumped off the back of the boat and swam for the bottom of the sea."

"But the blast . . ."

"Yes, it tumbled me into the reef," he said, lifting his arm to reveal the ragged, cut flesh. "But I'm here."

"Yes, you are." Enele turned toward the rest of his men. "Behold the hero!"

Everyone clapped again.

"This is a good omen," Adam said.

"Yes," Enele agreed. "It is indeed. Now let's get the boats emptied and these doors locked."

In spite of their exhaustion, the Tuvaluans finished transporting all the munitions and supplies into the depository, finishing just an hour before sunrise. Enele had them place the machine guns up on the fourth floor, then met with his war council: Nazil, Zeel, and Adam, who were going through their inventory of weapons and distributing them around the compound.

"We have everything salvageable inside," Adam said.

"All right. Let's lock the place down. Have Raphe rouse his soldiers and tell them they're on guard now."

Before going to sleep, Enele climbed back up to the fourth level and looked out over the ocean between Plutus and Nike. The rising sun cast a beautiful, rose-gold glow over the water as the sun rose from the sea. In other circumstances it was his favorite time of day— the promise of a new beginning. But now it seemed to hold only the promise of doom.

PART ELEVEN

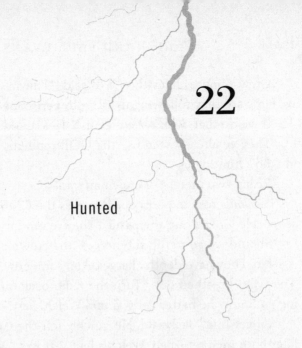

22

Hunted

"We're almost to Fiji," Welch said to Jack. "Wake everyone. Tell them to prepare to disembark. We don't have much time onshore, and they'll want to get some real air."

"Yes, sir."

"Wait," Welch said. "I'll do it myself. I'm going to take a shower. You and Zeus have the Conn."

"Yes, sir."

About twenty minutes after Welch left, Jack pointed to the panel. "What's that?"

"We're approaching vessels," the COB said. "And they're approaching us."

"Commercial or military?"

"I can't tell." He turned to a crewman. "Rig for silent running."

"Secure for silent running."

"Start evasive maneuvering. Back out to sea, two knots."

A few minutes later the COB said, "They're definitely following us. How are they following us? Rise to periscope level."

"If we do that, won't they see us?" Jack asked.

"They've already seen us," the COB replied. "I want a better look at who's hunting us."

"Rising two meters," a crewman said.

The *Joule* rose to periscope depth as the COB walked to the periscope. He looked out, then said, "They're military."

"Should we go to full submerge?" the crewman asked.

"No. They have depth charges. And somehow they're tracking us." The COB breathed out. "Turn the radio back on. They may be hailing us. Someone better get Captain Welch. Fast."

"I'll get him," Jack said. He quickly left the Conn. A few minutes later both men returned. Welch's hair was wet. "What is it?"

"We're being hunted by military vessels."

"How many?"

"Three. One's a battleship."

"Can we outmaneuver them?"

"No."

"Then we'll submerge."

"They have depth charges."

"They can't hit what they can't see."

"That's the problem. They're tracking us, sir. It's as if they have our GPS."

Welch gritted his teeth. "Hatch." He walked over to the periscope and looked out. "Who are they?"

"I don't know."

"Get everyone to the Conn," Welch said to Jack. "Now."

Jack hurried off to the bunks. Ostin was the first to emerge from the bunk room. He was followed by Jack and the others.

"What's going on?" Ostin asked.

"We're being hunted," Welch said.

"By who?"

"We're not sure yet," the COB said. "But their flag has a Morse."

"What's a Morse?" Jack asked.

"It's a lion with a fish body," Ostin said. "It's also the symbol of the Philippine Navy."

"How do you know that?" Welch asked.

"He knows everything," Jack said.

"He's right," the COB said, turning away from the periscope. "I recognize the number sequence on the boat. They are Filipino."

Just then the *Joule*'s radio snapped with crisp static, followed by a voice with a heavy accent. "Mutineers of the *Joule* vessel, on behalf of the Philippine government we order you to surface immediately and surrender yourselves. If there is any resistance, we have been given orders to sink your vessel."

"Will they really do it?" Tessa asked.

"Do you want to find out?" Zeus asked.

"They'll do it," Welch said.

"I say we surface," Zeus said. "When they try to take us, we attack. They don't know what we can do."

"Since when does Hatch have control of the Philippine Navy?" Quentin asked.

"He has control of their country's electricity. Ergo, he has their navy as well," Welch said.

"This is sounding a lot like Peru," Zeus said.

"Soon the whole world will be like Peru," Welch said. "Everyone beholden to the Elgen for their energy." He turned to the COB. "Tell him we're surfacing."

The COB lifted the microphone. "This is COB Quinn of the ES *Joule*. We are following your orders. We will surface where we are."

There was a pause; then the voice returned. "You have five minutes."

"Copy that." He set down the mic. "We've got five minutes. What do you want to do?"

Welch looked around at the anxious faces of the teens. "We don't know how deep their loyalties are, but we must assume they are working for Hatch. Prepare for the worst."

"If we're preparing for the worst," Nichelle said, "I'd rather die by explosion than be eaten alive by rats."

"Except we don't know if they'll turn us over to Hatch," Jack said.

"There are maritime laws," Ostin said. "They should take us to the Philippines."

"Governments break international laws all the time when their national security is threatened," Welch said.

"We can take them," Zeus said.

"What do we do?" Jack asked Welch.

"I think Zeus is right. We take the chance," Welch said. "Otherwise we're dead right here." He turned to the COB. "Surface."

"Surfacing," the COB said.

"They're filling the deck with armed sailors," Ian said.

"How many?"

"Maybe a hundred."

Welch looked around at the group. "This is it. Don't move until everyone is up top and I give the command—then let loose on them with everything.

"Quentin, I want their ships blacked out—communications, cameras, everything. Taylor and Tara, I want complete confusion. Tara, make everyone look the same, so they don't know who to shoot at."

"Who do you want everyone to look like?"

"Their commanding officer," Welch said. "Whoever is calling the shots. That will really mess with their minds." He turned back. "Zeus, Torstyn, hit those soldiers with guns first. Jack and Ostin, grab their guns and return fire. McKenna, I want your brightest flash; blind them if you can." He turned to Cassy and Tessa. "Tessa, I want you with Cassy. I want you two to freeze everyone—just like you did when you rescued us at the school in Taiwan."

"I can do that," Cassy said.

Welch put his hands behind his back. "We'll hit them so fast, they won't know what's happening to them."

"Then what?" Ostin asked.

"We disable their ships. Then we'll fuel the *Joule* and sail for Australia." He looked around. "Any questions?"

No one responded.

"All right, then. Wait until my command. Good luck."

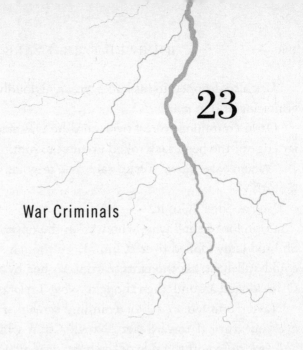

23

War Criminals

Welch was the first to climb up the tower to the *Joule*'s deck. He was greeted by more than seventy guns, every one of them pointing at him. He was followed by Ian, Jack, Quentin, and Torstyn. Then Tara and Taylor, Nichelle, Abigail, McKenna, Ostin, Zeus, Tessa, and Cassy.

Before Welch could shout out the command, all the electric youths fell to the deck, frozen with pain.

"RESATs," Quentin groaned to Ian. "You didn't see them?"

"No, man. They were disguised."

Everyone had fallen to their knees or stomachs except the Nonels—Ostin, Jack, Welch, and the Elgen crew. Suddenly Ostin dropped to his knees, then his stomach, groaning out loudly in pain as he rolled closer to the side of the deck.

Jack looked at him with a perplexed expression.

"Fall down," Ostin shouted as loud as he dared. "Near the edge."

Jack also dropped to his knees, groaning loudly as he held his side, grimacing as if in pain.

Ostin continued to roll over until he was about a yard from the far edge of the boat. Jack rolled up next to him.

"When I say 'now,'" Ostin said, "we're going to roll off the side. Got it?"

Jack nodded. "Got it."

Ostin looked at Taylor, who was on the opposite side of the boat. She suddenly looked over at him. Even though she was in pain, she could still hear his thoughts, carried to her by the wet steel deck. Ostin looked around, then thought, *Now, Taylor.*

Taylor erupted in a bloodcurdling scream. For a brief moment everyone turned toward her. "Now!" Ostin whispered fiercely. He and Jack rolled off the side of the boat, dropping twelve feet into the water. With Taylor's distraction, no one noticed their disappearance. They swam underwater, reemerging on the other side of the *Joule*, clinging to the boat beneath a small metal fin.

"What now?" Jack asked.

"Just stay close to the boat. It will pull us in to Fiji."

"How do you know it's going to Fiji?"

"It's out of fuel."

"They could tow it back to Tuvalu," Jack said.

"Let's just hope they don't."

While Jack and Ostin held their place, the Filipino sailors swarmed the *Joule*'s deck, handcuffing Welch and the *Joule*'s crew while soldiers walked among the youths, strapping RESATs to them.

Since neither Hatch nor the navy knew how many people were on the boat, no one even suspected that Jack and Ostin were missing. A patrol of six sailors climbed down the Conn, looking for anyone left behind. They returned fifteen minutes later with Kiki.

"She's the only one left. She says she's the cook. She's Fijian."

"Take her too," the commander said. "We'll let the Elgen sort them out."

The Glows, Welch, and the *Joule*'s crew were marched single file onto the largest of the ships, then taken belowdecks, where they were separated by gender and locked in four separate cells in the boat's brig.

"I want to speak to your leader," Welch said from behind bars.

The man he spoke to wore a bright white shirt with several gold bars and gold tasseled epaulets on his shoulders. "I am the leader. I am the ship's captain."

"I demand to be taken to the American embassy. You've illegally taken us prisoner."

"We've done nothing illegal. You are war criminals. We are returning you to stand trial."

"We've done nothing against your country. The Philippine courts will free us."

The captain shook his head. "Yes, but we are not taking you to the Philippines. We have been ordered to return you to the location of your crime. We are taking you back to answer to President Hatch of the Hatch Islands."

PART TWELVE

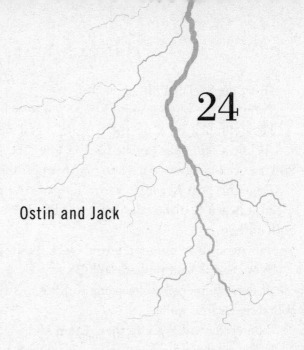

24

Ostin and Jack

By the time the navy boats started off, Ostin and Jack were already exhausted from the ocean waves slamming them up against the side of the *Joule*. Fortunately, Jack had found some narrow stainless-steel rungs that ran down the side of the ship to hold on to; otherwise they would have already been too tired to tread water.

As the navy boats' engines revved, Jack and Ostin lowered themselves back into the water so they wouldn't be seen by anyone on the departing ships. As the ships moved out of eyesight, the *Joule* began to vibrate in a low, steady hum as its engines began to churn.

"We need to climb up onto the side of the boat," Jack said.

"That's too risky," Ostin said. "Someone might see us."

"Have you ever tried to hold on to a waterskiing rope after you fell?"

"I've never water-skied before."

"Trust me, you can't hold on."

Ostin did the physics in his head. "You're right."

They climbed back up the narrow, metal rungs until Jack, who was below Ostin, was perched just a few feet above the waterline. Still, an occasional wave tried to pry them off the side of the boat.

Then the boat began to move forward. As the *Joule* picked up speed, it began to plane, spraying a steady stream of salt water against both of them.

"How good a swimmer are you?" Jack shouted.

"Not good," Ostin replied. "Why?"

"If they submerge, we're going to have to swim to Fiji. It's probably three or four miles."

"I don't know if I can do that," Ostin said.

Jack thought a moment, then said, "Don't worry about it. We'd probably get eaten by sharks anyway."

"You're all kinds of sunshine today," Ostin replied.

About five minutes later Ostin pointed toward the eastern horizon. "That's Fiji. We're getting close."

"What's the plan?" Jack asked.

"Why are you asking me?"

"Because you always come up with the plan. I'm the brawn; you're the brains."

Ostin looked ahead at the approaching island, then said, "First priority is not getting caught. We'll have to jump off before we reach port, then swim in."

"We'll look weird, walking out of the ocean all wet."

"We'll just look like dumb tourists who fell off a boat," Ostin said.

"Then what?"

"We'll need to somehow get a boat to get back to Tuvalu."

"How do we know they'll take them to Tuvalu?"

"Hatch would have insisted."

"How do we know Hatch was behind it?"

"They had RESATs."

"Oh," Jack said. "You're right. But we'll need more than a boat. We'll need weapons. Maybe an army. Does Fiji have an army?"

"Yes. It's small. Thirty-five hundred soldiers. But Hatch probably owns them, too."

"He owns everyone."

"Not everyone," Ostin said. "At least not yet." Ostin thought for a moment, then said, "We don't need an army. We already have one."

Jack looked at him. "Yeah? And where are you hiding it, your pocket?"

"The Tuvaluan people. They're like a bomb that just needs to be detonated. It could be like the eighteenth-century French Revolution when the people stormed the Bastille fortress for weapons. The Tuvaluans could attack Hatch at the Starxource plant. Enele is probably already planning that. We need to somehow find Enele. He's the key."

"I like Enele," Jack said. "He's got that Polynesian warrior blood in him. But we're still going to need a boat first. And a place to stay."

"Food would be nice too," Ostin said. "I'm starving."

Just then a fish jumped out of the water, hitting the side of the boat and then smacking against Ostin. Ostin swatted it away, almost losing his grip.

Jack laughed. "Why'd you do that? You said you were hungry. That was sushi-grade fish."

"I'd rather have a hamburger."

Jack shook his head. "If I see one swimming down there, I'll let you know."

About three hundred yards from the dock, the *Joule* slowed to a wakeless speed. Ahead of them, there were dozens of commercial fishing boats in the harbor, as well as a few large tankers.

"That's the port of Lautoka," Ostin said. "Lautoka is the second-largest city in Fiji."

"We better jump off soon," Jack said. "Before someone on one of those boats spots us." He climbed down to the edge of the water. "You good to swim that far?"

"I'm good," Ostin said.

"Let's go," Jack shouted, jumping into the water.

Ostin held his nose and jumped in after him. When he came up, Jack was about thirty feet from him. The *Joule* was already a good distance away from them both.

"Come on," Jack shouted, swimming toward the shore. Ostin started after him, surprising himself at how much better a swimmer he was than he used to be. Fighting the Elgen was like training for the Olympics.

When they were about a football field away from shore, Jack stopped and treaded water, waiting for Ostin to catch up.

"Let's swim over there by those sailboats," Jack said. "Less likely anyone will see us."

"Lead the way," Ostin said, panting.

Jack reached the shore first, lifting himself up onto the wood-planked dock. Ostin arrived just a few minutes later. Jack reached down and pulled him up; then they both fell back onto the dock, panting.

"Nothing ate us," Ostin said.

"Did you see that hammerhead shark swim beneath you?"

Ostin's eyes widened. "No."

"Me neither," Jack laughed. He closed his eyes and asked, "Pop quiz. Would you rather be eaten by a shark or Elgen rats?"

Ostin was quiet a moment, then replied, "A shark."

"Me too," Jack said.

"You know, the Fijians used to eat people. They called these the Cannibal Isles."

"You already told us that."

"I did?"

"On the plane on the way here."

Ostin said, "That seems like a year ago."

"At least," Jack said.

They lay for a few more minutes as the sun dried them. The salt water stuck uncomfortably to their skin.

"I need to wash off," Ostin said.

"Maybe they've got showers over on that beach."

Jack stood, then helped Ostin up. They were walking across a small grass strip toward the beach when a large native man asked in a British accent, "Are you two okay?"

Ostin and Jack turned to see who was talking to them. The man was muscular and at least three inches taller than Jack. "We're fine, thanks," Ostin said.

The man grinned. "Usually we put on swimsuits before we take a swim."

Ostin pretended to laugh. "We weren't planning on swimming. We were out fishing and our raft sank."

The man looked at them quizzically. "Really? Your raft sank? How did that happen?"

"A shark bit it."

Jack said, "A great—"

"Bull shark," Ostin said, knowing that there had not been a reported sighting of a great white in Fiji for many years.

"There are many bull sharks near this reef," the man said. "They can be aggressive. You're lucky you're still alive."

"We are," Ostin said. "But we lost everything. Our raft, our fishing poles, our cell phones. Even the bag with our wallets."

"That's too bad," the man said, studying them. "Perhaps I can help you. That's my house right over there. The green one. You can clean up. I can find you some dry clothes." He looked at Jack. "Mine would fit you." Then he looked at Ostin. "I'll get you some clothes from my sister."

Jack hid his grin.

The man stuck out his hand to Jack. "I'm Vishal."

"Vishal?" Jack repeated.

"Yes. Almost every man in Fiji is named Vishal. It's far too common."

"I'm Thomas," Ostin said.

"Thomas? That's also a popular Fijian name."

He turned to Jack. "What is your name?"

"Moki?" Jack said, making it sound more like a question than an answer.

Vishal's brow furrowed. "Moki? That's a peculiar name. Are there many Americans named Moki?"

"No. My mother was, like . . . Swedish."

Ostin rolled his eyes.

"I didn't know 'Moki' was a Swedish name. Very peculiar. It's my pleasure to meet you, Thomas and Moki."

"Our pleasure," Ostin said. "Thanks for your help."

"Glad to help. Follow me."

Ostin and Jack walked a few yards behind him.

"Why did you say your name was Moki?" Ostin whispered.

"Why did you lie about your name at all?" Jack replied.

"We don't know if he works for the Elgen."

"Would an Elgen guard offer to help?"

"He would if it were a trap."

Vishal led them to his house. "Where are you two staying?" he asked Jack.

Jack turned to Ostin. "What's the name of that place?"

"Suva," Ostin said.

Vishal looked at him curiously. "You rafted all the way from Suva?"

"No, we rafted from Nadi."

Vishal seemed more satisfied with this answer. "There are many boat rentals in Nadi. So many tourists. I have friends in that business. Which company was it?"

"Don't remember," Ostin said. "I just remember where they were located."

"And where was that?"

Ostin paused, then said, "On the beach."

A slight grin crossed Vishal's face, and he stopped in front of a small stucco house. "We are here. Come in. Please." He opened the door, and Jack and Ostin followed him in. The house was simple, with only a few pieces of furniture. There was a large cross on the wall.

"Excuse me a moment, please," Vishal said. He left the room.

"You're a good liar," Jack said. "I've never been very good at it."

"Thank you," Ostin replied. "I think."

Vishal returned with two towels and some shorts and a T-shirt for Jack. Jack held up the T-shirt. It read:

I'M FIJIAN

BUT YOU CAN CALL ME

AWESOME

"Thanks," Jack said. "That *is* awesome."

"You probably wish to wash the salt water from your skin. You can shower first if you like. The bathroom is right there."

"Thank you." Jack went in to shower. Vishal lay an open terry cloth towel on the couch for Ostin to sit on, then sat down in a wicker chair across from him. "So, Mr. Thomas, where in the U.S. are you from?"

At first Ostin was thrown by his own alias and looked around to see who Vishal was talking to. "Thomas? Oh, right. I'm from, uh, Idaho."

"Uh-Idaho," Vishal echoed. "What state is that in?"

Ostin looked at him blankly, then said, "California."

He nodded. "I know California. Hollywood. Disneyland. Richard Simmons." He stood. "Just a minute."

After he was gone, Ostin looked around the room. There was no art and only two framed photographs. As he examined one of them more closely, he realized that the picture inside was really just the stock photo that came with the frame.

A moment later Vishal walked in carrying a bowl and a teacup. "I brought you some Fiji grass tea and fish soup." He set the cup and the bowl on the coffee table.

"Thank you," Ostin said, sitting back down. He quickly slurped down the soup while the man watched him. After Ostin had finished the soup, Vishal said, "You were hungry. I'll get you more." He took Ostin's bowl, then walked back out of the room. Just then, Jack walked out of the bathroom. He was dressed in the shorts and T-shirt that Vishal had given him, and his long hair was wet and pulled back.

"Seriously, that shower was life-changing," Jack said. "Where's Vishal?"

"He went to get me some more soup."

Jack sat down next to Ostin. "Is it good?"

"Yeah. But I'm so hungry, I'd call roadkill gourmet."

Vishal walked into the room carrying a bowl and a plate of reddish-purple chips with a white dip. "Mr. Moki, you are done."

"Yeah. Thanks. It's good to get the salt water off. I hope it's okay that I just left my clothes hanging in there. I washed them in the shower."

"That will be fine." He set the bowl and plate in front of Ostin. "This is *rourou*," he said. "Do you know *dalo*?"

Ostin examined the chips. "Taro chips?"

"Yes. And tapioca." He stood. "I will get food for Moki now." Vishal again walked out of the room.

"You guys been talking?"

"Yes."

"About what?"

"Not much," Ostin said as Vishal walked back in carrying more tea and soup. He set the food in front of Jack. There was a fish head on top of the soup, the eye looking straight up at him.

"That looks . . . delicious," Jack said.

"Thank you. I have one more thing." He went back to the kitchen, returning with a plate of toast spread with butter and mango jam. He put the toast on the table, then sat down across from them. "I hope that's satisfying."

"It's more than satisfying," Jack said. "Thanks."

"So, Moki, are you also from California?"

Jack looked up. "California?" He glanced at Ostin. "Uh, yes."

"Where in California?"

"Same as Ostin," he said.

Vishal's brow furrowed. "Ostin? In Texas."

Ostin quickly interjected. "Sometimes *Moki* calls me Ostin instead of *Thomas* because I used to live in Austin, Texas."

"Oh," Vishal said.

"Oh, right," Jack said, suddenly realizing his mistake.

"But now he also lives in Uh-Idaho."

Jack just blinked. Ostin's lies were getting weirder all the time, and he was having trouble keeping up with them.

Ostin finished eating the second bowl of soup, then said, "I think I'll shower now."

"I'll find you some clothes," Vishal said, standing. "There's an extra towel in there."

"Thank you." Ostin went into the bathroom, locking the door behind him.

The room was small—a porcelain toilet, a sink, and a shower-bath. There was a pink plastic curtain with pictures of tropical fish, and Jack's clothes hung dripping across the shower rod.

Ostin took them down, then took off his own clothes, tossing them into the bathtub and turning on the water. A light flow of warm water streamed out, and he climbed in, letting the water cover him as he lifted his clothes up onto the back of the tub to form a makeshift pillow. Finally he lay back and closed his eyes, water bouncing off his face and chest. He was exhausted, mentally as well as physically. Fear and stress can take a greater toll than physical exertion, and that was the case right now. Suddenly his tears began to mix with the falling water.

It was the first time he'd truly been alone since the battle of Hades, and his thoughts immediately turned to Michael. He quickly pushed the memories out. He missed his friend, but right now it was more than he could handle. He couldn't believe that after all they'd been through, he'd really lost him. And now he might lose McKenna and the rest of his new friends as well. These days, he couldn't believe much of anything in his life. Everything was surreal. He felt like Alice in Wonderland, falling down the rabbit hole. And, like Alice, he hoped that he would just wake and find that it was all a bad dream, and then run over to Michael's house for epic waffles and video games. But it wasn't a dream. And those simple, carefree days were as far gone as his innocence. Nothing was simple anymore. And nothing was carefree.

His thoughts floated to McKenna. She was his first girlfriend, his first kiss, his first love. She was pretty much his first everything. The idea of her being hurt by Hatch made him insane. He knew that it was more about saving her than vengeance on

Hatch—not that he didn't want that, too—that was driving him back to Tuvalu. He had to save her—or die trying. Then he pushed those thoughts away as well. It was all too much to make sense of. Way too much, even for a brain the size of his. He fell asleep in the bathtub.

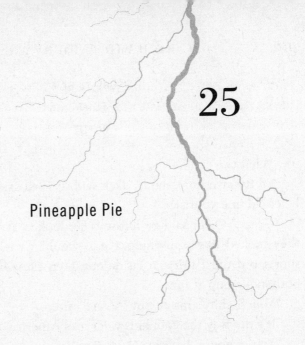

25

Pineapple Pie

Ostin woke to the sound of knocking. "Hey, *Thomas*," Jack said. "You alive in there?"

Ostin looked around, trying to remember where he was. "Yeah. Sorry. I fell asleep."

"Save some water for the fish."

"I'll hurry." Ostin got up and quickly washed himself with a bar of soap, rinsed out his clothing, and then hung them up on the rod where Jack's clothes had been. He turned off the water and got out, hung Jack's clothes back up next to his own, then dried himself off with a towel.

"Did Vishal come back with some clothes?" Ostin asked.

"Yeah, I put them on the floor outside the door. You're going to love the shirt."

Ostin opened the door, reached out, and grabbed the clothes. Folded on top was a pink cotton T-shirt that read:

PROUD TO BE A

FIJIAN

HOTTIE

"What the . . ."

"Pretty awesome, right?" Jack said. "Vishal said it's the only thing he could find your size."

"Great," Ostin said to himself. He looked at the shorts. At least they looked like something a guy would wear. He pulled on the shorts, put the T-shirt on inside out, then came out. Jack and Vishal both looked up at him.

"Your T-shirt's inside out," Vishal said.

"It's the way the cool kids wear it in America," Ostin said.

"You're not in America," Vishal said.

"That's okay," Ostin replied. "I'm not one of the cool kids either."

Jack grinned.

Vishal suddenly stood. "If you'll excuse me now, I need to go back to work."

"Vishal leads shark dives," Jack said. "For tourists."

"In parts of Fiji, the shark is worshipped as a god," Vishal said. "Perhaps the one who bit your raft was a great god bringing you to me."

"Perhaps," Ostin said. "Thank you for all your help."

"You're welcome. I'll be back around seven o'clock. I think maybe you both need some rest. I have a big bed in that room. You can sleep. When I come back, we'll get some dinner. In the morning I can drive you to Suva."

Jack raised his eyebrows. "Suva?"

"Yes. Your hotel."

"You don't have to do that," Ostin said.

"It's no problem. It's only one hundred and eighty-seven kilometers. About a two-hour drive each way," Vishal said.

"We'll just take a bus," Ostin said.

Vishal raised his hand to silence their protests. "It's no problem. I have friends in Suva that I would like to see. It will be a nice day for a drive. In the meantime, help yourself to anything you'd like to eat. There is pineapple pie in the refrigerator."

"Thank you," they both said in unison.

After Vishal walked out of the house, Jack said, "I can't believe he's just leaving us alone in his house. We could totally rip him off."

"They're trusting people," Ostin said.

"They'd have to be to fall in with the Elgen."

"Maybe Vishal is Elgen."

"Stop that already," Jack said. "That's just paranoid. When was the last time an Elgen fed you anything besides Rabisk?" He stood. "Anyway, he's gone and I need sleep before stealing a boat."

"Me too," Ostin said. "Some of that pineapple pie and sleep."

They walked into the kitchen and helped themselves to large pieces of pie. After they'd eaten, they went into the bedroom. They both stood there looking at the bed.

"Never slept in the same bed as a guy," Ostin said.

"No big deal," Jack said, sitting down and taking off his shoes. "In the old days, gold miners used to sleep like six guys to a bed. Probably sounded like a log mill, with all that snoring. You ever share a bed with anyone?"

"No. Maybe with my parents when I was little."

"When I was little, we only had room for three beds. My parents took one, my sister took one, and I shared a bed with my brother. And he wet the bed."

"I could have lived the rest of my life not knowing that," Ostin said.

"Yeah, now he's a marine." Jack looked at him. "You don't wet the bed, do you?"

Ostin looked at him. "No."

"Good. Because I just got dry clothes."

They slept soundly for several hours. It was after sundown when Jack woke to the sound of someone entering the house. Instinctively his first thought was of danger. He lay quietly with one eye opened, focused on the door, watching it slowly open.

Vishal stuck his head inside. "Hello?" He turned on the light. "Wake up, gentlemen. Or you won't sleep tonight."

"What time is it?" Jack asked.

"What day is it?" Ostin asked.

Vishal smiled. "It's the same day it was when you came to my beach. And it's dinnertime. I will take you out to dinner. Do you like pizza?"

"We love pizza," Ostin said, suddenly feeling more awake.

"I thought so. Americans love their pizza."

26

Kava Kava

Jack and Ostin followed Vishal out to his car, a white passenger van with the words SHARK REEF DIVERS printed on the side beneath the gaping jaws of a large shark.

"That picture on your van probably scares away customers," Ostin said after they climbed in.

Vishal said, "Only a few. But it makes it more exciting for the ones who really want adventure."

"Has anyone ever been attacked by a shark?" Jack asked.

"One of our clients? No. We hit them with a pole if they get too close."

Ostin looked confused. "You hit the clients or the sharks with the pole?"

Vishal laughed. "Whatever works."

Vishal looked both ways, then pulled out of the gravel parking lot into the road. He turned on the radio to a local radio station. He

157

drove the van about three miles to downtown Lautoka, parking near a sign that read: GIUSEPPE'S PIZZA INN.

The intersection next to the restaurant had been closed off, and one of the streets was crowded with pedestrians.

"What's going on there?" Ostin asked.

Vishal turned to look. "It's the night market. Would you like to walk through before we eat? It's only a few blocks."

"That would be great," Jack said.

"Good," Vishal said. "I think you'll find it interesting."

They walked past the restaurant to the end of the block, then crossed the street, joining the colorful, pressing throng of humanity wandering through the market. Music blared loudly into the warm, moist air, and the road was lined with scores of brightly colored tent awnings illuminated with strings of electric lights.

The street merchants sold a wide range of merchandise, from phone cases and cords to T-shirts and brightly colored bolts of fabric.

Ostin found a T-shirt he would have bought if he had any money. It read:

I'm FIJIAN
. . . but I won't eat you.
Probably.

While the majority of the crowd were Fijian natives, there were foreign tourists as well—mostly Asian but some Americans and Europeans. The entire market smelled of food: candied nuts, barbecued meats, fried food bubbling in large metal fryers, and sweets and pastries too numerous to count. There were large tables filled with fruits: pineapples, coconuts, green bananas, and some that even Ostin couldn't identify. There were all kinds of teas and fruit juices, and some people drank through straws from hairy coconuts.

"Moki, Thomas," Vishal said, standing in front of a small food stand. "Come try this." He handed Ostin a plastic bowl with a fork. Ostin took a bite, then handed the bowl to Jack.

"That's good," Ostin said. "What is it?"

"It is called *kokoda*. It's sometimes called Fijian ceviche. My friend here makes it."

Jack tried it as well. "I like it." He turned to Ostin. "I thought you didn't like raw fish."

"Only when it's still swimming," Ostin said. "Or still breathing."

"The acid in the lemon cooks the fish," Vishal said. "If you would like to continue on, I would like to talk to my friend for a minute."

"Sure," Jack said. "We'll stay on this street."

Vishal walked behind the booth's back wall as Ostin and Jack walked on.

"How are we going to get to Tuvalu?" Jack asked.

"I'm still thinking about it," Ostin said.

"You better think fast. We leave for Suva in the morning."

"I'll figure something out."

Jack looked at him. "Do you think they've reached Tuvalu yet?"

"No. It's only been a day."

"Maybe we should steal a plane," Jack said.

"Then we'd have to kidnap a pilot, too," Ostin said.

They walked a little farther on, until Ostin stopped next to a display of carved wooden forks. "Hey, look. *Iculanibokola*."

"Ikoo-what?"

"Cannibal forks."

"Yes," Vishal said, suddenly walking up to them. "They are a reminder of Fiji's past. These islands were once known for cannibalism." He lifted one of the forks. "Have you ever wondered what human flesh tastes like?"

There was something different about Vishal's voice, an edge to it, and a chill rose up Ostin's spine. "Not once," Ostin said. "Not something I want to know."

"Regardless, I am told that it tastes mostly like pork but is indistinguishable from veal. In the ancient Fiji days there was no refrigeration, so the victim had to be kept alive as long as they could be, to keep the meat fresh."

"Excuse me while I throw up," Ostin said.

Vishal laughed. "Please, not here." Then he walked to the next booth.

As Ostin turned back he suddenly froze. "Jack . . . I mean, Moki . . ."

Jack set down the fork he was holding and looked up. "Yeah?"

About thirty feet in front of them were two men in Elgen guard uniforms.

"Be calm," Ostin said, looking very uncalm. "Just act like tourists."

"They don't look like they're looking for anyone."

"See the patch on their shoulders? Chinese characters with the skull and dragon. Same as the guards at the Taiwan Starxource plant."

Jack stole another glance at them. "The Lung Li?"

"No. The regular guards. Don't stare at them."

Vishal suddenly turned back. His gaze darted back and forth between Ostin and Jack. Then he said, "Is it the men in uniform that concern you? Don't worry, they are not soldiers. They are just security guards for the Elgen Corporation."

"Oh," Ostin said. "What kind of corporation is that?"

"They build electric power plants."

"Never heard of them," Ostin said.

"Curiously, it's an American corporation, but I don't think they are in America. Too much politics. But lately there are many Elgen guards in Fiji," he said, his voice lowering. "*Many*. Over the last few days I've seen more than ever before. There must be some kind of gathering."

"Must be a Starxource plant convention," Ostin said.

Vishal looked at him peculiarly. "Perhaps." He lifted one of the cannibal forks, then said, "Are you ready to eat?"

"Yes," Ostin said, ignoring his reference to the fork. He couldn't figure out why Vishal was behaving so differently. His instincts told him to run.

"Follow me," Vishal said. As they retraced their steps to the main boulevard, Vishal said to Ostin, "Are you okay?"

"Yes. Why?"

"You seem upset."

"I'm just tired."

". . . And hungry," Jack said. "He gets cranky when he's hungry."

"'Hangry,' we call it," Vishal said.

"That's what we call it too," Jack replied.

When they got to the restaurant, there were several large groups of people outside waiting to get in.

"Looks like there's a long wait," Jack said.

Vishal opened the door. "Not for us."

As they walked in past the groups, a man standing at a host table looked up. "Vee," he said. "So good to see you."

"And you, Kena. As usual, you are busy tonight."

"Always busy with the night market," he said. "But never too busy for you, my friend." He looked at Ostin and Jack. "And your friends."

"American," Vishal said. "California."

"California," he replied. "Good pizza. Come with me." He grabbed three menus and stepped into the crowded restaurant. The three of them followed the man to a table. Kena sat them, then signaled for a server. "Lice will be right with you."

"Thanks," Vishal said.

After he walked away, Ostin said, "Our server's name is Lice?"

Vishal looked at him. "Yes. Is something wrong with that?"

"No," Ostin said. "Nothing."

"This place is packed," Jack said.

"Yes, they have good pizza. Look at the menu. Bacon Cheddar Ham, Taco Pizza, Buffalo Chicken."

"Look," Ostin said. "They call this one 'PizzaMax.' I love PizzaMax."

"What's PizzaMax?" Vishal asked.

"It's a pizza place in Meridian, Idaho," Jack said.

Vishal looked confused. "In Uh-Idaho, California?"

"Yes," Ostin said, glaring at Jack. "In *California*."

Jack breathed out in exasperation. They ordered a Meaty Max pizza and a Bacon Cheddar. It seemed like months since they'd had bacon, which in Jack's previous life had been one of his staples. His best friend, Wade, used to experiment with bacon creations, until one day he brought Jack a bacon ice cream shake, which just about ruined Jack's love for bacon and ice cream.

In addition to the pizza, Jack and Ostin ordered cheese bread and two large sodas. It was a lot of food even for them, but they were hungry and not sure when they would eat again.

Forty minutes later, after they had downed both pizzas, Vishal said, "I have something else for you to try."

"I don't think I could eat another bite," Ostin said.

"You won't have to," Vishal said. "It's a drink."

"Really, you don't need to."

"I insist," Vishal said. He got up and left the table.

"I'm so full," Ostin said. "I don't think I can put anything else down."

"Well, you better," Jack said. "It would be rude not to. Especially since he's getting it just for us."

A moment later Vishal returned carrying a bowl and a glass of coconut milk. He set them down on the table in front of them. Inside the bowl was a thick black liquid.

"This is something very special," Vishal said. "It's a Fijian specialty." He pushed the bowl toward Ostin. "You try it first."

Ostin's stomach groaned, just looking at it.

"Please," Vishal said.

Ostin glanced up at Jack, who narrowed his eyes at him.

"All right. I'll try anything once." He put the bowl to his lip, grimaced, and began to drink. He immediately stopped, his face contorting in pain. He had to force himself not to spit out what was in his mouth. When he had gotten it down, he said, "What is this?"

Vishal grinned darkly. "What do you think it is?"

"It tastes like goat phlegm."

"You've tasted goat phlegm?" Vishal asked.

"No," Ostin said, wiping his mouth with a paper napkin.

"Then how do you know what it tastes like?"

"I was making a point."

"Here," Vishal said, handing Ostin the glass of coconut milk. "Drink some of this. It will take away the bitterness."

"Thanks," Ostin said. He took a drink, then said, "'Bitter' is kind. More like 'intensely gross.'"

"You're being rude," Jack said.

"You try it," Ostin said. "See if you like it." His eyes suddenly widened. "Whoa, my lips are going numb."

Vishal smiled. "That means it's good."

Jack lifted the bowl. "My brother in the marines had to eat raw birds once. This is nothing." Jack tilted back the bowl. He drank more than Ostin but also gagged, setting the still full cup in front of him. "What is that?"

"You didn't like it?"

"No, sir."

"No, I didn't think you would. Non-islanders aren't used to Kava Kava."

Ostin looked at him. "Wait. This is Kava Kava?"

"You've heard of it?" Jack asked, then said, "What am I saying? Of course you've heard of it."

"'Kava' means 'intoxicating pepper,'" Ostin said. "It's a powerful tea. It can even cause hallucinations. It's banned in some countries." Ostin lifted the bowl again and, plugging his nose, took another drink. Then he sat back in his chair. He suddenly felt more relaxed than he had in months. "That feels good." He sounded funny saying it, as his lips felt like they were the size of loaves of bread.

"Yes," Vishal said. "It's very relaxing. Have more."

Jack took another small drink and gagged again. "Still tastes like dirt."

"Even the natives who were raised with it don't like the taste," Vishal said. "But it feels so good. A small price to pay for a second on the lips."

Ostin took another sip. A moment later he said, "I swear my chair is vibrating. Is it just me, or is the room getting bigger?"

"That's the kava," Vishal said. "How do *you* feel, *Moki*?"

Jack rubbed his forehead. "My ears are ringing." He took another drink. "Man, I haven't felt this good since . . . Heather Jennings."

"Who's Heather Jennings?"

"This angel . . ."

Ostin closed his eyes. "Wow. This is . . . so . . . peaceful. I . . .

feel . . . so . . . peaceful. It's the kavalact . . . kavalacto . . . kava . . . "

"Kavalactones," Vishal said. "They are the compound responsible for kava's psychoactive qualities."

"Psychoactive," Ostin said. "I like that word. I've always liked that word. I like big words. They're like those foot-long sandwiches. . . ."

"You sound drunk," Jack said.

"The people here call it getting *krunked*," Vishal said.

"Krunked," Jack repeated. "That's a funny word."

"It's a compound," Ostin said. "'Kava' and 'drunk.'" He suddenly leaned forward and yawned.

"Now, don't go to sleep on me," Vishal said.

"Sorry."

"So, tell me, Thomas. What were the two of you out fishing for?"

"Fishing?" Ostin said. "When did we go fishing?"

"Fishing," Vishal said. "That's what you said you were doing when I found you. Fishing in your raft."

Ostin laughed a little, then said, "Oh, right. We weren't really fishing."

"No?"

"We didn't even have fishing poles," Ostin said.

Jack shook his head. "We didn't even have a raft."

"Yes, I know, Jack," Vishal said. "I watched the two of you jump off a very odd-looking boat and swim to shore."

"Hey, you said Jack's real name," Ostin said. "How did you know his real name?"

"You are very poor liars, Ostin, from Meridian, Idaho. Very poor. Tell me, where were you coming from?"

"Hades," Jack said.

"Hades?" Vishal looked at them quizzically. "The mythical Greek hell?"

"No. Hades in *Tuvalu*."

Vishal immediately stood, knocking his chair back in the motion. His face was dark. "Do not speak of Tuvalu here," he said in a hushed but angry burst.

"Hey, it's cool," Ostin said. "No harm, no foul. It's just a bunch of islands—"

"It's time to go," Vishal said. "Do not speak to anyone." He grabbed Ostin by the arm. "Now."

"Wait," Ostin said, grabbing the bowl of kava. "I'm not done."

"Yes, you are," Vishal said.

"Where are you taking us?" Jack asked.

"Home," Vishal said.

"I don't believe you," Jack said. "I'm not going."

"Yes, you are," Vishal said.

"Who's going to make me?" Jack asked. "You and what army?"

Just then a massive islander walked up behind Vishal. As large as Vishal was, their host was dwarfed compared to the newcomer. The man was almost a foot taller than Vishal and nearly twice as wide. He looked like a mountain of muscle. The man wore dark-lensed aviator sunglasses even though it was night.

"Oh," Jack said, looking the man up and down. "That army."

"Wow. You're a really big dude," Ostin said. "Like, can you even fit in a car?"

"I think he came to beat us up," Jack said. "He looks like he's going to beat us up."

"I don't want to get beat up," Ostin said.

"Whether you get beaten up or not," Vishal said, "depends on how cooperative you are. That begins by you getting up and walking out with me right now."

"I'm going," Ostin said, practically bounding from his chair.

"I'll go," Jack said. "I'm in no condition to put up a fight. Actually, I've never fought a mountain before. Definitely would lose."

The man grabbed Jack by the shirt and lifted him.

"Hey. Easy, man; it's not my shirt."

He walked Jack out behind Ostin and Vishal.

"Where are we going?" Ostin asked.

"For a drive."

"That's not good," Ostin said. "In the movies, that's what the bad guys always say before they kill you. That or 'go for a swim.'"

"Then let's hope we don't go near water," Vishal said.

"Kinda hard when you're on an island," Ostin mumbled.

The two men put Jack and Ostin in the backseat of the van. Then the large man sat in the first bench seat, between them and the door.

"Look," Ostin said. "Big dude *can* fit in a car. But, technically, this isn't a car. It's a utility van. You could probably fit a bull in here." He looked around. "Maybe a small bull."

"Quiet," Vishal said.

"Sorry," Ostin said. He looked at the man who practically took up the entire seat. "Hey, Big Dude. Do you have a name? Or does everyone just call you 'Big Dude.'"

"His name is not your concern," Vishal said.

"That's a really weird name," Ostin said.

"Be quiet," Jack said. "Before he punches you."

"He's not going to punch me."

"Then I will," Jack said.

The large man turned around. "My name is Alveeta," he said, speaking for the first time, in a voice much higher than either of them expected.

"Alveeta," Ostin said. "Nice name."

"Yes. Now shut up, or I will hit you."

"Yes, Alveeta, sir."

Jack and Ostin were nearly asleep when they reached an aluminum-sided warehouse near the harbor where they'd come ashore. Vishal got out and opened a chain-link gate, pulled the van through, and then parked behind the building. He shut off the van, then turned back, looking at Ostin and Jack. "We're all going inside. For your sakes, remain quiet."

"Yes, sir," Jack said.

"So let it be written," Ostin said. "So let it be done."

"Shut up," Vishal said.

"Yes, sir," Ostin said. "It's the kava."

Vishal came around and opened the door. Alveeta climbed out first. "Come out. Now."

"Yes, sir," Jack said.

As they got to the building's metal door, Vishal turned around and said to Jack and Ostin, "Let me introduce you to our friends." He took out a key and unlocked two locks, then opened the door and stepped inside. He turned on the light as Ostin and Jack followed him in.

"I don't see anyone," Ostin said.

Alveeta shut the door behind them, and Vishal opened a side door. "Look in here, please."

Ostin took a step inside the room, then froze. There were three Elgen guards sitting at a table.

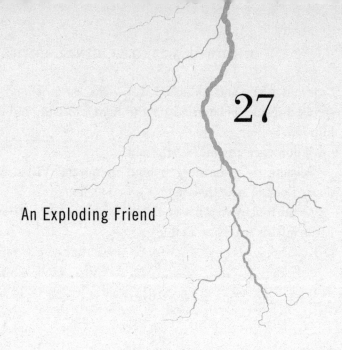

27

An Exploding Friend

"**Y**ou're Elgen," Jack said, suddenly feeling more coherent.

"Of course we are," Vishal said, shutting the side door. "Who did you think we were?"

"We didn't think you were anyone," Ostin said.

"Everyone is someone," Vishal said. "Alveeta, tie their hands behind their backs."

As Alveeta took a thin nylon cord from his pocket, Ostin realized that this had been their plan from the beginning.

"You said you had never heard of the Elgen," Vishal said to Ostin. "Then you made a comment about a Starxource plant."

"That was pretty stupid," Ostin said. "Especially for me."

"And that was before the kava," Jack said.

"What are you going to do to us?" Ostin asked.

"That depends."

"On what?" Ostin said.

"On how cooperative you are. You will answer our questions honestly, or we'll let our Elgen friends know who you really are. Something tells me that you wouldn't like that."

"How will you know if we're being honest?" Ostin asked.

"We'll interrogate you separately. If we get different answers, we'll know that one of you is lying."

"That's a good idea," Ostin said.

Jack shook his head. "Don't tell them that's a good idea."

"I'll take you first," Vishal said to Ostin. He led him into a side office. There was a simple card table with a metal chair in front of it.

"Sit," he said.

"Yes, sir." Ostin sat.

"We'll begin at the beginning. Who are you?"

"You know who we are."

"I know your first names and where you're from, but that's not knowing who you are, is it? Why did you come to Fiji?"

"The first time or the second time?"

"So you've been here before?"

"Yes, sir."

"The first time."

"To get to Tuvalu."

". . . And the second time?"

"To get *away* from Tuvalu."

Vishal nodded. "What brought you to Tuvalu?"

"You. The Elgen."

"You wish to be an Elgen like us?"

Ostin looked at him like he was a moldy doughnut. "I'd rather be fed to rats."

"That can be arranged. Who are you that you have business with the Elgen?"

"I'm with the Electroclan."

"What is that?"

"It's the resistance against the Elgen."

Vishal looked surprised. "You are young to be a member of a resistance."

"It wasn't my choice. We were dragged into it."

"By whom?"

"You. The Elgen."

"Explain."

Ostin took a deep breath. "The whole story?"

"Just explain."

"It started when you made my best friend electric."

"Jack?"

"No. He's not my best friend. Well, he kind of is now, but my real best friend died."

"What do you mean, we made him electric?"

"You don't know?"

Vishal just looked at him. "Humor me."

"Elgen Inc. has a machine that alters the physical electrical properties of unborn humans. That's how you made seventeen electric children."

"Are you electric?"

"No. Neither is Jack. We're the only nonelectrics. Nonels. You know what that is."

Vishal looked at him for a moment, then asked, "Why were you on our boat?"

"We'd stolen it. But then the Philippine Navy captured us. Jack and I were able to escape."

"How?"

"Your guys were using RESATs to paralyze the electric ones. They didn't know Jack and I weren't electric, so we pretended to be paralyzed. Then, when no one was looking, we jumped off the boat."

"Where are the others now?"

"We think the navy took them back to Tuvalu. The *Joule* didn't have enough fuel to make it back, so it came to Fiji to refuel. We rode on the side of the ship until we got close to the shore, then jumped off."

"Why are all these Elgen guards coming to Fiji?"

Ostin looked at him curiously. "You don't know?"

"Just answer my question."

"There was a big battle. Most of the Elgen guards were killed. My guess is that Hatch is trying to reinforce the island before the natives find out."

Vishal suddenly leaned back. "You're telling me the truth?"

"Yes."

"We heard rumors that there was a big explosion. A flash that was seen for more than three hundred miles."

"Yes, sir."

"What was it?"

Ostin looked down. Suddenly his eyes welled up.

"Well?"

"You won't believe me."

"Try me."

Ostin slowly looked up. "That explosion was my best friend."

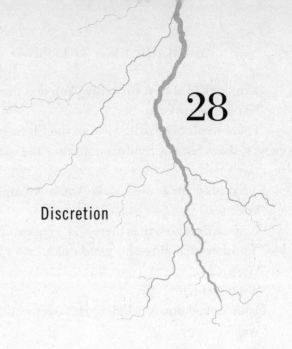

28

Discretion

Vishal gazed at Ostin for a long time before speaking. "What do you mean, the explosion was your friend?"

Even krunked, Ostin knew that whatever he said would not be believed. "My friend, Michael, had a special weapon. When it detonated, it wiped out almost all of the Elgen."

"I have heard the island is glass," Vishal said almost to himself. He stood. "If the Elgen are really that vulnerable, this is good news. It is important news."

"Wait," Ostin said. "Are you Elgen or not? Because now you're talking like you're not."

Vishal ignored his question. "If you're lying, it could cost the lives of thousands of my people. And I guarantee, it will cost you yours."

"I'm not lying. You can ask Jack."

"I intend to. And if you're lying, the punishment will fit the crime."

"I'm not afraid to die," Ostin said.

"Really?"

"I've accepted it," he said. "I've been lucky before. But luck always runs out. Eventually."

Vishal looked at Ostin. "How does a boy from Meridian, Idaho, end up in a battle for the island nation of Tuvalu?"

"I've asked myself that many times."

"And what's the answer?"

"The Elgen kidnapped my best friend's mother. We went to save her."

Vishal was quiet again.

"May I ask you a question?" Ostin said.

Vishal looked at him.

"Who are *you*?"

Vishal tapped his pencil on the table, then looked up at Ostin and said, "I am a Tuvaluan and the leader of the Tuvaluan resistance. I was sailing home from purchasing new scuba equipment in Fiji when I received an emergency radio broadcast that Tuvalu had been invaded. I returned to Fiji, only to find that all communication from Tuvalu had been knocked out.

"There were about two hundred of us Tuvaluans stranded here at that time, and maybe a hundred more who were in Australia or New Zealand and flying back. Against our counsel, a few went back to Tuvalu. We have not heard from them since. We all have family and friends in Tuvalu. We plan to rescue them. That is why your news is of such importance to me."

Ostin nodded. "That's why you found us."

"It was not a coincidence that I was there when you came ashore. I had received word that an Elgen boat was nearing Fiji. I was watching it through binoculars when I saw you jump off the side of it a few hundred meters from shore. I needed to find out who you were and what you knew."

"Why do you have those Elgen guards?"

"We have been capturing them to gain information and to keep them from joining the Elgen force."

"We should take their uniforms," Ostin said. "We've disguised ourselves as Elgen guards before. Now what are you going to do?"

"First I'm going to untie you," he said. He walked around the
table and untied the knots.

Ostin stretched out his arms, then rubbed his wrists. "Thank you."

"Tell me your plans," Vishal said.

"Jack and I are trying to get back to Tuvalu to rescue our friends."

"Then we have similar goals. We're both trying to get back to
Tuvalu."

"And we have a common enemy," Ostin added.

"Do my people know that the Elgen are vulnerable?"

"I don't think so. But they will. There's a man we fought with
named Enele Saluni. He was going to gather his people to fight."

Vishal looked at him with surprise. "You know Enele Saluni?"

"He fought in the battle of Hades with us."

"I feared Enele was dead."

"He almost was. We rescued him from the Elgen prison."

"Where is his grandfather, Prime Minister Saluni?"

Ostin frowned but didn't answer.

Vishal turned pale. "Then he is dead."

"No," Ostin said slowly, shaking his head. "Worse. Much worse."

Vishal leaned forward. "What have they done to that good man?"

"Hatch cut out his tongue, then put him in a monkey cage in the
center of Nike."

Vishal turned pale. "Who is this Hatch?"

"He's the Elgen leader."

Vishal shook his head. "What is Nike?"

"It's the name Hatch gave the main island. Funafuti. He renamed
all the islands. Like Hades."

Vishal's face turned dark with anger. "The Elgen are not worthy of
being called beasts," he said, choking on his words. "Where is Enele?"

"We gave his men the lifeboats from the *Joule* so they could
return to their homes. He planned to gather the natives and lead a
revolution against the Elgen, but he wouldn't know that the Elgen
have already begun rebuilding their forces."

"Then we must hurry to their aid before the Elgen are strong again," Vishal said. He looked at Ostin. "Will you fight with us?"

"Of course. We were planning to fight without you," Ostin said. "I need to rescue my friends. But first we need a way back."

Vishal stood. "If you will fight with us, I will take you back myself."

Jack was surprised to see the change in Vishal's and Ostin's demeanors as they walked from the office. They almost looked like friends.

"Alveeta," Vishal said. "Release Jack. These men are not our enemies."

Alveeta looked as surprised as Jack did. "How do you know this?"

"Because I have questioned him, and what he says adds up. And he knows Enele Saluni."

Alveeta looked at Ostin warily. "Why would you trust this boy? He has done nothing but try to deceive us since he arrived."

"As did we," Vishal said. "In such days, discretion is the better part of wisdom. Trust me, he is with us."

Alveeta walked over and untied Jack's hands. Jack rubbed his wrists. "What's going on, man?" he asked. "If you're not Elgen, who are you?"

Ostin said, "They're Tuvaluans. We're going to help them, and they're going to help us."

"We need to assemble everyone immediately," Vishal said to Alveeta. "The Elgen are vulnerable right now. That's why the guards have been gathering. The great explosion we heard about destroyed most of the Elgen forces. I'm going to put out the call." He walked back into his office.

After he was gone, Alveeta asked Jack, "Do you know Enele too?"

Jack nodded. "We fought together."

"Is he still alive?"

"He was the last time I saw him," Jack said. "You know him?"

"He was my friend," Alveeta said. "We went to grade school together."

"He fought bravely," Jack said. "He helped us hold the prison."

"You are fortunate to have fought with him. You get to know a man in battle."

"Something tells me you'll be getting to know us all better real soon," Jack replied.

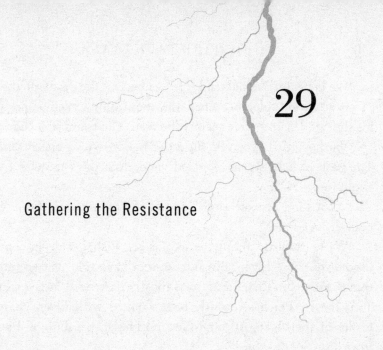

29

Gathering the Resistance

"It's a good thing we had that nap earlier," Ostin said to Jack. "I don't think we're getting any sleep tonight."

Jack watched the doors as more and more people filed into the warehouse. "I think you're right," he said.

Within an hour of Vishal's first phone call, there were more than fifty Tuvaluans gathered in the warehouse. By midnight there were more than two hundred. There were both men and women, but the majority were men.

"How many are missing?" Vishal asked, standing on a wooden crate to look over the crowd.

"I know of a few who have left Fiji," one of the men said.

"Where is Rynal?"

"I'm right here." The squat man behind the voice approached. "Sorry I'm late. What's this emergency?"

"We'll begin," Vishal said. He walked to the front of the room. "Your attention, please." When the room didn't silence, he took off his shoe and slammed it against the wall. The room silenced.

"We have just received the information we've been waiting for. The flash of light Rynal reported seeing four days ago was a verified explosion."

"What kind of explosion?" one of the men asked. "Do they have nuclear weapons?"

"We know little about the explosive," Vishal said. "Except it was used *against* the Elgen. But our sources have told us two important things. First, the Elgen army was mostly destroyed in the explosion. That is why Fiji has recently been flooded with Elgen guards. The leader of the Elgen, Admiral-General Hatch, is calling in his guards from around the world."

"There are many new guards in Vanuatu and Samoa as well," a woman said.

"My cousin in Tonga says the same," said someone else in the crowd, nodding.

"They are clearly calling them in," Vishal said. "Which only adds to the validity of the report. Second, Enele Saluni is still alive. He is gathering forces among our people. It is our hope to unite with him and help him overthrow the Elgen."

There was a notable rise in noise from the crowd.

"Where is he?" someone asked. "Where's Enele?"

"We're not sure," Vishal said.

Someone shouted from the crowd, "Who are these sources we'll be risking our lives for?"

"*A ia e fui talia,*" Vishal muttered to Ostin. "This man's name is Namase. He agrees with much difficulty."

"Who is it?" Namase repeated.

"I can't tell you," Vishal said. "Only that they will be going with us into battle."

". . . Or into a trap."

"It's not a trap," Vishal said.

"Do you know that? Who are these sources of yours? How could they know what's going on in Tuvalu? No one gets in or out."

"We did," Jack said, standing. "And it's not a trap. It's not going to be a cakewalk either, but if you want to take out the Elgen, this is the best chance you're ever going to get."

Everyone turned and looked at him.

Namase eyed him. "Who are you?"

"I'm Jack. I'm with the Electroclan."

"What's 'Electroclan'?"

"I know that boy," someone shouted. "He was with J.D. when they sailed to Tuvalu. J.D. never came back."

"J.D. was a traitor," Ostin said. "Why do you think the Elgen allowed him to sail to their islands?"

"They are not *their* islands," someone shouted. "They are *ours*! And our children's!"

"That's not what I meant," Ostin said. "J.D. was paid by the Elgen to deliver us to them."

"Why would the Elgen want you?" Namase asked.

"They don't want me. They wanted the rest of our group. The electric ones."

"The boy in the girl's shirt makes no sense."

"It's not my shirt," Ostin said. "The Elgen accidentally created seventeen electric children. They have been gathering them. We went there to rescue them."

"And how did you get out?"

"We stole their submersible boat. But before we got here, we were stopped by the Philippine Navy."

"I can verify that," Rynal said. "I flew over them. There were three navy ships, one of them a full battle cruiser. They had surrounded a strange-looking boat. They were taking people off of it."

"And I saw them jump off the boat," Vishal said.

"That's when we escaped," Ostin said. "We're the only two who weren't electric."

"Where is the boat now?" Namase asked.

"It left this afternoon," Vishal said. "I would guess back to Tuvalu."

Namase exploded. "You think we're fools? You think we believe this crazy story of submerging boats and electric children? Why would we listen to this boy in a girl's shirt?"

"Enough with the shirt already," Ostin said.

Vishal turned red in the face. "I don't care what you believe, Namase. Stay here with the cowards. But you'll never return to Tuvalu with your head up."

"*None* of us with a head on our shoulders will ever return to Tuvalu," Namase said. "And those of you fool enough to believe stories of electric children are just fools who are going to follow this man into slavery or death."

Suddenly a low voice from the back of the room said, "The electric children are real."

Everyone turned to see who had spoken. An elderly, silver-haired man stood against the back wall, leaning on a cane. One of his legs was in a cast. He was Maatia Maani, a respected Tuvaluan elder and former government minister. He had been meeting with Fijian officials when the Elgen attacked Tuvalu. But it was not respect for his government office that silenced the crowd; it was respect for his position as island elder. There were only three elders left in Tuvalu, and they were regarded with deity-like respect. Everyone silenced to hear what he had to say.

Maatia blinked as he panned the quiet room with his ancient, dark eyes. "The electric children this young man speaks of are real. I have seen them with my own eyes."

He said something to the young man next to him, then began limping forward, leaning heavily on his cane, with the young man at his side. The crowd parted for him as he hobbled to the front of the room. When he reached the front, he bowed slightly to Vishal, then turned back to face the crowd.

"A month before the Elgen attack, I was riding my bicycle on Funafuti near the Elgen power plant when I came upon two Americans, a boy and a girl about these young people's ages," he said, pointing at Jack and Ostin. "They were throwing stones at a dog. Hurting the dog. I told them to stop. They were very disrespectful and told me to mind my own business. They called me many names that I think they did not think I would understand. I told them that they had poor manners and should respect the elderly.

"The young woman said to me, 'Maybe you should respect the *young* or you might get hurt.' Then she reached out her hand, and like magic my bike was pulled out from under me, as if she were a powerful magnet. I fell hard to the ground. That is how I broke my leg." He frowned. "They both laughed when I fell. They enjoyed that a great deal."

Indignation rose in the room.

"They will pay," someone shouted. "Who are these youths?"

Maatia raised his hand to silence them. ". . . After I fell, the young man walked over to me. He smiled at me; then he put his hand over my bicycle. Electric sparks came out of his hand. He cut my bicycle in half. I thought I was watching a demon."

"I saw the bicycle with my own eyes," the young man next to him said. "It was cut in two pieces. The metal was melted in a way I'd never seen before." He turned back to the elder. "My apologies for interrupting, Elder."

"Thank you for sharing your testimony." The old man looked around. "I have seen many peculiar things in my life but nothing as peculiar as those two youths."

"That would be Kylee and Bryan," Jack said. "They're two of Hatch's Glows. They're bad news."

"There were seventeen kids born with electric power," Ostin said. "Each of their powers is different. Some of them are with the Elgen, like Bryan and Kylee; the rest are now against them. But now the Elgen have captured all of them. After what they did to his army, we're pretty sure he'll kill them."

Vishal turned to the crowd. "Do you believe me now? Or will you deny the testimony of Elder Maani and these young friends who have already risked their lives fighting our battle for us?"

"No," Namase said humbly. "My apologies."

Vishal looked around the room. "Time is against us. Every day the Elgen force will grow in strength. We must sail as soon as possible. Nikhil, you have the fastest boat. Alveeta, the Americans and I will

go with you and your crew. We will find Enele, then radio everyone
to join forces."

"Do we have weapons?" Jack asked.

"We have some," Vishal said.

"The Elgen have enough weapons to equip a large army."

Vishal looked at Jack as if he were unimpressed. "Then we will
have to borrow theirs."

The Tuvaluans spent a sleepless night gathering weapons and supplies
for the three-day journey to Tuvalu. As the dawn sun began to rise
above the turquoise blue South Pacific, there were, in all, one hundred
and sixty-four men and eight women who had volunteered to fight.
The remaining forty-six women and twelve men joined together to
make a plan to slow the Elgen guards' departure from Fiji to Tuvalu,
using Fijian travel regulations. This was Elder Maani's idea.

"Even the smallest of us can keep ten or more Elgen guard from
joining the battle through paperwork and regulations or whatever
means available," the elder said. "Oftentimes in war, more damage is
done by a bureaucrat with a pen than a soldier with a rifle."

One of the young women added, "Or a woman with a smile. It
was a pretty woman who kept the British from attacking the American colonial army when they were at their weakest."

The elder nodded. "A pretty face is a powerful weapon indeed."

While the Tuvaluans made their preparations, Ostin and Jack spent
most of the night with Vishal, writing notes on the island maps,
detailing what they knew of where the Elgen strongholds were. The
most important question they couldn't answer was where Enele was
and how they would find him.

"If I were him," Jack said. "I would first rescue my grandfather."

Ostin shook his head. "I don't think so. Nike is the Elgen's stronghold. With a force that small, even surviving Elgen guards could stop
them. I think Enele is patient. He will gather men and weapons first,
then free his grandfather. Prime Minister Saluni has already been
imprisoned since Hatch took over. What's a few more days?"

Alveeta nodded. "I think little Ostin is right. The Enele I know is not one to let his heart outrun his brain."

Ostin looked at the map of Tuvalu. He put his finger on Hades, then moved it down. "If I were him, I would go to where the largest potential number of soldiers were located." He touched the map. "That would be here, the closest island, Nanumaga. That's where the Elgen grow their food. It will be filled with hundreds of young, strong workers. They'll also need food and water; both would be plentiful there. The only thing they won't have is weapons."

"Then where?" Jack said.

Ostin studied the map again, then said, "The next closest island is Nui, the Elgen's science island, where the *Volta* is docked. But there's nothing there for them except scientists. Like I said, they may gather people on Nanumaga, but without weapons they're not soldiers. The most likely way for them to secure weapons would be to sail south to Vaitupu. That's where the Elgen train their guards and dock their warships. Before the battle of Hades it would have been suicide to go there, but I'm guessing that it's probably only guarded now by a skeleton crew of a few dozen guards."

Jack said, "Enele's forces would probably land there after dark, when they are less likely to be seen."

Ostin's forehead furrowed. "Not necessarily. The Elgen have advanced night-vision technology, which would give them the advantage. If they attack during the day, they're on equal ground. Or might even have the advantage since they are better hunters and know the land better."

"So the real question," Vishal said, "is, would Enele think of all that?"

"How long would it take them to get from Nanumaga to Vaitupu?" Jack asked.

"That depends on what boats they are able to secure from Nanumaga. If there are none and they keep the *Joule*'s tenders, it will take them two days."

Jack nodded. "After Vaitupu, where would he go?"

"The only other island between Vaitupu and Funafuti is Nukufetau," Ostin said, "the one Hatch renamed Plutus. That's where the

Joule was docked. But there's no reason for them to go there, so I'm guessing that Enele would bypass it and sail directly to here"—Ostin drew his finger in an arc around the east side of the island—"landing on the northeastern side of Funafuti."

"That side of the island is very much jungle," Alveeta said.

"Yes. If they have many people, it would give them the cover to land and move in toward the Starxource plant. And," Ostin said, looking at Jack, "rescue his grandfather."

"I do not think they will stop in Vaitupu," Vishal said. "Family is all in Tuvalu. Enele might stop in Nanumaga for supplies, but then he would go to Funafuti to rescue his grandfather."

"But would he go without weapons?" Ostin said as he looked away from the map.

"Would they not find weapons on Nanumaga?"

"Where there are Elgen, there are weapons," Jack said.

"If we sail to Vaitupu and they've already started to attack Funafuti, we will be too late to help," Alveeta said.

Ostin rubbed his head. "We could really use Ian right now."

"Who is Ian?" Vishal asked.

"He's one of the electrics," Jack said. "He can see for miles and miles."

"I can see for many thousands of miles," Alveeta said.

Ostin looked at him. "You can?"

"Yes. Every night I look up at the stars."

"Not what we meant," Ostin mumbled to himself.

"All right," Vishal said, looking exhausted. "We sail to Funafuti and hope he is there."

"What do you think of that?" Jack quietly asked Ostin.

Ostin rubbed his chin, then said, "I just hope that Enele is a better strategist than Vishal."

With the exception of those still loading the boats, the Tuvaluans met for a final time in the warehouse.

"*Talofa*," Vishal said to those gathered before him. "Many centuries ago our people defended themselves from the people who came by canoe from the Fijian islands. Today we come from the Fijian islands not to steal our lands but to reclaim them, the land of our ancestors' bones. *Konei, e o ai? E o koulua.* These lands are ours, not the Elgen's. The spirits of our ancestors will travel with us. We go not by canoe but by modern boats. But the spirit is the same.

"Rynal will fly ahead of our boats and send us reports of any Elgen activity. We'll stay far enough apart from each other to not arouse suspicion, but close enough to be of protection to each other. We may encounter other boats as the Elgen guard arrive. Those who stay behind will do what they can to stop those coming from Fiji, and they will let us know what boats make it off the island, so that we can look for them. We will sink them before they make it to Tuvalu.

"When we reach Niulakita, you will dock on the southeast shore and wait until you receive word from me. We will go ahead of you to Funafuti, seeking Enele and his warriors. When we find them, we will alert you before we attack the Elgen stronghold. Not a minute before." He looked over the tired but impassioned patriots. "There is much danger ahead. I fear that much blood will wet the soil of our home. But we will be courageous and we will not fail." He pounded his chest. "Tuvaluans, be of great strength."

The group returned the greeting, likewise striking their chests. "Be of great strength."

"That was a good speech," Jack said as Vishal walked back to him.

Vishal did not smile. "Let's hope it's not my last."

The group moved silently out of the warehouse. Ostin and Jack followed Vishal, Alveeta, Nikhil, and two of his crewmen out to Nikhil's boat. There were already three other crewmen on board.

In all, there were twenty-one vessels in the Tuvaluan armada. They were mostly commercial fishing or transport ships, with the exception of Nikhil's boat, which was a high-speed commercial touring yacht called the *MAS*.

"What's 'MAS' stand for?" Ostin asked Vishal as they boarded.

"I don't know. Nikhil won't tell anyone."

Nikhil overheard the question. "It means whatever you want it to."

"What does it mean to you?"

"That's for me to know."

Ostin climbed aboard the boat. When Nikhil was out of earshot, he asked Jack, "What do you think it stands for?"

He shrugged. "'Maniac at steering wheel.' How about you?"

"Well, in Spanish '*más*' means 'more.' But MAS is also an acronym for the disease macrophage activation syndrome, which, as you know, is a life-threatening complication of rheumatic disease. But then I thought, why would he name his boat after a disease, especially one that occurs much more frequently in juveniles than adults?"

Jack looked at him in wonder. "Does your brain ever want to, like, explode?"

"Brains don't explode. Unless you want to define an intracranial aneurism as an explosion; arguably a rupture could be called—"

"Stop, stop," Jack said, holding up his hand. He walked down a stairway belowdecks, talking to himself. "I wish someone would explode my brain."

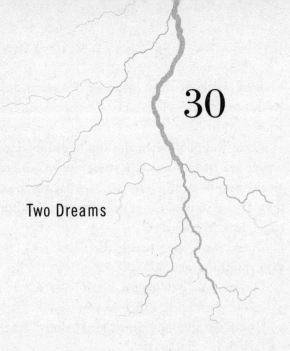

30

Two Dreams

The sun had just begun to creep above the horizon as the boats, one by one, headed out to sea. The sea was as calm as it had been the day Jack and Ostin had arrived in Fiji. Vishal spent most of the day in the cabin with Captain Nikhil, studying maps and communicating with other boats. By the end of the first day, the fleet was spread out more than ten miles. No Elgen were spotted, but there was one incident that slowed the fleet down. One of the older boats broke down and had to be abandoned, its passengers, cargo, and fuel distributed among the other ships.

The atmosphere on the *MAS* was tense, and most of her occupants kept to themselves. The beautiful weather felt like a lie, since everyone knew there were war clouds ahead. It seemed that with each mile the tension grew still greater. At one point, Jack took one of the guns they'd stored belowdecks and went to the back of the boat to shoot. The diversion didn't last long because Nikhil sent one of his crew back to tell Jack to stop wasting ammunition.

Ostin was glad when the sun began its descent into the rippling-orange sea and he and Jack went belowdecks to the berths. Ostin lay on the middle of three bunks; Jack lay on the bottom. An hour after they'd gone to bed, Ostin rolled over in his bunk toward the outside edge. "Jack. You awake?"

There was a long pause, then Jack said, "If I said *no*, would that stop you from talking?"

"That would be illogical, because—"

"Stop," Jack said. "What do you want?"

"I was just thinking they should almost be there by now."

Jack didn't respond.

"What do you think Hatch will do to them?"

Jack was silent for a moment, then said, "I don't want to think about it."

"Me neither. Do you think *we're* going to live through this?"

"I don't know."

"What's your gut feeling?"

"You don't want to know," Jack said.

"I really do."

"I didn't think we were going to live through the battle of Hades."

"Me neither. If it wasn't for Michael, we wouldn't have."

Jack sighed. "How many guards do you think Hatch will bring in?"

Ostin thought it over. "The short answer?"

"Sure."

"However many he needs to feel safe."

"What's the long answer?"

"At last count there were seventy-two operating Starxource plants. I've never seen less than twenty guards at each plant we've been in, but they run 24/7, so if they keep eight-hour shifts, triple that number. That would make for four thousand three hundred and twenty guards at plants. If Hatch keeps a skeleton crew on each plant and pulls in two-thirds of them, that would be approximately two thousand eight hundred and eighty guards on their way to Tuvalu. Of course that's all speculation."

Jack groaned. "Almost three thousand highly trained, armed guards against one hundred seventy-four of us. I don't like those odds."

"Last time we fought them off with less."

"Yeah, and we had the Electroclan."

". . . And Michael," Ostin said.

"That's why we've got to find Enele and his army," Jack said.

"What if we don't find them?"

"Then we go with plan B."

"Plan B? What's plan B?"

Jack said softly, "We are the army."

Ostin rolled back over and closed his eyes. He didn't want to ask any more questions.

Not surprisingly, neither Jack nor Ostin slept well that night. Ostin didn't fall asleep until after three in the morning. He woke several hours after sunrise to see Jack sitting on the bunk opposite him eating something.

"What's for breakfast?" Ostin.

"Coconut granola bars." Jack threw him one. "How'd you sleep?"

Ostin began to unwrap the bar. "Bad."

"Me too," Jack said.

"I had the weirdest dream. The weirdest part was that it seemed so real. I could almost swear it was real."

"That's bizarre," Jack said. "I did too. Tell me yours first."

"I was lying in bed when I suddenly saw Michael. He was just standing there, his feet a few inches off the floor. And I could kind of see through him, except he was so bright. Like a fluorescent lightbulb."

"Hold on," Jack said. "You dreamed that Michael was, like, floating in the air, right here next to us?"

"Yes."

"That's the exact same dream I had. Except, in my dream, he gave me a message. He said we would find Enele on . . . He said two places, one started with an *N*, the other with an *P*. Sounded like a planet . . . Pluto."

"*Plutus*," Ostin said. "He said to find Enele we needed to go to the island Hatch calls Plutus, the one the Tuvaluans call Nukufetau. He said Enele was sent there by . . ."

". . . Elder Malakite . . . ," Jack said.

"Malakai," Ostin corrected. "He went to talk to him before going to war."

"Dude, we had the exact same dream. Except it was like you said, it didn't seem like a dream."

"Maybe it wasn't a dream."

"What do you mean?"

"Maybe that really was Michael."

Suddenly Jack's expression changed. "Stop," he said. "Don't even go there. Michael's dead. Just like Wade and Tanner and Gervaso."

"But what if he isn't?"

"I *said*, stop it," Jack said angrily. "It's just wrong."

"Then explain the dream."

Jack took a deep breath. "I can't."

Ostin climbed out of his bunk. "Just a minute." He walked out of the room, returning a moment later with a pen and piece of paper. He wrote something down on the paper, then folded it into a square.

"What are you doing?" Jack said.

Ostin handed the paper to Jack. "I'm telling you, I don't think it was just a dream. At the end of the dream, just before Michael left, he said something very specific. Do you remember?"

Jack thought for a moment, then said, "Yes."

"What did he say?"

"He said something like, 'You will be attacked. But hold on. I will be there when I can.' Then he said, 'Look for the . . .' It was a really weird word, sounded like '*hurry at you*.'"

Ostin said, "Open the paper."

Jack unfolded the piece of paper. Ostin had written:

You will be attacked. Hold on.
I will be there when I can. Look for the Uira te Atua.

Jack looked up. "How did you do that?"

"It wasn't a trick," Ostin said. "That's what he said to me too."

Jack was speechless.

"What if Michael isn't dead, just *changed*?"

"What do you mean, changed?"

"Energy can't be created nor destroyed; it just changes from one form to another. Just like chemical energy can't be destroyed, but it can be converted into kinetic energy."

"I don't know what you're saying," Jack said. "What's kinetic energy?"

"It's energy in motion. For instance, if you take nitroglycerin, a chemical compound, and detonate it, like in dynamite, you've changed chemical energy to kinetic energy."

"What's your point?"

"Hear me out," Ostin said. "This is just a *what if*, but before Hades, Michael was becoming more and more electric—he was becoming more *energy* and less *matter*. What if, then, when the lightning struck him, it completed the process and he became pure energy?"

"And then he couldn't be destroyed," Jack said.

"No. He was converted to kinetic energy, which changed to thermal energy, like a nuclear blast."

"But then, after the explosion, he's gone."

"Not really," Ostin said. "What if he is trapped in some kind of energy field and he's trying to reestablish himself? Taylor said he appeared to her but didn't say anything. We both saw him and he spoke to us. That means his consciousness is still attached to his energy. It also means he's starting to figure himself out."

"Then Michael is . . . energy?"

"We're all energy," Ostin said. "Michael's just *pure* energy. Einstein believed that energy could be turned into matter, which, in 1997, was proven when a linear collider, using a high-powered electron beam and an electric field, was able to collide the photons in a way to produce matter."

Jack shook his head. "I have no idea what you just said."

"What I just said is that I believe that Michael is pure energy trying to convert himself back into matter."

"You mean, you think Michael's trying to come back?"

Ostin looked at him. "I think he already has."

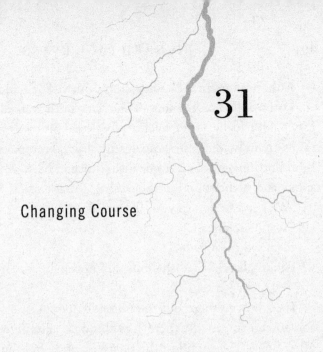

31

Changing Course

"The problem now," Jack said, standing up from his bunk, "is how do we tell Vishal we need to change destinations?"

"We just tell him the truth," Ostin said.

Jack frowned. "The *truth*? You want to tell Vishal that Michael appeared to us like a ghost? He'd have us thrown overboard."

Ostin thought on that. "Yeah, he wouldn't go for that."

"We could tell him that we suddenly remembered that Enele told us he was going to Nukufetau."

"We just suddenly remembered? He's not going to buy that. That's not something you'd forget." Ostin thought a little more, then said, "I think we just tell him that we both had the same dream."

"A dream. How's that any different from a ghost story?"

Ostin shook his head. "These native guys put a lot of stock in dreams."

After a moment Jack said, "Can't hurt." Then added, "Too much."

Ostin pulled on his shirt. Then they both walked up to the boat's cab. Nikhil was wearing aviator sunglasses and was seated in the captain's chair, holding the wheel. Vishal was seated a few meters from him. Both men looked tired. Vishal turned back as they entered. He spoke above the sound of the ocean. "What's up?"

"We need to talk to you," Jack said.

"Yeah? Go ahead."

"Can we go outside?"

Nikhil glanced at Vishal but said nothing.

"Sure," Vishal said.

He followed them out the portside door. It was another clear day, and to the southwest there was the pale silhouette of one of their other boats. The sound of the boat's engines and the hydroplaning of the boats on the waves was the only real noise.

"What's on your minds, guys?"

"We think we need to change destinations," Jack said.

Vishal looked back and forth between them. "We already went through this. What are you up to?"

"Nothing," Jack said. "It's just . . . last night we both had the same dream." He looked at Ostin. "You explain."

"We dreamed that our friend Michael came to us in the night. He told us both the exact same thing."

Vishal looked at them skeptically. "Which was . . . ?"

"That we will find Enele on Nukufetau."

Vishal shook his head. "Why would he go to Nukufetau? There is no reason at all for them to go there." He frowned. "We already spoke of this back in Fiji. It was either Vaitupu or Funafuti. We're sticking with Funafuti."

"But we had a dream," Ostin said.

"A dream?" Vishal said, his voice sharp with annoyance. "Shall I lead these people to their deaths because of a dream you had? We've made our plans. We'll follow them."

"It was a dream we *both* had," Jack said.

"Okay, shall I lead them to their deaths because of a dream you both had?"

Jack shook his head. "You've got to admit that's weird."

"In the world of dreams, everything is weird."

Ostin said, "In the dream, our friend said that Elder Malakai sent Enele to Nukufetau."

Vishal's expression suddenly changed. "Who did you say?"

"Malakai. The elder."

"How did you know that name?"

"It was in the dream," Jack said.

Vishal suddenly looked worried. "'Malakai' is a name only known by a few. You could not have known that name."

"In our dream, Michael told us that Enele had gone to see Malakai in Nui."

Again Vishal looked surprised. "How did you know that the great elder was on Nui? That is information that had been kept very secret."

"The dream," Ostin said. "He said Enele went there to get Malakai's blessings before going to war."

"That is our way. We consult the elders before battle. Just as we did in Fiji." Vishal looked back and forth between the two of them. "Did he say anything else?"

"He said something about the *Uira te Atua*."

Vishal turned white. "How do you know that phrase? It is sacred, in an ancient language, known only to a few."

"We told you," Jack said. "That's what he said in the dream."

"We're not making this up," Ostin said.

"No," Vishal said. "No one could have made that up."

Jack looked at Vishal seriously. "What do you think?"

Vishal took a deep breath, then breathed out slowly. "I think we better change course to Nukufetau."

PART THIRTEEN

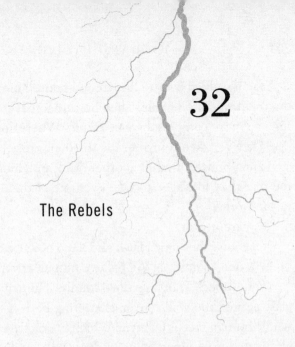

32

The Rebels

EGG Amon walked anxiously into Hatch's office, carrying news he didn't want to share. "Admiral-General, sir, I've two messages to deliver."

Hatch looked up from the financial report he was reviewing. "Give me the bad news first."

Amon took a deep breath, subconsciously preparing for Hatch's explosion. "We've just received notice that the *Edison* has been sunk."

Hatch stared at the EGG in disbelief. "By whom?"'

"The rebels."

"The rebels?" Hatch's face began to turn red. "The rebels were on unarmed, slow-moving cattle ships. The *Edison* is a Kirov-class anti-ship, anti-submarine battle cruiser." Hatch slammed down his fist. "You don't sink a battle cruiser with a cattle boat!"

"It was a suicide attack, sir. One of the rebel boats was filled with explosives and managed to get behind the *Edison*."

Hatch walked over to his bar and poured himself a Scotch, downing the drink in one gulp. Then he turned back to Amon and, speaking in a more composed voice, asked, "Where are the rebels now?"

"They've taken refuge inside the depository."

Hatch poured himself another drink and drained it. "You're telling me that they managed to take over one of the most secure buildings in the world?"

"Apparently, sir."

"Of course they did," Hatch said. "And how, exactly, did that happen?"

"We don't know, sir. We believe human error."

"You think?!" Hatch groaned loudly. "Human error!" He threw the glass against the wall mirror, shattering both it and the mirror. "The whole human race is an error. Which is exactly why the sooner we've eliminated the human being from this planet, the better. What is the status of the rebel boats?"

"The *Edison* managed to take out all the rebel boats except the *Proton*, the smallest of the agricultural boats. They also have a few lifeboats and rafts."

Hatch looked at the map of the islands he'd mounted on the wall. "Plutus is within range of our Apache helicopters. I want you to order an attack on whatever they're floating on. We don't have the men or time to wage war on them right now, but at least we can strand them on the island. We'll make the island itself a prison, like Alcatraz in San Francisco. Once we've rebuilt the guard, we'll take the rebels apart. On our timetable, not theirs."

"Yes, sir."

"You said you had two messages."

"Yes, sir. I've also received notice that Captain Shool of the Philippine Navy has reached Nukulaelae."

"Where?"

Amon realized his error and slightly bowed. "Excuse me, Admiral. I meant the island of *Dionysus*, the island *formerly* known as Nukulaelae."

"It's about time. Is the *Joule* with them?"

"No, sir. The *Joule* was delayed with refueling. She'll be arriving four hours later."

"And she's safe?"

"Yes. She is being accompanied by one of the Filipino battle cruisers."

"Very well."

"They made good time, sir. Less than fifty hours."

Hatch went back to his report without comment. Amon continued to stand at attention. After another minute Hatch asked, "What is it, EGG?"

"Will you be greeting Captain Shool, sir?"

"No," Hatch said. "It's still too dangerous for me to leave the plant."

"Sir, someone must greet him. It's protocol."

Hatch looked up from his papers. "I had no intention of leaving him unattended, EGG. You and a contingency of guards will greet the captain and bring him back to the plant along with their prisoners."

"Yes, sir. You mean Welch and the Glows."

"That's exactly who I mean." Then a slow, angry smile spread over Hatch's lips. "You have no idea how excited I am to see Welch again. And my Glows. My only problem is deciding what I am going to do with them. So many traitors, so many possibilities."

"Yes, sir."

"On second thought, EGG, maybe I will greet the captain. I want to see Welch's face when he comes off the ship. Radio me when they are docking."

"Yes, sir."

"You can go, EGG."

"Yes, sir," Amon said. Then he spun around and quickly walked away.

Two hours later, Hatch, flanked by Amon and a half dozen guards, greeted the Filipino captain as he walked down the gangplank onto the Elgen dock.

"Captain Shool," Hatch said, stepping forward. "Welcome to the Hatch Islands."

The captain saluted. "Admiral Hatch. It's an honor."

"The pleasure is mine, Captain. You have our prisoners?"

"Seventeen of them, Admiral. Including the one you call Welch."

Hatch smiled. "Congratulations, Captain, on a well-executed operation. Such competency will not go unrecognized. I will see to it that President Bautista is informed of your success."

"Thank you, sir."

"Where are your prisoners now?"

"They're still in the brig awaiting your orders."

"Very well. Have Welch brought to me immediately. In chains, of course."

"Of course, sir."

Captain Shool turned to one of his guards and spoke quickly in his native tongue. The guard ran back up the gangplank into the boat.

"It seems that all went well with the capture of the mutineers."

"Yes. The machines you gave us were quite remarkable. They paralyzed all of the youths except one."

Hatch looked at him. "Which one?"

"There was a young Fijian woman who was the ship's cook."

"How many teens did you capture?" Hatch asked.

"Twelve."

"Twelve," Hatch repeated. "I guess they didn't all make it off of Hades, then."

At that moment two burly, heavily armed Filipino soldiers walked down the plank, escorting Welch between them. Hatch looked up at him with a grim smile. "There he is."

"The one you call Welch," Shool said.

"*Traitor* Welch," Hatch said.

The soldiers dragged their prisoner in front of Hatch.

"So the prodigal returns," Hatch said.

"Not by choice," Welch said.

"I expect not. What traitor wants to be held accountable for his cowardice?"

"One man's traitor is another man's hero."

"Don't fool yourself, Welch. You're no one's hero." He looked him over. "You've looked better. You didn't really think you could escape, did you?"

"I didn't think we could decimate your army either, but we did, didn't we?"

Hatch sneered. "Michael Vey did. And, frankly, it was worth the loss just to be through with him." Hatch turned to EGG Amon. "Take your former colleague and lock him up in Cell 25."

Welch looked at Hatch and said, "You're not going to win."

Hatch smiled. "I already have, David." He turned to Amon. "Take the traitor away."

"Yes, Admiral."

"What would you like done with the others?" Shool asked.

"The Glows," Hatch said. "Put them under full guard, and EGG Bowen will lead you to the prison. We'll hold them until they stand trial."

"Yes, Admiral."

Shool again issued an order to his men, then turned back to Hatch. "Should we deactivate the machines you gave us?"

"The RESATs? No! Never turn off those machines!"

The captain was taken back the intensity of Hatch's reaction. "As you wish, Admiral."

"You don't understand," Hatch said. "If you turn off the RESATs, you'll have a much bigger problem than you could ever imagine."

Shool looked unimpressed. "They're just teens, Admiral."

"No, Captain. They're not 'just' anything. You have no idea what you're holding in your brig. Had you attempted to take those 'teens' without the machines I provided you, they would have taken you *and* your ships."

The captain looked at Hatch cynically. "You hold us in contempt, sir. My soldiers are decorated, well-trained fighting men of the highest caliber."

"I meant no disrespect, Captain. I'm sure your men are the elite of your navy. You just don't know what you don't know. These youths are not ordinary humans. They are a science experiment gone awry. In the last week those youths have killed more than four thousand of my men and wiped out the whole of my navy."

Shool looked at him with amazement. "I had no idea, Admiral. Why was I not informed of this danger?"

"If you have to walk a tightrope without a net, it's better not to know how high up you are, if you know what I mean. What about the *Joule*'s crew, COB Quinn and his men?"

"They're being held in the brig as well. Would you like me to release them?"

"You'll release them to ZC Denkers," Hatch said. He signaled for the Zone Captain. "Denkers, Captain Shool will be releasing the COB and his men into your custody. Take them to the bowl and have the crew prepare them for dinner."

"Yes, sir," Denkers said.

From Hatch's order the captain assumed the Elgen COB and his men would be guests at the dinner, not be the meal.

Hatch turned back to the captain. "Please, come inside and avail yourself of my hospitality. We have an officers' club that has no parallel in this part of the world—companionship and the finest European food and drink, including some of your local favorites—coconut wine, Tondenia premium rum, and San Miguel for your men—as well as a few imported specialties. Have you ever tasted Karuizawa, Captain?"

The captain almost laughed. "The Japanese whiskey? No, sir. That's a bit above my pay grade."

"At forty-thousand dollars a bottle, I would think so," Hatch said. "Or the officers of the Philippine Navy would be the envy of the world. I have a lovely forty-eight-year-old bottle in my office that you and I will open tonight to celebrate your success. Now, if you'll excuse me, I have other matters to attend to."

"Of course. Thank you, Admiral, for your kindness. I will look forward to seeing you tonight."

Hatch started to walk away, then suddenly stopped and turned back. "Captain, have you ever seen how a Starxource plant operates?"

"No, sir. It is my understanding that the operation is top secret."

"Yes. But you, of course, have top secret clearance. Tonight you will get a rare view of what few have ever seen. Trust me, you'll never forget it." With that Hatch turned and walked away.

PART FOURTEEN

33

The Dinner Jacket

Welch had never been more than a few feet inside Cell 25, but he knew enough about it to fear it. He never imagined he would someday occupy it. The infamous cell was designed to bring its occupant the maximum amount of stress, fear, and pain. Hatch sometimes used Tara to create an added dimension of terror, but even without her contributions it was horrible. He wondered how long he would be able to endure it.

While Welch was locked away by Amon and three guards, the Electroclan was taken to the dungeon with the RESATs strapped to their chests and their hands chained behind their backs.

In spite of Hatch's orders to keep the youths separated, there weren't enough cells to give everyone his or her own, so McKenna and Cassy were kept in the same cell, as were Zeus and Torstyn. Once in the cells, their chains were removed but the RESATs were only turned down, not enough for them to use their powers, but enough to allow some relief from the overwhelming pain that made it difficult to breath and kept their hearts pounding at more than a hundred and fifty beats a minute.

Cassy was the only one who had never been inside a Starxource plant. About ten minutes after being locked in the cell, she said, "At least there's food." On a side table extending from the wall was Rabisk. Cassy picked up a biscuit.

"I wouldn't eat that," McKenna said. ·

"What is it? And what are these little fibers covering it?"

"It's Rabisk."

"What's Rabisk?"

"It's what they feed the rats. It's made of ground-up rats. Those fibers are rat hair."

Cassy dropped the biscuit, almost throwing up. After a moment she asked, "Do you think they're going to feed us to the rats?"

"Don't think about that," McKenna said.

"Where do you think Jack and Ostin are?"

McKenna spun around. "Shhh! They're listening."

Cassy looked around the room, then said, softly, "Sorry. This is new to me."

McKenna walked over to Cassy and put her mouth up to her ear. "They're probably making a plan to save us."

McKenna had barely finished whispering when from each corner of the room came an audio blast as loud as the horn of a diesel truck, loud enough to almost knock them over. It was followed by a voice from the overhead speakers. "Prisoners of Cell 17. No talking is allowed. Stay away from each other or you will be punished."

McKenna stepped back. "Like we're not already being punished?"

The horn blasted again, followed by a sharp pulse in the RESAT, dropping both girls to their knees.

"Enough already!" Cassy shouted. "We get it!"

Out of all of the surviving Electroclan, Taylor was the least affected by the capture. She had already hit her emotional bottom, and she no longer cared what happened to her. She had lost Michael and with him all hope in their cause. She didn't know if her parents or brothers were still alive, and if they were, she assumed that Hatch would find them all and kill them. It wasn't a question of *if*, only *when*. No matter what Hatch did to her, she was already broken. Not even the rat bowl held any terror, as there was simply no more pain she could add to what she already felt. As she lay back on the cell's hard mattress, she heard someone call her.

"Taylor."

She looked over. Michael was standing near the door. Or, at least, what seemed like a projection of Michael, since the image quivered and shimmered in places.

"You're not really here . . . ," she said, rubbing her eyes. "I know you're not really here." She buried her face in her hands.

"It's not over, Taylor. Don't lose hope."

Taylor looked up, expecting the image to be gone. Instead Michael was just staring at her.

"Why are you tormenting me like this?" she screamed.

The vision faded.

Taylor rubbed her eyes again as she lay back on the mattress. "I really am going crazy."

The youths had been locked up for about seven hours when an alarm went off in the cells, followed by a voice coming from the ceiling speakers.

"Enemies of Hatch Islands. Prepare for transport. Elgen guards will be at your rooms shortly. Stay away from the doors or you will be punished." The message was followed by a sharp increase in the RESATs' amp, dropping all of the youths to their knees. Within a few minutes, two guards appeared at each cell, walking them to an electric cart and driving them to a separate part of the building, the curved observatory deck above the bowl. It was the same room where Prime Minister Saluni had been humiliated and dragged away as the rest of the Tuvaluan government learned of Hatch's plans to take their country. The bowl was closed off by a metal screen, leaving the room lit by stark, overhead blue and white LED lighting. There were several long tables set with china, crystal, and silverware in preparation for the evening's feast in honor of Captain Shool.

Cassy, who had been separated from McKenna, was the last to arrive. Everyone else was already kneeling on the floor, their hands cuffed behind their backs and chained to a ring on the floor.

Cassy was brought over to the last vacant spot, a space between Quentin and Nichelle, and locked down. After the guard stepped away, she looked over at the set tables, then asked Nichelle, "Hatch is having us for dinner?"

"Be careful how you ask that," Nichelle said.

"Hatch has lost his mind," Quentin said. "Word was he was planning to eat Michael when he caught him."

"He's crazy," Cassy said.

"Yeah. He is," Nichelle replied.

"How did you guys live with him all those years?" Cassy asked.

"When you're raised in an asylum, crazy is normal," Quentin replied.

Cassy frowned as she looked around the room. It seemed nicer than the other parts of the plant she had been exposed to. It was less industrial. There was padded carpet. The walls were paneled in stained wood, and bronze light fixtures provided soft illumination. "Where are we?"

"We're next to the bowl," Quentin said.

"The *bowl*," Cassy repeated. She had only heard of the bowl. Still, the very mention of it made her shudder.

"Are they going to feed us to the rats now?"

"No. They don't feed from here," Quentin said. "This is where you watch the rats feed."

A light alarm beeped and the massive wall divide began to move. As the two parts separated, the light from the bowl flooded the room in brilliant, oscillating orange hues. Within less than a minute the walls had completely parted, exposing a broad panoramic view of the rat bowl. The rats glowed crimson and orange. They were being moved by the continual sweep.

Cassy looked at the scene with awe. "Oh . . ."

"That's the bowl," Quentin said to her. "That's where the rats produce electricity. You should see it when they're about to feed."

"It's hideous," Nichelle said.

Cassy just stared. "It's strangely beautiful."

"Only from this side of the glass," Quentin said.

Suddenly a voice filled the room. "My Glows, my Glows." Everyone except Cassy recognized the voice coming from a speaker near the center of the room. It was Dr. Hatch. "Welcome back to Elgenland."

"You're psychotic!" Torstyn shouted.

"Considering your present circumstance, Torstyn, you should be more careful with your tongue, unless you'd like to lose it. But I digress. You of the Electroclan cult caused quite a mess of things the last time you were here. You murdered thousands of my men. I'm sure you weren't planning to be back so soon. But make no mistake, you will be spending the rest of your lives here. How *long* the rest of your lives are, and the quality of those lives, depends solely on how well you cooperate with my instructions.

"Which leads to why I had you brought to the bowl. The reason is simple. Motivation. At the end of the week, one of you, along with former EGG Welch, will be fed to the rats. I have not yet selected which one of you it will be. You're all so special that it's going to be difficult choosing just one of you, but if any of you wish to help sway me with your defiance, it will certainly be appreciated."

The youths glanced back and forth at one another. Suddenly an alarm sounded from inside the glass. A chute, almost twelve feet wide, slowly began protruding from the wall. It continued to extend to more than thirty feet, then abruptly stopped. Slowly it began to lower until it was just six feet above the bowl's floor. Immediately the rats swarmed beneath it, the brilliance of their coats growing into bright orange and yellow until they glowed like molten lava.

"They're about to feed," Quentin said softly.

Hatch continued. "I would like to use this demonstration to

remind you all what's at stake. For those who have witnessed this before, forgive the redundancy, but when it comes to teaching, a refresher never hurts. Personally, I never tire of watching them feed. Please, your attention to the bowl."

An amber light began flashing as a door at the mouth of the chute began to open.

"What do you see, Ian?" Quentin asked, forgetting that the RESATs that took away their powers had taken away Ian's sight.

"I don't see anything," Ian said. "I'm blind."

"Sorry, man," Quentin said. "I forgot."

Something slowly emerged from the door. It took a moment for Cassy to understand what she was seeing. "They're feet," Cassy said. "Human feet."

"Indeed, young lady," Hatch said. "When your compadre, Vey, decided to go all supernova on us, his flash blinded most of my guards. Fortunately, I was wearing my protective glasses."

"Shame," Torstyn said.

"A second mark on Torstyn," Hatch said. "Congratulations, Torstyn. You are now well in the lead in the race to the rat bowl."

"I was already scheduled for your bowl, you nutcase."

"Oh, I'm going to enjoy watching those little beasts rip the flesh from your bones, Torstyn. But as I was saying. Nearly all of my personal guards were blinded by the flash. Unfortunately. A blind Elgen guard is about as useful as an armless boxer. Of course, being loyal Elgen, they apologized for their state and promised that they would do whatever they could for our cause. I assured them that, in spite of their situation, they could still provide some benefit. They were genuinely excited about that prospect. You are about to see a few of those men give their all."

The body began to move out of the door until it was entirely on the chute. The man was alive, bound at the ankles and knees, with his arms tied against his waist and chest.

"You've got to admit this is pretty cool," Hatch said. "Look at those rats scurrying to feed. Of course there's really no way that we could ever know what their favorite food is, but from the increase in their excitement and subsequent electrical output, it's pretty clear that they prefer fresh meat over Rabisk. They certainly do look excited, don't they? The rats, that is. The human doesn't look like he's having as much fun."

"You're sick!" Abigail shouted.

"Be quiet," McKenna said to her.

"We hear from the gentle Abigail. Torstyn, you have some competition. But with your fiery temper, you're up to the challenge."

Torstyn clenched his jaw but said nothing.

As the conveyor lowered, the rats gathered more closely together in anticipation, until they formed a large hill of rat, with those on the top jumping for the belt.

As the man slid down the chute, he continued to struggle against the straps that held him. Then, as his feet extended over the edge of the chute, the first of the rats, in a wild frenzy, flew at him. Within seconds they were swarming around him as he screamed in pain.

"You're lucky you get to see this in person," Hatch said. "I could put it on YouTube and get a billion views."

Within two minutes the man's rib cage was exposed as the rats ate his internal organs.

"It's the simple pleasures," Hatch said.

Abigail began shaking. McKenna leaned into her. "Don't say anything."

"You'll notice an improvement to the process. Since the rats can't digest fabric, what's left of the clothes wreaks havoc on the Rabisk machines. So we tried something new. We created what we refer to as 'the dinner jacket.' Not what most exclusive diners are looking for, this jacket is actually edible. It's made of dried vegetable and fruit textile. It's like wearing apricot leather. It's nothing you're going to want to serve to guests, but the rats like it.

"They say clothes make the man, and you are what you eat. I think we just proved both statements correct. But I digress. Our dinner guests are waiting. Contestant number two. You might recognize this one."

As the conveyor started again, the first man's bones dropped into the bowl and were quickly covered by the teeming swarm. The second man was screaming loudly enough that they could hear him even above the frenzied squeal of the rats. Cassy recognized the man as one of the crewmen from the *Joule*—the one who had tried to kiss her. She turned away.

"No fair looking away," Hatch said. "Turn back, or I'll slow down the chute so he can suffer more."

Cassy forced herself to watch. Even before the man was completely consumed, the third man began rolling down the chute, another crewman from the *Joule*.

"Now notice what he's wearing," Hatch said. He suddenly laughed. "I sound like I'm an announcer at the Miss Ratworld fashion show: our third lovely contestant is wearing an inedible creation by Christian Dior." He laughed again. "I was saying, the third guard was a little more defiant than I preferred, so he didn't get the dinner jacket. He got the leather corset. The significance? The corset protects his vitals. So that means the rats will have to burrow through his body to get to the really juicy stuff. It also means that he will be fully alive and feeling all of it. Some of these unlucky corset wearers not only get to see their own bones; they can see rats burrowing under their skin."

Abigail gagged.

"I know, it sounds unpleasant. It is, of course. Far more so than you could imagine. But I point out his attire because the one of you whom I choose to feed to the rats will be wearing the same thing— leather armor. I think with all this buildup and anticipation, it would be a shame to have it over so quickly."

"Just take me!" Quentin shouted. "You deranged madman."

"Noble Quentin," Hatch said. "Cool your tongue before I cut it off like I did to the other inhabitant of the monkey cages, which is exactly where I'm returning you. I hope you're not too disappointed."

Quentin gritted his teeth. "I'm good. I like monkeys."

"Ah, I miss that. That's one of the things I always liked about you, Q. Your unabashed sense of humor. Joking in the face of terror. What a remarkable gift. You would have made a grand king, maybe even my successor if you hadn't gotten so . . . stupid."

"I could never fill your shoes, Hatch," Quentin said. "Actually, I couldn't fit my feet into them, they're so small. What do they say, small shoes, small . . . brain."

Tara laughed.

"That's one for you, Tara. And you, Quentin, you jest with the boldness of a man whose fate is already decided. But just because your fate is sealed, don't believe that I can't make it worse. Trust me, I can always make it worse. There are other things I can cut off besides just your tongue. And, if not to you, perhaps I could arrange something for your girlfriend, Tara."

Tara blanched.

"I'm sorry, sir," Quentin said.

"I thought that might get to you. And for the record, Frank, the young man formerly known as Zeus, isn't in the running for the bowl either. His destiny is with something as unspectacular as the sprinkler system in the courtyard. He will be tied to a chair. Then, as each sprinkler makes its rounds—you know the sound, *cha, cha, cha, cha*—each time that water hits him, it will burn like acid. It will likely take hours to finish him off. Imagine that, burning him alive with water. What a fascinating twist. We're all very excited about this. We plan to record it for posterity.

"In fact, the guards talked me into having him installed with a heart monitor so we can call the exact time of death. They're doing that because they've already started putting down bets on how long he'll survive." Hatch's voice lowered. "I give you forty-five minutes."

Tessa's eyes filled with tears as she looked at Zeus. Zeus just looked down, defeated.

The alarm began to beep again. With the meat devoured, the rats' brilliance had already started to fade. The sliding doors began to close on the bowl.

"Show is over," Hatch said. "Got to save some for later. I hope you enjoyed it. More important, I hope it inspired you. You will now be taken back to your rooms. Get some rest, if you can. I will be meeting with you in the morning. And I have a very big surprise for you. All of you. Sleep well, Glows." The speaker clicked, and the room went silent.

The guards unhooked the youths, then took them all back to their cells.

"What do you think his surprise is?" Tessa asked Quentin.

"No idea," Quentin said. "But I can wait to find out."

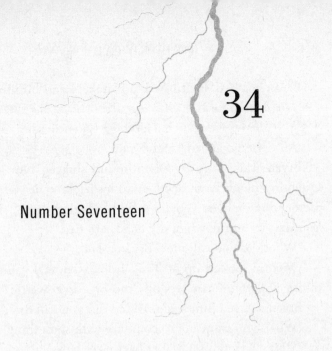

34

Number Seventeen

Just an hour after sunrise, the Electroclan was brought back to the same room above the bowl. It was the one room designed so that all of them could be chained down together. After the guards had again chained them to the floor, the lights were turned off. The room was lit only by the dim combined glow of the youths.

It was a full hour later when a door opened and a voice spoke from the darkness. "I'll never get tired of seeing that." Dr. Hatch stepped forward, followed by two guards, Bryan, Kylee, and a young woman none of them had ever seen before. "You really are remarkable creatures," Hatch said. "Granted, trying to control you is like herding cats, but as physical specimens, you are truly remarkable."

"Hey, Q-tip," Bryan said to Quentin.

"Hey, moron," Quentin said. "Still wetting the bed?"

Bryan blushed. He turned to Hatch. "Can I hit him?"

"No," Hatch said.

"You always were such a lapdog," Quentin said.

"All right, go ahead," Hatch said.

Bryan walked up to Quentin and slugged him in the stomach. Quentin's hands were tied behind his back, so he was unable to completely double over. When he could speak, he said, "What a coward. You wait to hit me when my hands are tied?"

"What did you call me?" Bryan asked.

Quentin looked up at him. "I don't know. I called you so many things. Did you mean 'lapdog,' 'moron,' or 'coward'?"

Bryan slugged him again. "What did you call me?"

"What, you want me to come up with something else?"

"Stop it," Hatch said. "Get back over here."

Bryan slapped the top of Quentin's head, then walked back.

"Chicken," Quentin said.

"I told you I had a surprise for you this morning. I think this one is really going to blow your minds."

"Who's the girl?" Zeus asked.

"You always were one to jump the gun, Frank. This young lady is the surprise I promised you. Come up here, darling. Let's give these Glows a look at perfection."

The young woman stepped forward. She looked to be the same age as them, only there was something older about her. She was tall and shapely and had long black hair that fell to the middle of her back, with a magenta streak running down the middle. Her face was narrow and pretty, with pale skin and radiant blue eyes. She wore tight designer jeans and knee-high leather boots. She carried herself with a confidence that could be construed as arrogance or cruelty. It was obvious that she looked down on the other Glows as inferior.

"It's been written that the first will be last and the last will be first," Hatch said. "You knew there were originally seventeen electric children. You've met sixteen of them. Let me introduce you to number seventeen. Zara."

The youths all looked at her, wondering where she had come from.

"Did you know about her?" Tara asked Quentin. Quentin shook his head.

"I remember her," Nichelle said.

"No, he must have just found her."

"No, I didn't just find her," Hatch said. "In fact, the opposite was true. I knew her before any of you, except Nichelle. Zara was the second child we found. Nichelle is right. Even though you don't remember, most of you have met her. Quentin, you were five years old when the two of you played together. But that didn't last. Zara was so unique, I decided to keep her to myself. No one but me knew about her. A good card player never shows his hand."

He turned back. "Say hi to your siblings, Zara."

"Yeah," she said, staring at them as if it were the last thing she wanted to do.

"There you go," Hatch said. "I know what you're all thinking. What can she do? What's her power? This is why I kept her apart. She can do it all. While Nichelle can diminish your power, Zara can replicate it."

"Vey could do that," Zeus said.

"There is no Vey," Hatch shouted. "Vey is dead. While Zara, as you can see, is very much alive. And, like those of you who once were with me, she has been trained and sharpened like a deadly tool."

"You're a tool," Torstyn said.

"Another mark on Torstyn's run for the bowl," Hatch said. "You're not making this hard for me."

"Looking at you is hard for me," Torstyn said.

"Well, don't worry. You won't have to for much longer." He turned to Zara. "As I was saying, Zara can replicate your powers. But the best part is, anything you can do she can do even better. So, this morning we're going to take some inventory. Zara, if you will . . ."

Zara began to rise off the ground.

"Great," Tessa said. "She can fly."

"She's not flying, per se," Ian said. "It's magnetic repulsion. It's like the opposite of Kylee."

Zara floated to the end of the line, where McKenna was chained. She held out her palm in front of McKenna's face.

"Zara," Hatch said. "This first Glow is McKenna."

As Zara looked at her, Zara's hand turned to fire. Then she turned it into an intense flame so hot that even McKenna tried to push away from it.

"That's fun," Zara said. "Light and heat. That could be very useful."

"That is correct," Hatch said. "And next to her is a Glow I've wanted to meet for a very, very long time. No one told me you were so attractive, Cassy. What do you young people say, 'hot'?"

"I'm going to throw up," Cassy said.

"So where have you been hiding, Cassy?"

"I've never wanted to meet you," Cassy said. "And where I've been is none of your business."

"Every aspect of your life is most assuredly *my* business," Hatch replied. "And you will tell me where you've been. You should know by now that I *always* find out what I want to know."

Zara put her hand over Cassy's head. "Wow. She's a powerful one. She could kill everyone in this room with a thought. Everyone but me, of course. I'm definitely going to hang on to this one."

"Very good," Hatch said. "You do that. Going down the line, this next one is Abigail."

"Abigail." Zara held out her hand. "Boring. Taking away others' pain but not your own. What a waste of electricity. Moving on."

Abigail turned away from her.

"Next," Hatch said with disgust, "is Frank, the Glow once called Zeus."

Zara held her hand above Zeus's head for a moment. Then she turned and fired a lightning bolt so intense that it split apart the lectern at the front of the room. "Sorry, Admiral-General. I don't always know my own power."

"It's not your power," Zeus said. "It's mine."

"What's yours is mine, and what's mine is mine," Zara said. "Sucks to be you, little man."

"When I get out of here . . ."

"The only way you're getting out of here," Hatch said, "is when your heart stops beating. Move on. The girl next to him is Tesla."

"Tessa," she said.

"Tessa, Tesla," Hatch said. "What's in a name? Doesn't matter anymore. You can call yourself Bob for all I care."

"Why would I call myself Bob?"

"This one's power feels a little weird," Zara said. "So this one amplifies others' powers. In fact . . ." Zara stepped back a few paces. "I can pick up different powers at the same time. She could definitely come in handy."

"So glad I'm useful," Tessa said.

"You should be," Zara replied. "That means you might live longer."

"Next is Ian."

Zara stepped up to him and smiled. "Oh, that is cool. I can see . . . everything. Do you know how many rats you have around here?"

"We breed rats," Hatch said.

"I'm not referring to the electric ones," Zara said. "This power is not only useful. It could be a lot of fun. Oh, look at the guards . . ."

"Next up needs no introduction. Torstyn."

Zara nodded. "So that's what microwaves feel like." She pointed her hand across the room at a picture of Hatch, and the frame began sparking. "That's pretty dangerous. I can see why you keep this one locked up."

"Dangerous but stupid. Next to him is Nichelle."

Zara closed her eyes as her hand fluttered around Nichelle's head. "So that's what you do. You're basically a black hole."

"I'd love to shove something up your hole," Nichelle said.

Zara laughed. "Crass little emo. I could use her power against any of these losers and kill them with it."

"Next is Tara."

"Tara," Zara said. "I've heard of you." Zara suddenly changed her appearance to look exactly like Tara. She then changed to look like Dr. Hatch, Justin Bieber, and then Michael Vey.

"Stop that!" Taylor shouted.

Zara turned back into herself, then stepped past Tara to Taylor. "So you're the other half of the twins. You don't like that, mind-scrambler? You and Vey were tight?" As she moved closer to Taylor, Zara began to grin. "Oh my, oh my, oh my. That is going to be so useful."

"What's going to be useful?" Hatch asked.

Zara turned back. "The prettier twin can read minds."

Hatch looked at Taylor in amazement. "'Oh my' indeed. That explains a lot. Will the revelations ever cease?" Hatch said, "Take her power. Now."

"Yes, sir." She turned back and held her hand a few inches above Taylor's head. "Done."

"We're going to find out some things right now. We'll start back here with Cassy. I thought she was dead. Let's find out where she's been hiding. Or who's been hiding her and where."

"I'll never tell you," Cassy shouted.

Zara walked over and held her palm over Cassy's head. "She's been in a secret compound in France."

"Stop it!" Cassy shouted.

"She's very afraid. She doesn't want you to know that she's been living with the one they call the voice."

"Has she, now?" Hatch said. A broad smile crossed Hatch's face. He turned to the two guards next to him. "Bring her to the interrogation room. We're going to have a little discussion."

"Stop it!" Cassy shouted. "Leave me alone."

"You're asking me to walk away from a diamond mine," Hatch said. "Come with me, Zara. Bryan and Kylee, you're dismissed."

Hatch and Zara left the room.

"C'mon," one of the guards said to Cassy.

"No!" Cassy screamed.

"Leave her alone!" Abigail shouted.

"You're coming one way or another," the guard said.

"I'm not going."

"Not your decision," the guard said. The two guards unchained Cassy, then lifted her, carrying her down the hall to a small, mirror-walled office where Hatch and Zara were sitting. They dropped Cassy in a sobbing heap onto the floor.

"Shut the door," Hatch said. "Then take the others back to their cells." He pointed at one of the guards. "You stay."

"Yes, sir."

Hatch sat back in his chair. "You can read her from here?" he asked Zara.

"Yes, sir."

"Then we'll start." He leaned toward Cassy. "All right, hot little Cassy. You're being recorded, so everything you say will be captured. And I think you have a lot to say. I know I have a lot of questions."

"I won't tell you anything," Cassy said. "You can't make me talk."

"You don't have to talk," Hatch said. "You just need to think. So let's begin with a softball question. Tell me, Cassy, who is the voice?"

Cassy struggled with her restraints. "You can't make me tell you."

Zara turned to Hatch and nodded. "Got it."

"I'm afraid you already did, sweetheart. Who is it, Zara?"

"Some man named Dr. Coonradt."

Hatch almost gasped. "Coonradt? I didn't see that coming. Well, well . . . Dr. Coonradt is supposed to be dead. How clever of him. The doctor was a very intelligent man, but I don't see him starting a revolution. Where is Coonradt holed up?"

Zara turned back to Cassy. "France."

"It's hard to believe I was so close to him all along. Tell me about the compound. Where is it exactly?"

"Please let me go."

"I will once I've milked you for all you know. Now, where is this compound?"

Zara shook her head. "She's trying to think of different things."

"Just wait for her to slip. There's no better way to get someone to think of something than to tell them not to think of it. Tell her not to think of a pink flying monkey, and what have you got?"

"She just thought of a pink flying monkey," Zara said.

"Exactly. Now, pretty little Cassy, tell me exactly where we'll find the resistance's compound."

Cassy closed her eyes and bowed her head.

"She's reciting Bible verses," Zara said.

"Interesting," Hatch said. "I like Bible verses. Do you like the Psalms? How about this one? 'They gaped upon me with their mouths, as a ravening and a roaring lion. I am poured out like water, and all my bones are out of joint: my heart is like wax; it is melted in the midst of my bowels. My strength is dried up like a potsherd; and my tongue cleaveth to my jaws; and thou hast brought me into the dust of death.'"

"Stop it!" Cassy shouted.

"I can see it all," Zara said. "I need something to draw with."

"Get her a pad!" Hatch shouted to one of the guards.

The guard found a pad in the desk and carried it over to her. Zara immediately began drawing. "There's just one outer wall. The building's a mansion. It's three stories high. I can draw it."

"How is it protected?"

Zara hesitated. "Mostly by her. There are fourteen guards. They're well trained, fairly well armed, automatic weapons, UZIs, nothing we can't take out."

"Keep drawing," Hatch said. After fifteen minutes she showed him a picture of the European compound.

"Is Coonradt the head of the resistance?"

Cassy shouted out in pain. "Stop it!"

"No," Zara said. "He's second in charge. There's someone above him." She thought a moment, then said. "It's Vey. Not Michael Vey."

"Sharon Vey?" Hatch said, sounding skeptical. "She's the heart of all this?"

Zara shook her head. "No. Not Michael's mother. His father."

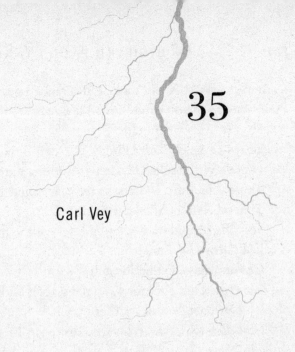

35

Carl Vey

Hatch slammed his fist down on the table with delight. "Jackpot! This is too much. You're telling me that Carl Vey is *also* alive?! And I thought Coonradt being alive was a mind-blow. That's unbelievable news. Well played, Vey. Well played. From the very beginning he's been orchestrating the rebellion from his grave!"

Cassy closed her eyes as tears streamed down her cheeks. She had just betrayed the one secret that had kept the resistance alive.

"Where is he?" Hatch asked. "Where's Vey?"

Zara turned back. "She doesn't know. It's their prime secret."

"Ask her who does know."

Zara struggled briefly with Cassy's thoughts, then said, "Dr. Coonradt. He's the only one who knows."

"Then we'll start with him. So, Cassy, where's the rest of the resistance based? It can't all be in France because we found one of their bases in Mexico and burned it down."

"Stop it!" Cassy shouted.

"There's a ranch," Zara said.

"I know. We attacked it. There's nothing left."

"There's another. The first ranch was called Time . . ."

"Timepiece Ranch," Hatch said.

"Yes. The second one, where the rest of the resistance is right now, is called Christmas Ranch."

"Clever. Where is that located?"

Zara closed her eyes for a moment, then said, "It's on the east side of Zion National Park in southern Utah."

"Utah," Hatch said. "Who would ever think to look in Utah?" He smiled. "Now, Cassy. Tell us everything you know about Christmas Ranch."

"I don't know anything about it," Cassy said out loud. "I've never been there."

"She's telling the truth," Zara said.

"Ask her who knows."

Zara got up and knelt in front of Cassy, gently stroking her fingers through the sobbing girl's hair. Then Zara slowly looked up. "Pretty much every one of the Glows but her."

When Hatch had finished interrogating Cassy, he smiled. "Beautiful. Just beautiful. Thank you, Cassy. You told us everything we need to know to end this nonsense for good. I'm so glad your friends were thoughtful enough to send you."

"I hate you!" Cassy screamed.

Hatch looked at her stoically. "Of course you hate me. You wouldn't be here if you didn't. But I don't hate you. You're just a product of your upbringing. But I made you. You could say I'm your biological father. Or your god."

"You're not a god. You're the devil."

Hatch shrugged. "One man's devil is another man's god." He leaned forward. "You might want to be more careful about how you judge others, since you just betrayed everyone you have ever loved. After we arrest Dr. Coonradt, I'll be sure to let him know that it was you who led us to him."

"You're sick," Cassy sobbed.

Hatch laughed. "Guards, take her back to her cell. And see to it that she doesn't try to hurt herself. I'd like to keep her around for a while."

Hatch stood. "I've got to go." He turned to the guard. "Start bringing the Glows in one by one. Don't bother with my Glows, just the ones who came here from the resistance. Start with Ian and Frank. Ian because he's seen the most and Frank because he's a detail man. I want Peters and Heinz up here interrogating them with Zara. I want to know everything about this Christmas Ranch by twenty-one-hundred hours. I want a complete map, schedule, everything. I'll be back in ninety minutes."

"Where are you going?" Zara asked.

"I've got a date with a bottle of Karuizawa."

When Cassy got back to her cell, she was sobbing hysterically. McKenna put her arm around her. "It's okay, honey."

"No, it's not. Nothing's okay. I've given away everything. *Everything*. I didn't know they could do that. I never should have come. I've ruined everything."

PART FIFTEEN

36

Welcome Aboard

Hatch had Captain Shool escorted up to his office on the second floor.

"How is business?" Hatch asked the captain.

Captain Shool smiled. "Business? Do you call *war* business?"

"War is big business," Hatch said. He brought the bottle of Karuizawa out of his liquor cabinet and held it up for the captain to see. "Imagine, this liquid costs more per ounce than gold." He opened the bottle and poured liquid into two shot glasses.

"Admiral-General . . ."

Hatch held up his hand to stop him from talking. "Please. Enjoy this moment. Such pleasures are far too rare."

Both men lifted their glasses and drank.

"Magnificent," Hatch said. "Worth every penny."

"Indescribable," Captain Shool said.

"Then let me pour you another." Hatch refilled the captain's glass, then his own. After they had drunk the second glass, Hatch's face had a red glow. "Did you know that the distillery where this nectar was produced was on the slope of an active volcano?"

"No, Admiral."

"Unfortunately, it is no more. The distillery was closed more than a decade ago, which makes this magnificent liquid all the more valuable. Life is like that. The most precious things are fleeting. Do you agree, Captain?"

"Yes, I agree."

Hatch again lifted the bottle to top off the captain's glass.

"Thank you, Admiral, but I think I've had enough."

Hatch smiled and poured the glass anyway. "Can you have enough heaven?" He laughed. "I think not." He filled his own glass again. "So, as I asked before, how is business?"

"It is well, mostly."

"Mostly?"

"You know. I'm a soldier, not a politician. The politics are as capricious as the sea."

"I understand," Hatch said. "I have a solution for that. I would like to make you a proposition."

"A proposition?"

"Yes, Captain. I have recently lost my best ship captains."

"How could you lose them all, sir?"

"Very unexpectedly," Hatch said, lifting his glass. "What do you know of these criminals you brought me?"

"I was not told much, except that they were terrorists."

"Terrorists," Hatch said. "Indeed. They were involved in a suicide bombing that destroyed most of my army." He put the top back on the bottle of Karuizawa. "My point in telling you this, Captain, is that I am looking to hire." Hatch took a slow sip as he studied the captain's face. "I don't know what you know about the Elgen Corporation, but we are poised to become not only the largest and most profitable corporation in the world, but also the most powerful. If we were a country, our GNP would make us the twelfth most profitable in the world, somewhere between Australia and Mexico."

"That is remarkable, Admiral."

"Yes, it is. I am, by trade, a scientist as well as a businessman. Which means I don't assume anything. I hypothesize, then prove. I research. And I've researched your career, Captain. You are from Quezon City, the most populous city in the Philippines. Your father was a bureaucrat, your mother, who is Vietnamese by birth, was a professor of international law. You have never been married; you have been quoted as saying that you are married to the navy."

Captain Shool smiled. "That is all true, Admiral."

"You were also the captain behind one of the most controversial operations in all of Philippine history, as you put down the president's rival with a significant number of civilian casualties."

Captain Shool downed the rest of his glass. "I was following orders."

"Exactly," Hatch said. "Exactly. Which makes you precisely what I am looking for. I'm impressed with what you have accomplished. I'm impressed with your obedience in following unpopular orders. I'm impressed by your attention to detail and precision, and how successfully you carried out this mission. As such, I would like to offer you the position as head of the Elgen Navy."

The captain looked stunned. "Sir . . ."

"Before you answer, consider this. You will have a life of power, privilege, and, most important, purpose. I will quadruple your current salary and give you a million-dollar signing bonus if you agree right now. That is in American dollars, or the equivalent of a million dollars in any currency you wish. But my proposal is only good if you accept it now, before you leave this room."

Captain Shool was quiet for a moment, then said, "I cannot abandon my crew here. I would need to sail back and inform my superiors."

Hatch smiled. "See, exactly why you are perfect for the job. Of course, Captain. I would expect that. But before you go, I do have a favor to ask, one that may benefit your crew."

"What is that, sir?"

"The coup that took place in our nation is not completely put down. The rebels have taken refuge inside our national gold depository just sixty kilometers from here. Unfortunately for us, I built the depository to withstand any land assault."

"Of course you would," the captain said.

"Being indestructible is, of course, only of value if you have control of the building. But, currently, I do not. I could use a battleship right now to . . . *correct* the situation."

"I understand, Admiral. But to engage in battle I would have to have the permission of my superiors."

Hatch took the top back off the bottle of whiskey, then said, "Unless, of course, it was only a training exercise. It's not often you get the opportunity to engage in a real-life shelling of infrastructure. Far too costly."

Captain Shool thought for a moment, then said, "It could be done."

"Excellent," Hatch said. He poured another two glasses of Karuizawa and handed the first to the captain. "If you will accept my offer, please celebrate with me with a toast."

"I will," Captain Shool said, and took the new glass.

"To my new chief admiral of naval operations. Welcome aboard, Elgen."

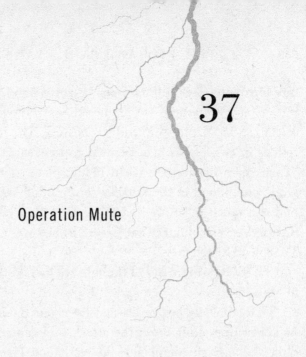

37

Operation Mute

Since Cassy had never been to Christmas Ranch, she couldn't reveal much about it. Zara and Hatch's war ministers grilled Ian, Taylor, Zeus, Nichelle, Abigail, and McKenna for several hours on the specifics of the ranch headquarters. The Elgen learned how the property was laid out, the level of security, where their weapons were kept, their routines, and, most important, where they would find Sharon Vey. By the time they finished their interrogation, they knew everything they needed to destroy the ranch once and for all.

After concluding his meeting with Captain Shool, Hatch called a council of the EGG—the four who were in Tuvalu and the rest by video around the world.

"Gentlemen," Hatch said. "The resistance has made a fatal error and handed us the rope we need to hang them. Yes, we are weakened, but, fortunately, we still have guards abroad and, as luck would have it, not far from where we require them." He walked to an electric screen, and a map of the world appeared. "The last of the resistance resides in two places." He pointed to the map with a laser pointer. "Their main headquarters and hiding place of the voice is here, a secret compound in the northeastern mountains of France. The second is a ranch in southern Utah, where the resistance council and Sharon Vey are hiding. That is where they went after we destroyed Timepiece Ranch."

"Sir," EGG Amon said. "I thought we had destroyed the resistance in Mexico."

"Unfortunately, we've learned from our interrogations that they had been tipped off about the attack, and contrary to our belief, we didn't kill a single member of the resistance. There was no one there to kill."

"But we lost men in the attack. . . ."

"Yes, we did," Hatch said. "The resistance was defending the ranch by remote to create the appearance of a battle. We have a clever adversary." Hatch turned back to the council. "We'll send Captain Smythe and his men from our Baja base to Christmas Ranch to bring back Vey, then destroy the ranch and all its inhabitants."

"Who will we send to their French compound?" EGG Amon asked.

"The Domguard."

The EGGs looked at one another.

"Do you have a problem with that, EGG Amon?" Hatch asked.

"No, sir," Amon replied. "That's precisely what I would recommend."

"Good. Because it's what we're going to do."

The Domguard, also known as the Order of the Amber Tunic, was the most elite of the Elgen special services and was considered even deadlier than the Lung Li. They received the highest level of combat training, comparable to military special ops, the Navy SEALs, Army Rangers, or Marine RECON.

The Domguard were stronger and larger than the other Elgen

guards. But it wasn't just their physical presence that made them stand out. Their attire was unique, consisting of a black-silk uniform with an insignia of an all-seeing eyeball, with the pupil in the form of the *taijitu*, the black-and-white yin-yang sign.

In addition, the Domguard wore an amber-colored cloth belt, signifying the Amber Tunic, an ancient occult society. Amber had special significance for the Elgen scientists and the Elgen in general. In fact, before the Elgen company was incorporated, it was, for a time, called Amberz. The word "electricity" came from the word "*elektron*," the Greek name for amber. An early Greek philosopher noticed that amber, when rubbed by silk, would become magnetized and attract objects. That invisible power was called electricity.

In reality, the EGGs knew little about the Domguard, which was Hatch's doing, since he reserved the force to serve as his personal guard and troops, loyal only to himself. If there were ever an attempted coup within the Elgen, it would be the Domguard who would crush it and restore Hatch to power.

When Hatch had returned to the Tuvalu plant from Hades, one of the first things he had done was put the Domguard on alert to be prepared to fly to Tuvalu. But he hadn't given them the order yet, as they were currently his only troops in Europe, and with Schema, the former Elgen chairman, still abroad, Hatch couldn't afford to leave that part of the world completely unattended.

"We're still analyzing all the data we've received from the Glows and finalizing attack strategies," Hatch said. "But here are the basics. To avoid the possibility of them warning each other, causing us to lose this priceless opportunity, we must simultaneously attack both strongholds. Since there's an eight-hour time difference between the two locales and a night attack is always to our advantage, we plan to attack their French headquarters at four thirty a.m. using night vision. This would put our attack on Christmas Ranch at eight thirty p.m. mountain time, an hour after sunset."

Hatch stepped back from the board to better emphasize his point. "I'm calling the French operations Operation Mute, since we're finally silencing the voice. I'm calling the Utah sortie Operation

Christmas Eve, for obvious reasons. Our objective is to bring back Coonradt from Europe and Sharon Vey from America."

"What about the Glow Grace?" EGG Bosen asked. "Is she being held at the ranch?"

"Yes, she is. What about her?"

"Don't we want her back?"

Hatch shook his head. "No. Only silenced. She can die with the rest of our enemy." Hatch stood. "While we finalize the specifics of the attack plans, I want both forces moved into striking position. Bring the Domguard up from Rome into Turin, and the Apache Guard in Baja up into northern Nevada. I want them ready to strike at a moment's notice. EGG Amon, I leave it to you to get them in place."

"Thank you, sir."

"What of the rebels?" Despain asked.

"They are, for the time being, stranded on Plutus and holed up in the depository, a situation we will soon remedy. Captain Shool of the Philippine Navy has agreed to shell the depository and deliver our army to the island to reclaim our property. He has also agreed to come on as our new chief admiral of naval operations."

EGG Despain clapped, followed by the other EGGs. "Well done, sir," he said.

"Thank you." Hatch looked around the table at his council. "Does anyone else have anything to add?"

Amon raised his hand. "Yes, sir. I thought it might be appropriate, at this time, to invoke the words of the Elgen handbook. 'A new day has dawned, not just for the world but for us. Rise up to this morning of a new dispensation, the *novus ordo glorificus Elgen*, and personal glory will follow.'"

"Thank you," Hatch said. "And allow me to complete the charge. *'Elgen, I salute you!'*"

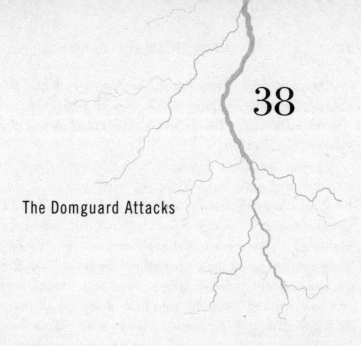

38

The Domguard Attacks

Hatch considered it a gift of fate that the Domguard were still stationed in Rome, so close to the resistance's European compound. The Domguard flew two Black Hawk helicopters from Rome to Turin, then refueled and waited for their final orders from EHQ. The order to attack came at two in the morning, and the helicopters lifted into the moist night air, flying north over the Italian Alps toward France. Unlike the Apache attack helicopters that the Elgen had used in the assault on Timepiece Ranch, the Black Hawks were designed for speed and troop transport, which at the moment was what was required.

The sun was still an hour from rising when the two helicopters descended in unison a quarter mile north of a thick forest of spruce and fir trees that surrounded the resistance's compound. The heavily wooded forest that had served to conceal and shelter the resistance now worked against them, as it provided cover for the Elgen force.

On their flight from Rome, the Domguard had been given a complete briefing on their mission, as well as electronic plans of the compound's layout and security—a detailed sketch derived from Cassy's thoughts.

Twenty-five Elgen Domguards, using night-vision goggles, surrounded the compound. They set explosives and simultaneously blew up three different sections of the outer wall and the outside guard booth, killing the guard on watch. The blasts set off the compound's first alarms and effectively divided the resistance's security forces, as they broke up to cover the three breaches in the walls.

The resistance's headquarters relied more on secrecy than security, and without Cassy to help defend the installation, they were undermanned and outgunned. They were vulnerable. The wall breaches were a diversion and a trap, resulting in twelve of the resistance's guards being taken out immediately by the waiting snipers.

It was a quarter past two in the afternoon in Tuvalu when the Domguard started their attack, and Hatch, along with his EGGs—Amon, Grant, Bosen, and Despain—watched the covert operation unfold in his office, the attack playing out on twelve different monitors, captured by the night-vision cameras the Domguard wore on their helmets. It was like watching a video game except that the action figures—and the blood—were real.

The Domguard moved silently to surround the exits of the French château, the soft, rubberized soles of their boots barely making a sound on the mansion's black cobblestone driveway.

Samantha Scholes, Dr. Coonradt's personal assistant, had heard the explosions and, wearing only her nightgown, walked out onto the patio to see what was going on. She was immediately grabbed from behind by one of the Elgen guards. Since Hatch had ordered the guard to avoid noncombat casualties, Samantha was zipped up in a specially designed body bag and left in the yard.

The body bags, called PEQs by the Elgen (an abbreviation for "polyethylene quod"), were an ingenious Elgen invention. They were basically pocket jail cells. The bags were lightweight, less than a pound, and folded up into a canister the size of a flashlight. The bags effectively bound, blindfolded, and muffled their victims, allowing just enough oxygen for the occupant to breathe if she didn't put up too much of a fuss—which worked well to control the captive inside. Since the bags were puncture resistant—resisting twelve hundred pounds per square inch—no one, even with a knife, could get out until they were let out. The bag's zipper was located on the outside of the bag, so it didn't even require a padlock to secure the occupant.

The compound's final guard was stationed on the main floor of the mansion in the video surveillance room. He was neutralized as he ran up the stairway to alert Dr. Coonradt of the danger.

Dr. Coonradt's room was at the end of the corridor on the home's third level, the wide, wood-paneled walls lined with deer and elk antlers. Coonradt had been up until two in the morning in communication with the board at Christmas Ranch and, upset that the Electroclan were still unaccounted for, had taken a sedative to help him sleep. The sleeping aid, in addition to the earplugs he wore, left him so isolated that, in spite of the explosions and alarms, he was still asleep when the three Domguards entered his room.

Dr. Coonradt was easily subdued by the powerful guards and handcuffed. Then a needle was shoved into his jugular vein, injecting him with methohexital—a barbiturate that rendered him completely unconscious in less than fifteen seconds. He was then placed faceup on the bed for Hatch to identify. It had been years since Hatch had seen the scientist, and seeing him brought back a flood of anger.

"That's him," Hatch said. "That's coon-rat. Bring him to me."

The guards radioed for transport; then they slid Dr. Coonradt into a PEQ. A guard carried him out of the room, with a guard in front and back, their weapons drawn, prepared for any resistance.

As they were descending the third-story stairs to the second floor, another occupant of the house walked out of his bedroom into the hallway. The man in shadow kept close to the wall, working his way toward the stairway. The guards crouched and silently watched him, giving command time to identify the individual. When Hatch realized who the man was, he was as thrilled as a child finding a new bicycle under the Christmas tree.

"That's Schema," Hatch said, his voice shrill with excitement. "Bring him to me." Hatch then said to the EGG, "If there were a god, besides me, I'd say he was on our side."

The guards ordered Schema to his knees, and Hatch's former boss knelt without resistance—in part because he was still half-asleep and terrified, but also because he had subconsciously resigned himself to the fact that he would someday be captured by the Elgen who had put a million-euro bounty on his head.

Schema was also injected with the barbiturate and placed into another PEQ. Then the two men were carried out of the mansion.

With the compound cleared, the first Elgen helicopter landed in the yard next to the house, and the Domguard stowed their precious cargo inside. Ten other guards hurried in after them; then the helicopter quickly took off.

The second helicopter landed a minute after the first had cleared the space, and the remaining fifteen guards climbed inside. Then she too lifted off, leaving the compound smoking and violated, and Samantha wriggling helplessly in her PEQ bag, looking like an oversize, rubber caterpillar. After years of battling the resistance, the entire operation had taken less than forty minutes to complete.

The Black Hawks could cruise at speeds upward of 183 miles per hour, so it took less than three hours to return to Turin. Dr. Coonradt and Schema both woke during the flight, but since they were still confined in the PEQs, they were unable to resist or communicate. That too was Hatch's plan. Hatch was worried about Dr. Coonradt's intelligence and his power of persuasion, so the guards had been ordered not to communicate with their prisoner.

After refueling in Turin, the helicopters flew to Rome, where Coonradt and Schema were transferred to an Elgen jet. Once on board, they were let out of the PEQs but handcuffed and hooded. They were flown to Dubai, where the jet refueled; then Hong Kong; and then to their final destination in Funafuti, where Hatch was waiting.

39

Christmas Ranch

While Operation Mute was being carried out on the other side of the world, Captain Smythe, the same commander who had led the attack on Timepiece Ranch in northern Mexico, had commenced his own operation.

Smythe's helicopter squad had been static since the Timepiece attack, awaiting a transport to Tuvalu, which would require a boat since it was much too far for the helicopters to fly. Again, fate seemed to favor the Elgen. After three delays caused by weather, the squad was still in Mexico and ready for the mission Hatch was sending them on. The helicopter squad not only had experience in attacking the resistance's ranch, but they were also the only unit within three thousand miles of the target.

The two operations were launched simultaneously. Prior to the attack, Smythe's squad made the 375-mile flight to northern Nevada, where the helicopters landed at a private airport and refueled. From there it was only 160 miles to Christmas Ranch. If all went according to plan, they would fly in from the south over the Vermilion Cliffs and attack the ranch just after nightfall.

At seven forty-five p.m. mountain time, Captain Smythe received GPS coordinates for the ranch, detailed attack plans, and orders to attack. The eleven Elgen helicopters flew across the Nevada border, closely following the rugged desert canyon terrain. It took them just thirty-four minutes to reach the ranch, the only structures within miles of the national park.

With Gervaso and the youths gone and no advance warning, Christmas Ranch was ripe for picking, even less well defended than the European headquarters, with only three men on guard duty: two guarding the outer roads and one on the water tower.

The Elgen's attack orders were simple: capture Sharon Vey, then destroy the ranch and all its inhabitants. The battle plan was to silently take out the water tower guard, then drop three teams of jumpers to capture Vey. (The guards had pictures of Sharon taped to their forearms.) Once she was secured, they would attack the ranch by air with their full payload of Hellfire missiles and napalm.

"This is Elgen One. Destination is one mile ahead," Captain Smythe said. "Prepare jumpers. Release on my command."

In the dark, Smythe's helicopter dropped lower than the rest until it was only slightly above the tree line. It quickly approached the west side of the ranch, carefully following the contour of the land until it was about twelve hundred yards from the water tower, and an Elgen sniper with a night-vision scope silently took out the watchman.

The helicopter quickly gained altitude, then did a flyby over the quiet ranch. There were enough commercial tour helicopters flying over Zion that the helicopter's presence did not alarm the ranch's inhabitants, but Smythe wasn't taking chances. Still, there was no movement below, and most of the buildings were dark.

"Drop jumpers," Smythe said.

At ten thousand feet, twelve paratroopers jumped with Ram-chute parachutes from four of the helicopters. It was higher than their usual drop, as the helicopters were still hoping to avoid detection. The Elgen jumpers free-fell until about two thousand feet before pulling their chutes and landing just fifty yards south of the water tower, three hundred yards from the main ranch house. Only one of the Elgen had a problem as his chute caught in a cedar tree and he had to cut himself down.

Captain Smythe in Elgen One continued north to the resistance's road outposts, where he flew down on the two guards, neutralizing them with machine-gun fire.

The ranch had gone dark earlier than usual. It had been a hard day, and Sharon Vey had been crying for most of it. It was over a week since the Electroclan had been heard from, and the resistance had convened a meeting to discuss a possible rescue mission even though the odds were that the Electroclan was already dead. The meeting was emotional and tense, and nothing had been decided. The Lisses were beside themselves, and Mrs. Liss had screamed at the board. Sharon was angry at herself that she hadn't stopped her son from participating in a suicide mission.

She was alone in her room getting ready for bed when the guards kicked open her door.

"That's her," a guard said, pointing his pistol with a silencer. "Scream and I shoot."

The guards put Sharon in a PEQ, radioed the helicopter for pickup, and then carried her out back to where they had landed, waving a green laser into the air to signal the helicopter their position.

A few minutes later a chopper descended. The two troopers threw Vey inside, then climbed in themselves. "Fly," the guard said.

After they were a thousand feet in the air, Captain Smythe came to the back of the Apache and unzipped the PEQ enough for Sharon to put out her head.

"Who are you?" Sharon asked.

"I'm Captain Smythe."

"Elgen?"

"How many enemies do you have?" Smythe asked.

"Where's my son?"

"You don't have the clearance to know that."

"Where are you taking me?"

"You don't have the clearance to know that."

"What can you tell me?"

"I can tell you that it's time to say good-bye to your friends." He reached back to the control for his microphone. "This is Elgen One. All helos cleared to launch Hellfire missiles on my command. Lethal force is authorized. I repeat, lethal force is authorized."

"Please . . . don't," Sharon said. "You don't have to hurt them."

"As a matter of fact I do." The captain said into his microphone, "All helos let missiles fly."

"Hellfire missiles away," came a multitude of replies.

From her window Sharon could see dozens of missiles streaking fire against the black sky, sixteen from each helicopter, scattering across the ranch in a broad swathe, blowing everything apart.

"Elgen Nine and Eleven, fire napalm," the captain said.

"Elgen Nine. Roger that, One. Napalm firing."

"Elgen Eleven. Napalm firing."

More missiles struck the ground, only these lit up the sky with a row of flames three hundred yards long and more than a hundred feet high, the tops of the flames curling with the helicopters' down-draft.

"God's wrath," Captain Smythe said. "Thank you, Nine and Eleven." The captain set down the microphone and turned back to Sharon. "Are you a God-fearing woman, Mrs. Vey?"

Sharon said nothing, though tears streamed down her cheeks. Her lips were tight with anger.

"You might not believe this," Smythe said, "but I was an altar boy. Saint Vincent's in Cherry Creek, New Jersey. I even thought of becoming a priest someday. Imagine that."

Sharon looked at him hatefully.

"I'm still spiritual. I just chose a different way to do God's work. Something a little more . . . deliberate." He took a deep breath. "Look at that down there. It's biblical. The 'heavens shall pass away with a great noise, and the elements shall be dissolved with fervent heat, and the earth and the works that are therein shall be burned up.'" He shook his head. "We are the destroying angels. Unfortunately, your friends are no more." He lifted the microphone. "This is Elgen One. Mission accomplished. All helos return to Vegas base. Let the beer flow, boys. Tonight it's on me."

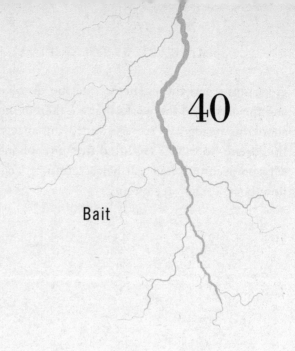

40

Bait

The Apache helicopters landed in Vegas, and Sharon Vey was moved to the Elgen's Gulfstream jet, which was waiting for them on the runway, fueled and ready for take-off. Drenched in her own sweat, Sharon was taken out of the PEQ, handcuffed, and then handed over to the two guards who were waiting to escort her to Tuvalu.

The flight from the U.S. to Tuvalu was a little more than five thousand miles, with only one stop in Honolulu, less than a third of the distance that Dr. Coonradt and Schema were flown. The Gulfstream landed a full twelve hours before Dr. Coonradt arrived.

The guards, at Hatch's instruction, had informed Sharon of the success of Operation Mute and the capture of the voice. He wanted her completely broken and hopeless before she arrived. The jet had also briefly circled Hades, and the guards had made Sharon look down at the charred and still smoking island.

"What happened down there?" Sharon asked.

"You'll find out soon enough," the guard next to her answered cryptically.

Twenty-two minutes later the jet touched down on the Nike runway. Hatch, with his newly received information about the whereabouts of the Tuvaluan rebels, was no longer worried about leaving the Starxource plant, and he, along with six of his guards, met the plane as it landed.

The jet taxied up to where Hatch stood, and the door opened. A guard was the first to emerge, followed closely by the still handcuffed Sharon and then another guard. Her eyes flashed when she saw Hatch.

"Where's my son?" she shouted.

Hatch grinned. "It's good to see you too, Sharon. When was the last time—Peru?"

"Where is he?"

"I knew you'd ask. That's why I had the pilot make a brief flyover of Hades. Did you look out the window?"

"Where's my son?"

"That's what I'm trying to tell you. That smoking, burning island? That's your son. At least what's left of him. He went supernova on us and destroyed the island. He killed thousands of my men. He killed his friends. Like a suicide bomber with a nuclear weapon strapped to his back. You've got to hand it to him, he really went out with a bang."

"You're lying."

"I wish I was. But we both know I'm not. Michael killed some of my best soldiers and sank almost all of my boats. In its own way, it was a valiant last stand—a Hail Mary pass of epic proportions. So you can, at least, find solace in the fact that no one killed your son. He did it himself. Misguided as he was, you could even call him a hero."

"No!" Sharon shouted.

"I know it must be painful to hear all this, but it's about choice, Sharon. Michael's choice. Parents need to let their children make choices. And now you're going to make choices."

"Why did you bring me here? Why didn't you just let me die with the rest of my friends?"

"Leverage," Hatch said. "I needed a little leverage. Or perhaps I should say *bait*."

"Bait for whom?" Sharon said. "You've already killed everyone."

"Not everyone, Sharon. Not yet, at least. But, with your help, I soon will." He turned to her escorting guard. "Take her to Cell 9 in East Block."

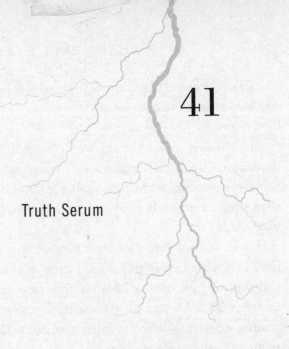

41

Truth Serum

Dr. Coonradt's plane landed at two in the morning. Hatch didn't meet him, not because he was worried about being out of the protection of the Starxource plant; rather he didn't want to extend the courtesy to Dr. Coonradt or disrupt his own sleep. Hatch gave the guards specific instructions. After the exhausting flight, Coonradt was not allowed to lie down to sleep; he was taken directly to a cell and strapped to a chair with the cell lights on. He was to be given nothing to drink, nor was he allowed to leave the chair for any reason, even to use the toilet.

"It smells in here," Hatch said, walking into the cell.

Coonradt looked at him angrily. "That's because you just walked in."

"No," Hatch said. "That's because you have soiled yourself." He walked over next to his prisoner. "So news of your death was premature."

Coonradt glared at him but said nothing.

"Really, Steven, I've got to know, did you honestly send your electric kids here to steal my boat?"

Coonradt didn't answer.

"I probably wouldn't answer either if I were you. It's hard to imagine such cowardice, even from you. Sending kids to do something you wouldn't do yourself. They should hate you more than they hate me. If you were half a man, you would have come yourself."

Hatch looked into Coonradt's eyes. "But that's all you are, less than half a man. Maybe I should dress you in a diaper and bonnet and put you on display." Hatch condescendingly patted Coonradt on the head. "You know, that might have possibility. I've considered creating the world's first human zoo. Someday it will be necessary, as humans slide off into oblivion. You would make a lovely exhibit. How amusing."

"You've finally gone mad, Jim."

Hatch's eyes flashed. "That's 'Admiral-General Hatch' to you."

Dr. Coonradt grinned darkly. "It's telling that you were less bothered by me calling you *insane* than by me not using your self-appointed title. Mental hospitals are filled with men who think they're kings or Jesus. Make no mistake, Admiral-General King of the World, or whatever lunatic name you want to call yourself, you're still just Jimmy Hatch from Minnesota, the megalomaniac. The only change I see in you is the extent of your psychosis."

Hatch punched him in the face, then grabbed his own hand in pain.

Coonradt reeled back as blood trickled down from his nose. "Why didn't you just kill me?"

"Everyone keeps asking me that," Hatch said, rubbing his hand. "I'll get around to it. Eventually. But after all this cat and mouse, where's the fun of that? Most important, there's information in your head that I need."

"I won't tell you anything."

"You'll tell me everything," Hatch said calmly. "I've got a little help." He pushed a button on his pocket microphone. "Send her in."

The door opened, and Zara walked into the room. Dr. Coonradt eyed her carefully, then, when she was a few yards from him, said, "Hello, Zara. How have you been?"

Zara looked confused. "How do you know who I am?"

"I know all my creations."

Zara froze. She turned back to Hatch as if for an explanation, but he just folded his arms at his chest. She said to Dr. Coonradt, "You didn't make me. Dr. Hatch made me."

"Jimmy Hatch? Yeah, right. Jimmy couldn't make a tuna sandwich let alone an electric human. So I'm assuming you borrowed Taylor's powers and you now read minds."

Zara again looked stumped. "How did you know that?"

"You don't have to read minds to know what Hatch is up to. . . . He might as well have a transparent skull. So ask him who made you."

Zara turned back to Hatch. "You lied to me."

"No, I didn't."

"I can read your mind."

"Dr. Coonradt was the scientist I hired to create the MEI. *He* worked for *me*. Therefore, his creation is mine."

"Actually, you didn't hire me," Dr. Coonradt said. "I was with Elgen Inc. before you darkened their lobby. But that's beside the point. What you said is illogical. It's like saying I own an iPod, so I'm a musician."

"Enough," Hatch said. "On with the interrogation, Zara."

"Yes, sir," Zara said. She walked behind Dr. Coonradt's chair so she wouldn't have to look at him. "I'm ready."

"Tell me, Doctor. Who is really behind this resistance?"

Coonradt looked down but said nothing.

"Nothing," Zara said. "It's some song in his head."

"Let me try this. Are you working with Dr. Carl Vey?"

"I got an affirmative," Zara said.

Hatch nodded. "So Vey isn't dead."

"No, sir," Zara said.

"Where do I find him?"

Zara hesitated. "He's not sure. Vey moves around a lot."

"How do you reach him?"

"There's a phone number. He's doing the song again." After five minutes Zara had a few numbers, but they were random. "He's just throwing out numbers."

"Okay, there's another way." He opened his desk and brought out a syringe.

"You just keep that in there?" Coonradt asked.

"I had it brought in special for you."

"Pentothal?"

"Nice guess. Truth serum."

"You know it's not reliable."

"What you say while on it isn't reliable. What you are unable to keep yourself from thinking is a different matter." He inserted the needle into Coonradt's arm and pressed the plunger. "That shouldn't take long."

Within a few minutes Coonradt was struggling to keep his head up.

"Grab a pen," Hatch said to his guard. "Keep at it, Zara."

"Dr. Coonradt, what is the phone number you use to contact Carl Vey?"

Zara began writing. "I got it. It's 33 . . . 555 . . . 5876 . . . 3214."

"Country code 33," Hatch said. "It's a French number." He took out his phone and dialed. It rang three times before a once familiar voice answered. "Steven, do you have word on Michael?"

"I have word," Hatch said. "But this isn't Steven."

There was a long pause. "Who is this?"

"You know who this is, Carl. It's your old pal Jim. I wanted you to know how much I enjoyed your funeral. I even sent flowers. Did you see them?"

"How did you get this number?"

"You know that for me to get this number everything would have to be brought down. And it has. It's over, Vey. Your resistance has failed. It's over, except for you."

"Where's Michael?"

"You sound like your wife," Hatch said. "So I'll tell you what I told her. Your son is no more. He turned himself into a bomb and did a whole lot of damage. Most important, he was killed on the mission that you sent him on. It's ironic, isn't it? For years he believed that he killed you, while in the end, it was you who killed him." Hatch sniffed. "He died not even knowing that you were still alive. And you call me evil."

"I don't believe you."

"Of course you don't. That would be far too easy and logical. Besides, the liar never believes others. So whose words would you accept?"

"Steven Coonradt's."

"I could get him, but he wasn't here when your son died, so he couldn't really say for sure. Who else?"

"Gervaso."

"No, I'm afraid you killed him as well. Would you like a list of survivors? The ones you didn't kill?"

"Let me talk to Ostin."

"Ostin. No can do. He too is on that list. Died in Hades."

"Get me Cassy."

"Cassy. Yes. That I can do. It will be a moment; she's in her cell."

"If you don't mind, I'll be hanging up," Vey said.

"Of course. You don't want us to track you, do you? Call back in, say, ten."

Vey hung up.

Hatch said to his guards, "Bring me Cassy." Then he added, "And Sharon Vey. I think it's time we reunited the happy couple."

Nearly ten minutes later Cassy was brought into the room. She froze when she saw Coonradt, who was softly babbling. "Hello, Cassy," he said.

Cassy started crying. "I'm so sorry."

Coonradt just mumbled.

The phone rang and Hatch answered. "You always were right on time, Carl," Hatch said. "As reliable as a Swiss watch. I love that about you. Now here's Cassy."

Hatch handed the phone to the girl. She took it cautiously and pressed it against her tearstained face. She swallowed. "Hello?"

"Is this Cassy?"

"Yes."

"This is Carl Vey."

"I know who you are."

"Where's Michael?"

Her voice cracked. "He's gone."

Vey's voice fell. "What happened?"

"He turned himself into a bomb."

Vey was quiet for a long time. Then he said, "Who else do they have?"

"They have everyone. Dr. Coonradt. Your wife."

"Sharon?"

"Aw, she ruined my surprise," Hatch said, grabbing the phone from Cassy. He turned to his guards. "Take hot little Cassy back to her cell." He lifted the phone. "You heard that, Vey. I have *every*one. Everyone who's still alive, at least. Just try calling your French château or your Christmas Ranch, you'll find no one's home.

"But now comes the moment you've been waiting for. I think it's time you talk to your wife and explain to her how you killed your son. It might be a bit tricky, seeing how she still thinks you're dead. But seriously, this is, like, big drama moment. This is going to be a treat."

"Just get her," Vey said.

"Really? You've been hiding for eight years, and suddenly you can't wait another minute to talk to her? Patience, Vey."

"Let me talk to Sharon."

"You will. We're just waiting for her to arrive." He put the phone on mute. "Where's Sharon Vey?"

"She's almost here, sir."

Two minutes later Sharon walked into the room. "What do you want?" she asked Hatch tersely.

"Someone sounds like she's having a bad day," Hatch said. He offered her the phone. "You have a phone call."

"Is it Michael?"

"Sharon, you're killing me. You have to accept that Michael is gone. It's someone else you care about."

She looked at Hatch, then took the phone. "Hello."

"Sharon."

There was a long pause. "Who is this?"

"It's Carl."

Sharon began to tremble. "No. You're dead."

"Honey, I'm not dead."

"I don't believe you. What did you say to me when you asked me to marry you?"

"I just said, 'Will you marry me?'"

"No. You said more."

Vey was silent a moment, then said, "I said, 'You could do worse.'"

Sharon began to cry. "Where have you been? You left us to all this."

"You don't think this has been killing me? I was saving your lives. Hatch was killing everyone who knew about the MEI."

"You didn't save our lives," Sharon said. "We're about to die. And you ruined the rest of them."

Hatch snatched back the phone. "You did not disappoint, old friend. So tell me, was that worth the wait? The bigger question is, will she ever forgive you? Of course, it's a moot question, since your time is short. You should know, she did fall in love with someone else in your resistance, but, not to worry, I took care of him for you. You can thank me for that later."

"What do you want from me?" Vey asked.

"You know what I want, Carl. I want you. I want you to surrender yourself to my guards and come to the Hatch Islands."

"Why would I do that?"

"Firstly, because you don't want your friends' blood on your hands. Because if you don't come, I will start killing them, one by one. Coonradt . . . Cassy . . . the entire Electroclan that your son started. . . .

"Secondly, you don't want your beautiful wife tortured and killed. Your lovely Rose of Sharon. Sharon the pain."

"How do I know you won't just kill them anyway?"

"You don't. You'll just have to believe me. But you can be assured that if you don't come, they will *all* die. I'm sure you won't have any trouble believing me when I say that. And I will video tape each of their final moments just for you. I will make them thank you for killing them just before they breathe their last breath. And, since I've destroyed the rest of the resistance, you will spend the rest of your life as a fugitive, running with a ten-million-dollar bounty on your head. For that much money your own mother would turn you in."

Vey was silent a moment, then said, "What do you want me to do?"

"You will fly to Rome immediately. There you will be greeted by the Domguard. They will bring you to me."

"All right."

"Very well. Let's see if you're a man of your word. You have twenty-four hours to be in the Domguard's custody before I start killing. Do you understand?"

"I'll be there."

"Good. I look forward to seeing you again. We all do." Hatch hung up his phone and smiled. "And the walls came tumbling down."

PART SIXTEEN

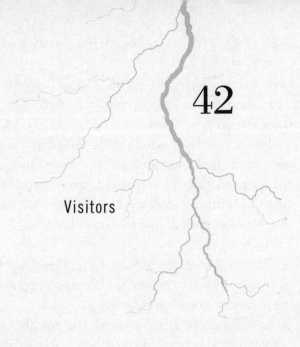

42

Visitors

It was the morning of the fifth day on Plutus. Enele looked out the gap in the fourth-story wall of the depository, toward his home island of Funafuti. It was four days since they'd sequestered themselves inside, and still no sign of an Elgen attack. It wasn't a question of if they would come, only when. The Elgen knew the Tuvaluans were there. There was no question of that, as the rebels were being regularly monitored by Elgen drones. Twice a day and once at night they'd come, always circling the island just out of gunshot range, watching for movement. But still no attack. Enele knew what Hatch was waiting for. He was rebuilding his army while Enele's grew weaker.

Hatch had all the time in the world. He had stranded Enele and his men on the island and guaranteed that they would remain there. Just six hours after Enele's army had finished carrying all their weapons and supplies into the depository, a fleet of Elgen helicopters—twelve fully-armed Apaches—flew in from the east. They passed over the depository in formation, then, circling back, commenced their mission.

It was easy to conclude what their mission was. They didn't fire once at the building; instead they focused their missiles and guns on the boats docked in the harbor. They performed their operation efficiently. Just fifteen minutes after they arrived, they were headed back to their base, leaving Enele's boats shredded, sinking, and burning in the harbor.

The ES *Proton*, the only real ship Enele had had left, was, missile by missile, blown to pieces, her burning wreckage scattered and floating in pieces around the harbor.

In addition to their missiles, the Apaches carried M230 chain guns mounted beneath the helicopters that fired 30mm bullets at the rate of 625 bullets a minute. The helicopters strafed the ground so thoroughly that even the smallest of Enele's rafts was so riddled by bullets that it looked more like a block of Swiss cheese than a flotation device.

Four days, Enele thought now. *When will it come?* Or maybe it wouldn't. Perhaps Hatch's plan was to just wait until they ran out of food and water. If the gods were generous, he and his men could capture rainwater for drinking, but food was a different matter. Even with rationing, Enele's army wouldn't survive more than two months.

Enele's thoughts were suddenly broken by something he hadn't heard in a while: the sound of boat engines. But they weren't coming from the east. Enele ran to the other side of the floor and looked out over the enclosed Nukufetau harbor. Amid the wreckage of their ships there were nineteen boats of different shapes and sizes headed their way. Enele grabbed his radio. "Adam, you see that?"

"Yes, sir. We've got visitors."

"Who are they?"

"I don't know. I'll go out to meet them."

"Be careful," Enele said. "Consider them hostile. Send some men up to me, and we'll cover you from here."

"Roger," Adam said.

A minute later four soldiers ran up the stairs. "We're here," the first said.

Following Enele's instruction, they pointed two of their machine guns out toward the harbor. Two of the boats had already docked, and their occupants started to disembark. None of them appeared to be carrying guns. Then Adam, flanked by six armed soldiers, walked up to them. The men spoke for a moment, then, to Enele's surprise, embraced.

"I'm going down," Enele said. "Hold your fire unless we're fired on." He ran down the stairs. As he reached the main floor, the front door opened. Adam walked in. "Enele. I have someone to see you."

Enele walked forward to see who it was. Standing just inside the doorway were Jack and Ostin. Enele immediately threw up his arms. "Jack! Ostin!"

"Enele," Jack said. They came together and hugged.

"What are you doing back here?" Enele asked. "I thought you had escaped."

"So did we," Jack said. "The Philippine Navy captured the *Joule*. We're the only ones who got away. We came back to save them and help you."

"Who are 'we'?"

"Our new friends," Jack said. He turned back and said, "Come on in, you guys."

Vishal, Alveeta, and the *MAS* crew all stepped inside the depository.

"In Fiji we met Vishal and Alveeta," Jack said.

Vishal and Alveeta stepped forward.

"Enele," Alveeta said. "Do you remember me?"

"Of course, my friend." The men embraced. "I haven't seen you since grade school. You look the same."

"I weigh the same," Alveeta said with a slight laugh. "I am here with Vishal. He is the leader of the Tuvaluan resistance. Now we will follow you."

"I'm Vishal," Vishal said, extending his hand. "It is an honor to meet you, Enele Saluni. You come from a great family."

"Where did you come from?" Enele asked.

"There were about two hundred of us who were out of the country when the Elgen attacked. We've been waiting for the right time. When Jack and Ostin told us that you were rallying our people, we knew it was time."

"I would someday like to hear how that came about," Enele said. "But we haven't time now. You have two hundred soldiers?"

"Almost two hundred, though we're not much for soldiers. We're mostly salesmen and professionals. But we are willing to fight and die for our country."

"That is good," Enele said. "We have an army. Did you see any drones as you came in?"

"No," Ostin said.

"Good. That is how they watch us. Come in. Have you eaten?"

"Yes," Vishal said. "Likely better than you. We have supplies and weapons on our boats."

"Adam," Enele said. "Take a hundred men and help our friends unload their boats. Then hide their boats wherever you can. There is a mangrove forest a mile north of here; they might be safe there. Then hurry back. I am convening a war council."

"Yes, sir," Adam said.

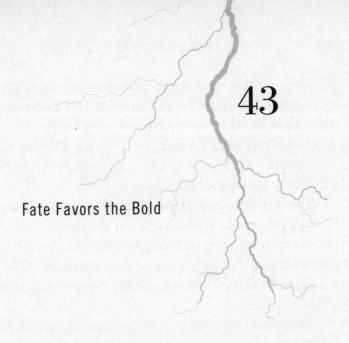

43

Fate Favors the Bold

Adam returned to find Enele seated around a long table with Jack, Ostin, Nazil, Tomas, Raphe, Captain Pio, Alveeta, and Vishal.

"You are just in time," Enele said. "How did it go?"

"We brought in about two hundred guns and ammunition and about a ton and a half of food."

"That is good," Enele said. "Now please close the door and be seated."

Adam shut the door, then sat down at the end of the table. Enele stood. His eyes looked tired but hard, and his voice was weary but clear.

"Soldiers of Tuvalu, this is our situation. We are stranded here. We have seven hundred and fifty-eight soldiers with weapons and ammunition. If we carefully ration, we have enough food to last perhaps just over two months. That is basic survival. We have new boats, but it would take several—at least four—sorties of all the boats to move our soldiers from here to Funafuti. It is doubtful that we could make so many trips without being seen by the Elgen drones and attacked before reaching land."

". . . And we are low on fuel," Vishal said. "We could not make the trip four times without refueling."

"There is that, too," Enele said. "This is our predicament. If the Elgen decide to wait us out, we are at their mercy. We will eventually run out of food, then be forced to either surrender or attack, with only a portion of our army against their strongest island. By that time it is likely that Hatch will have rebuilt most of his forces. I'm afraid it will not go well."

"That would be a highly uncharacteristic stratagem for Dr. Hatch," Ostin said.

The men looked at one another. "What did he say?" Adam asked Jack.

"He means Dr. Hatch probably won't do that because he doesn't like to wait." Jack looked around the table. "I'm learning to speak Ostinese."

Ostin continued. "It would be the logical thing to do, but it's not Hatch's way. He likes to strike hard with speed and force and take what he wants. Just like he attacked Tuvalu."

"Then why hasn't he attacked already?" Tomas asked.

"Because he's rebuilding his forces," Vishal said. "He is bringing in his guard from around the world. In Fiji there are Elgen guard everywhere. They are coming from Samoa and Taiwan and many other places."

"He has more than just guards," Jack said. "He's using other governments' militaries. Like the Philippine Navy that captured us."

Enele looked grim. "The elder was right. The evil one has already grown stronger than we realized." He breathed out slowly. "So, my friends. What do we do?"

"I have an idea," Raphe said.

Everyone turned to hear what he had to say.

Raphe was one of the youngest in the room and looked around

the table nervously. "I don't like the idea of sitting here waiting for them to come kill us. At night, the drones only pass overhead once. We could take two boats and sail them outside of the drone's flight pattern to the northeast shore of Funafuti. It is a wooded area. We could take a hundred people each night and slowly amass our army and weapons.

"We would leave enough men here, just a half dozen or so, to give the appearance that we are all still here. As you said, Hatch strikes with speed and force. He will send all his men to the depository, leaving none back. When he leaves, our army attacks the plant and captures it and all its weapons. Then we blow up the dock to slow their return. We will have the advantage, and we can call all our people to us. We will have thousands of soldiers."

"It will be a death sentence for those who stay," Adam said.

"I don't think so," Raphe said. "It is no more dangerous than for those who fight. The ones who stay here will lock themselves in with more food and supplies than they could ever use. If we fail and the Elgen destroy us and then come back to reclaim Plutus, our men can slip off in the night amid the many soldiers."

The room was silent. Enele looked around the table, then said, "What do you think?"

"It makes sense to me," Nazil said.

"And me," Tomas added. "I think if we just wait, we are playing into the Elgen's plans, not ours."

"Captain Pio?"

The captain nodded. "We can make the trips, but we still have the problem with fuel."

"We would have to find some in Funafuti," Raphe said. "Do we have enough to make two trips?"

"We do," Vishal said. "But if we're just taking two or three boats a night, we could take fuel from the other boats until we find more."

Enele looked at Vishal. "Vishal? Alveeta? What do you think?"

"I like the idea," Vishal said.

"Me too," Alveeta said.

"Jack?"

Jack looked vexed. "I think it's crazy." Everyone looked at him. "But what choice do we have? If we just wait here, we'll die for sure."

"Ostin?"

Ostin shook his head. "Jack's right, it's risky, but not riskier than doing nothing. It's a little like what we did in Peru. I need more time to process it."

"What do you think?" Adam asked Enele.

"I'd like to think it over as well," Enele said. "I think you are all correct in saying that to wait for the Elgen's time line is suicide. They won't attack until they are certain to achieve victory."

"There is one more possibility," Tomas said.

"What's that?" Enele asked.

"We could take the boats not to Funafuti but to the other islands and disperse our forces. We could then practice the *Bati Kadi*, attacking the Elgen as individual cells."

Enele thought for a moment, then shook his head. "No. Tuvalu is too small. Once the Elgen have rebuilt their force, they would hunt us down and exterminate us as well as all those who provided for us.

"Right now I am leaning toward Raphe's plan, but I must think more on it. Does anyone else have anything to say?" He looked around the room. No one spoke. "No? Then get your lunch; we will meet again in a few hours."

The men all stood to leave. As Jack and Ostin were about to walk out of the room, Enele said, "Jack, Ostin, please wait. I'd like to speak with you."

"Sure," Jack said.

Once everyone else was gone, Enele said, "Shut the door, please."

Ostin closed the door, and he and Jack sat down. Enele looked at Ostin. "What is it about the plan that you don't agree with?"

"I didn't say I disagreed. I said I needed more time to process it."

Enele nodded. "I need to ask you something very important."

"Yes, sir."

"How did you know to find us here?"

Ostin hesitated, unsure of how Enele would respond to the truth. Before he could answer, Jack said, "We had a dream."

Enele looked at him. "A dream?"

"Don't think I'm crazy," Jack said. "It happened."

"I don't think you're crazy. You're here; that's proof in itself. Was there anything more in the dream?"

Ostin and Jack glanced at each other, unsure of how much they should share. Ostin said, "There were a few things. We were told that we would be attacked by the Elgen. But . . . someone would help us."

"Who?" Enele looked incredibly eager. Still, Ostin was hesitant to answer.

". . . Why are you afraid to speak?" Enele asked.

Ostin fidgeted. "Because it sounds crazy."

Enele looked back and forth between them. "Tell me, friends. What really happened back at Hades? What caused that explosion?"

Ostin said, "We can't be completely sure, but we're pretty sure it was Michael."

"Michael Vey set off the explosion?"

Ostin shook his head. "Michael *was* the explosion."

Enele's brow furrowed. "Explain."

"Michael was one of the electric kids." When Enele didn't respond, Ostin said, "One of the Glows. Do you know what that is?"

Enele nodded. "Yes, I know about the Glows."

"But he was different from the others. Something about the way his body handled electricity. He could hold it."

"Like a battery," Jack said.

"Exactly, except, with his power, he could increase it. What I think happened, Michael knew we were about to be overrun, so he climbed the radio tower in order to get hit by lightning. That's when he sent us to the bunker. I think he was struck by lightning and managed to hold it. Maybe for just a fraction of a second, but long enough to amplify it. He turned himself into a bomb. And blew himself up along with everything else. It was like the biggest lightning bolt ever struck the island and blew everything away."

"That would explain why the sand turned to glass," Enele said.

Ostin nodded.

"So let me ask you this—perhaps it is what you are afraid of speaking. What do you know of the lightning god?"

"*Uira te Atua*," Ostin said.

Enele's eyes grew wide. "How do you know that name?"

"Michael told us in the dream. But we don't know anything about it. What do you know?"

"The elder told me that even though we had beaten the Elgen army at Hades, Hatch was not as weak as we believed and had already brought in other armies to serve him, which you verified today is true."

"Straight up," Jack said.

"He said that we should take shelter here, on this island, because we would be fiercely attacked. He said that there would be an opportunity for success when *Uira te Atua* came."

"What is the *Uira te Atua*?" Ostin asked.

"There's something you don't know?" Jack said.

"As smart as Ostin is," Enele said, "he could not possibly know the meaning of that word. The word is sacred and not often spoken in public. It is not even Tuvaluan. It's from a language even older than ours, long before there was writing, when our history was handed down in stories from the elders. The word refers to an ancient legend that someday a great one would come to save us in our troubles. *Uira te Atua*, the lightning god."

"The lightning god," Ostin repeated.

"The elder said that when *Uira te Atua* came to deliver us, we would know that it was time to expel the evil one and liberate Funafuti. Now you tell me that your friend, Michael, was struck by lightning and . . . comes to you in dreams?"

"We believe so," Ostin said.

"But he is dead?"

"Anyone else would be dead. But Michael's not anyone else."

"The dream we had," Jack said. "We're not sure it's a dream."

Enele slowly shook his head. "Do you think Michael could be . . . the lightning god?"

Ostin scratched his head. "I don't know. He's no god; he's just our friend."

"If he can hold lightning, he is a god. Perhaps not *the* God, but to us, a god all the same."

"So what do we do now?" Jack asked.

Enele shook his head. "I was hoping you could enlighten me."

"Logically," Ostin said, "Raphe's idea makes the most sense. But it seems counter to the elder's prophecy."

Enele thought for a moment, then said, "Perhaps it is a problem that people don't have faith in prophecy, so they try to make their prophecy happen, instead of trusting in it. Destiny is chasing us, not the other way around. We cannot guess destiny's mind nor her course. In such cases, we must move ahead and make the best decisions we can. Fate has always favored the bold."

Jack nodded in agreement. "I agree."

"Okay," Ostin said. "Then we'll follow Raphe's plan unless something else comes up."

"Then it's agreed," Enele said. "There's no time to waste. We'll send out our first boats tonight."

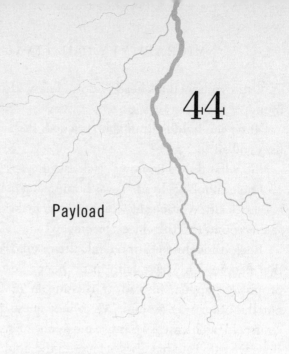

44

Payload

Enele's war council met again a little after sunset. They decided that since the first trip would be the riskiest, they would start with just one boat and ten men to find a place to gather in secret. The boat would leave right after the drone had passed by, since it had been coming fairly regularly at about three a.m. Captain Nikhil volunteered to take his boat and captain the first sortie.

"You are brave," Enele said.

"It is why I came," Nikhil said.

"You must get some sleep while the others prepare your boat."

"I'll take watch," Jack said.

Enele nodded. "If you are willing, I will leave you in charge of the fortress tonight."

"I'm willing," Jack said. "Good night."

"Good night," Enele replied.

As Adam and Enele walked to the sleeping quarters, Adam asked, "Are you okay leaving such a young man in charge of our defense?"

Enele looked at him. "Of course. In the last battle I worked for him."

Ostin and Jack went up to the open fourth floor. The stars shown brilliantly above them like a million pinpricks in a black velvet canvas. There were three other watchmen, one at each wall.

"Do you have any idea how close we are to our friends?" Ostin said.

"No."

"Really close. Just sixty miles. If we had a telescope, we could see Funafuti."

"They might as well be on the moon," Jack said, looking out. He turned back. "Do you think Ian can see us?"

"Yes."

Jack nodded. "Somehow that makes me feel good."

"If he's still alive," Ostin added.

Jack sighed. "Well, that *did* make me feel good." He walked over and looked out the west side of the floor. He could see the men preparing the *MAS*. He said back to Ostin, "Did you ever figure out what 'MAS' stood for?"

"'Men at sea,'" Ostin said.

"Could be," Jack said. "It's a lot better than what I just came up with."

"What's that?"

"'Mexicans and Spaniards.'"

Two hours later Vishal came up to the fourth floor carrying a woven basket filled with food. Seeing how Enele had greeted them, he had gained even more respect for the two young men.

"I brought you some food."

"Thanks," Jack said. "You should be sleeping."

"I know. I couldn't sleep."

Jack looked through the basket. There was salted fish and small loaves of bread. He took out a loaf and ripped it in half, then put a fish inside. "Look at us," he said to Ostin. "A raw fish sandwich in the middle of the night. Could you imagine eating something like this back in Idaho?"

"I can't even imagine Idaho," Ostin said. He turned to Jack. "Do you think we'll ever see Idaho again?"

Jack thought for a moment, then said, "Keep it in your mind, and you will."

Vishal looked back and forth between the two, then said, "You mean Uh-Idaho in California?"

Jack laughed. "We're not good liars."

"No. You're not."

Just then one of the other men shouted, "Drone!"

Jack walked over to the east wall. The drone was approaching. Jack lifted his radio. "The drone is approaching. Prepare for sortie, Alpha."

Ostin lifted his binoculars to examine the drone. "You may want to belay that order," Ostin said.

Jack turned around. "Why?"

Ostin handed Jack the binoculars. "That's not an observation drone. It's carrying payload."

Jack looked through the binoculars, then said, "We've got more than that." He quickly lifted his radio again. "Everyone, inside the compound. I repeat, get inside the compound. Abort sortie. Abort sortie. Nikhil, are you there?"

"I'm here, Jack. What's wrong?"

"Wake Enele. Tell him we've got an armed drone and a fleet of Apache helicopters incoming. The Elgen are coming."

45

Hellfire Missiles

The first wave of Elgen attack helicopters consisted of the same twelve Apaches that had taken out the rebels' boats. Jack guessed that the Elgen had spotted Vishal's flotilla and had come to sink his boats as well. But if the Elgen knew about the boats, they ignored them. Instead, for the first time, they fired on the building.

Two Hellfire missiles streaked across the night sky, exploding against the east wall of the fourth floor, filling the open room with smoke and spreading shrapnel and chipped stone within yards of where Jack and Ostin were positioned.

"Get below!" Jack shouted. "Everyone, go below."

They all hurried down to the mostly enclosed third level.

"Can those missiles knock down these walls?" Jack asked Ostin.

"Not one of them," Ostin said. "Maybe not a dozen. But they can chip away at it."

"We could use Tanner about now," Jack said.

"We could use the whole freakin' Electroclan," Ostin replied. "And Michael."

In spite of the machine guns Jack and Ostin and the Tuvaluans shot at them, the helicopters confidently hovered around the island for nearly forty-five minutes, some dropping as low as ground level. They blew up all of the outer fences, destroyed the depository's few vehicles, and fired six missiles into the thick metal walls of the loading docks, which dented them but didn't penetrate.

After the attack, Ostin and Jack sat back, exhausted, against the east wall.

"That was weird," Jack said. "It's like they came just to annoy us. Like mosquitoes. What do you think their objective was?"

"They took down the fences," Ostin said. "There's only one reason they'd do that."

Jack looked at him, awaiting the reason. "And that reason is . . . ?"

". . . Ground troops," Ostin said. "Boots on ground. I think they're softening us up for a full-on invasion." He looked up at the helicopters. "You watch. They'll do what we were going to do, except they don't have any reason to hide. They'll keep sending guards over here until they're ready to blow the walls."

"I thought you said these walls were impenetrable."

"Nothing's impenetrable," Ostin said. "The walls can hold off Hellfire missiles but not everything."

"Like what?"

"A battleship's cannons."

"Fortunately, Enele sank their battleship," Jack said.

"I'm sure Hatch will find another one eventually," Ostin said.

"You're so optimistic," Jack said, shaking his head. "So, if you were Hatch, what would you do?"

"What would I do, or what would I do if I were Hatch?"

"Both."

"I would have just starved us out," Ostin said. "But I'm not Hatch. If I were and didn't care about the lives of my men, I'd start sending men over. Then, when I had a large enough force, I'd either send a detonation team to blow a hole in the wall or, preferably, find a battleship."

"Why is that preferable?"

"With our weapons, it would be too easy for us to take out a detonation team and capture their explosives. But a battleship, we couldn't touch it."

"Why would you *start* sending men over? Why not send them all at once?"

"Because they don't have any ships large enough to transport all their men at once, so I'd send them in waves."

"But if they had a battleship, they'd be able to kill two birds with one stone."

"If by 'birds' you mean our resistance and all hope, yes."

Jack groaned. "Then what would you do?"

"Then, after we had breached the wall, I'd throw in grenades and smoke bombs to clear the way. Then I'd send in soldiers to take the building."

"Just like Hades," Jack said.

"Just like Hades," Ostin replied. "What would you do?"

"If I were Hatch, I'd punch a hole in the wall. Then I'd fire in a nerve agent, like sarin."

"You'd have to be sick to do that."

"'Sick' is Hatch's middle name," Jack said.

Ostin frowned. "Let's just hope he doesn't have any sarin."

A half hour later Enele came up to the third floor to inspect the damage.

"Are you okay?" he asked Jack and Ostin.

"Yes."

"Was anyone hurt?"

"Tomas got some shrapnel in his hand, but nothing too serious," Jack said. "He's got it wrapped up. How about below?"

"One casualty," Enele said curtly. "War council in thirty minutes." He turned and walked away.

Less then an hour later the same group from before was gathered for war council in the conference room. Everyone except for Adam.

"We're all here," Enele said.

"Where's Adam?" Ostin asked.

The room went quiet, except for Raphe, who was softly crying, his face concealed behind his hands.

"He's the casualty," Enele said, forcing himself not to show emotion. "He went out to get a better shot at the helicopters." His face fell. "They saw him." Suddenly the anger showed in Enele's eyes. "This is just the beginning. We must accept that the Elgen are preparing for an invasion. This is better than being starved out, but we must also prepare. We've taken full inventory of what weapons and ammunition we have. We are limited and cannot afford to waste, but I believe we have enough.

"To attack us, their biggest problem is getting inside. They can only do this with explosives. There are three ways they can accomplish this. They can drop a bomb from the air. They can, on ground, deliver explosives. Or they can shell us from a battleship. We are fortunate in this regard. They clearly do not have aerial bombs, or they would have used them on Hades. We do not know if they have land explosives, but we know we took all they had at Vaitupu, and Captain Pio then used them to sink their battle cruiser. But if they do have more, we will not allow them near the building. Lastly, we do not believe that they have a battleship; as I said, Captain Pio has sunk it. So, for now, we have a short reprieve. In addition to preparing our men for these three possible situations, how do we best use that time?"

"We never should have come here," Tomas said. "The old man was wrong. Now we are just papaya waiting to be picked. We should have followed our first plan and attacked Funafuti."

"We would have died on Funafuti," Nazil said.

"We'll die here," Tomas said. "At least we would have spilled some of their blood."

Enele said, "Where we are is all that matters now. We must deal with our present situation, not rethink the past choices."

Raphe raised his hand. "Sir, is it possible to still move toward my original plan?"

Enele was quiet a moment, then said, "Yes. I do not think we will have time to move the whole of our army, but it is still preferable. But the increase in drone activity makes it even more risky."

"At this point, sir, all options are risky," Nazil pointed out.

"Well said, Nazil," Enele said. "I would like to appoint Jack as my second-in-command in charge of keeping the Elgen away from the building." Enele looked at Jack. "Do you accept that responsibility?"

Jack nodded. "Yes, sir. I'm honored."

"I know you will succeed. Nazil, you will be in charge of the troops inside the building. I ask you to design a plan to hold off the Elgen should they gain access to the building. They will likely parachute in. In that case Jack and his men will be the first line of defense. If they blow a hole with explosives, I would expect them to take aim at our structurally weakest point—the metal gates of the loading dock. I believe that is why the Elgen helicopters targeted them, to test their strength. As we all saw, the gates are vulnerable. Perhaps not to Hellfire missiles, but certainly to something more powerful. Like a vehicle loaded with explosives. Jack, it is your responsibility to keep them away from the building."

"Yes, sir."

"Nazil, we must have a plan to protect the north loading dock if they manage to break through."

"Yes, Enele."

"If they are to shell us from the sea, it will be the eastern or southern side of the building that they will target."

46

Why Did the Elgen Cross the Channel?

The next four days on Plutus were quiet except for the drones. The Elgen had increased the flybys to every two hours. On the third day Jack took a shot at one just out of anger.

"That's not going to do any good," Ostin said.

"It did me good," Jack said. He put down the rifle. "What are they looking for?"

"They're just making sure we stay put," Ostin said. "Or trying to drive us mad."

"It's working," Jack said. "They're not bringing men over."

"Which means Hatch is waiting for a ship."

Then the drone did a second flyby.

"That's new," Jack said. He lifted his binoculars. "It's circling."

"Is it carrying payload?"

"No." Then Jack lowered his binoculars to the eastern horizon.

Then he groaned. "It doesn't need it." He turned back to Ostin. "You were right. Hatch found a battleship. And a few others."

Ostin lifted his own binoculars. "Oh no." A moment later he said, "Wait, we know those ships. I recognize the flag. They're Filipino." He lowered the binoculars. "They're probably the same ships that captured us in Fiji."

"Now the Filipinos are helping out," Jack said. "Why would they help Hatch?"

"Because he owns them," Ostin said, still looking at the ship. "It's got sixteen-inch cannons." He turned back to Jack. "We're so screwed."

It wasn't a direct hit, but the battleship's first shell exploded with a deafening boom that shook the entire depository. Even though the shell struck the rock shore twenty yards in front of the southeastern wall, it was big enough to rip away pieces of the outer wall and scatter rock higher than the depository. Smoke rose above the building.

Enele and Raphe came running up. "What was that?" Enele shouted.

"They've got a battleship," Jack said, handing Enele his binoculars. Enele looked out at the ship and shook his head. "There are four ships."

"They're the same ships that captured the *Joule*," Ostin said. "I'm sure the others are carrying soldiers."

There was another boom in the distance, and a second shell struck. This one caught a corner of the southeast wall. Jack ran over to the nearest opening and leaned out. "They've breached the wall. It's twelve feet up, too high for them to climb."

"They'll keep firing," Ostin said. "That particular battleship can hold nearly a thousand rounds."

"We are screwed," Jack said. "Maybe they'll just shell us into oblivion."

"If they hit this floor, it will kill us all," Raphe said, grabbing Enele. "We've got to evacuate this floor."

"No," Jack said. "Once they blow a hole in the wall, the soldiers are going to pour in. We need the machine-gun nest to stop them from getting inside."

"Then we can come back up after they've landed their men and have stopped shelling."

"He's got a point," Ostin said. "They'll stop shelling after they land their own men. We can watch from the third floor."

As they evacuated the fourth floor, Ostin said to Jack, "Why did the Elgen cross the channel?"

Jack looked at him. "Why?"

"To kill us."

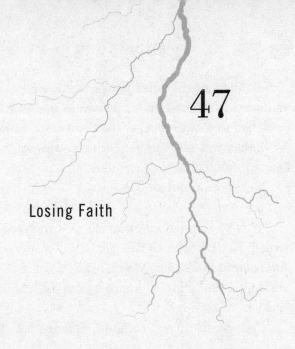

47

Losing Faith

As the ships neared the island, the shells fell with greater accuracy. The fourth and fifth shells struck within seconds of each other, creating a hole big enough for a dozen men to enter at once.

"They got their front door," Jack said.

"She's still coming closer," Ostin said. "And the other ships are turning north."

"That's where the dock is," Enele said. "They are preparing to land."

Then Nazil and Tomas came up to the third floor. "Enele, they've opened the wall," Nazil said. "Your orders?"

"My orders remain as before. We know where they are coming; prepare your men to hold the fortress."

"We are prepared," Nazil said. "We have a machine-gun nest in place."

Just then another shell struck. It was well placed and landed a few yards inside the hole they'd blown in the wall. It shook the building and filled the lower level of the depository with smoke.

"Enele, you need to get below to the vaults," Raphe said. "They can withstand the ship's cannons."

Enele didn't move.

"Sir."

"Why? So Hatch can put me in a monkey cage like my grand-father? No, I'll fight to the end. I will stand here when the *Uira te Atua* comes in his glory." He looked out over the ocean and the near-ing ships. "*Uira te Atua*, do not let our faith be in vain." Then he said, "Why is he waiting?"

"Because he is not coming," Tomas said. "Because it is all just myth."

"Do not speak so," Raphe said.

"We are doomed," Tomas said.

"Go below with your troops," Enele ordered.

"Troops," Tomas said. "They are basket weavers."

Nazil and Tomas left the floor.

Ostin said to himself, "Michael, if you're coming, now would be a good time."

The good news was that the battleship stopped shelling the deposi-tory. The bad news was that it was because the other three Filipino ships were about to dock and release their troops.

Looking out the north wall slot of the fourth level, Jack could see the ships lined up, the men on dock armed and ready to swarm the island. He estimated that there were at least several thousand soldiers just on the first ship, half Elgen, half Filipino. Hatch had efficiently brought in his guard from around the world. "Here they come." He turned back to Ostin. "It's déjà vu."

"Yeah," Ostin said. "Hades all over. Except this time, it's without Michael." He breathed out heavily as a gangplank began to extend from the ship.

"At least we'll be with him soon," Jack said.

"What do you mean?"

Jack pointed skyward. "In heaven."

"You think there's a heaven?" Ostin asked.

"There's got to be."

"Why is that?"

"Look around you. We know there's a hell. There's got to be balance, somewhere."

"What if there's not?"

Jack shook his head. "Then we'll never know, will we?"

Ostin's eyes filled with tears. "My poor parents."

"They've got their own problems. In some ways, we're the lucky ones."

"How's that?"

"When you're dead, you're free. No pain, no Elgen. No Hatch."

"No fear," Ostin said.

"Are you afraid?" Jack asked.

Ostin nodded. "Terrified. Are you?"

Jack looked at him. "I try not to think about it."

Just then one of the ships blew a horn.

"They do that before they unload," Ostin said.

"I need to make sure everyone is ready," Jack said.

He ran around the fourth floor, checking out his twelve riflemen and three machine gunners.

"This all the ammo we have?" Jack asked one of the machine gunners. In light of the growing enemy, the twenty-two boxes they had seemed inadequate.

"Yes, sir," the gunner replied. "We brought up all we have."

"All right. Don't waste ammo. We'll at least make them fight their way in."

Just then a door opened on the ship's second level and a second gangplank extended to the dock.

"What's that?" Ostin said.

Jack looked out at the boat. "They've got a tank. That's not fair."

"We are so screwed," Ostin said.

Jack looked at Ostin. "Remember that time when we caught you behind the school and Wade pantsed you, underwear and all?"

"I'll remember that until the day I die. Which is probably today, anyway. Why?"

"Sorry."

"You're apologizing now?"

"Yeah."

"Okay. I forgive you."

"And Wade?"

"I'll forgive him, too."

"Thanks."

"I don't forgive Mitchell."

"Well, he did let us hang out at his place when the Elgen were hunting us."

"That's true."

"And he paid for all that pizza."

Ostin sighed. "Okay. I'll forgive him, too." A moment later Ostin said, "Since we're doing this, I need to apologize too."

"For what?"

"Back when I found out that you were driving Michael and me to California, I told Michael that I didn't like you."

"Of course you didn't. We pantsed you."

"Yeah. Well, I also said if Wade was in a shark tank and asked for help, I'd throw in chum."

Jack laughed. "Good thing you didn't say that to my face. Back then I probably would have smacked you."

"I figured."

"Not that you did anything wrong, but I forgive you too. I think Wade would too."

"Thanks."

Jack and Ostin both looked at the tank sitting on the gangplank. "Our guns won't do a thing to that," Ostin said.

"See that tank in back?" Jack said. "The smaller one with the weird gun? It's not really a tank."

"What is it?"

"Really? I actually know something you don't know?"

"I don't know everything," Ostin said.

"You could have fooled me. It's an M132 armored flamethrower."

"An unstoppable flamethrower. That's not good."

"No. If they're smart, they'll drive it inside that hole they breached and push us back. The halls are wide enough for it. And if not, they'll just drive through them. We've got to tell Nazil to set the land mines."

"This is all kinds of happy," Ostin said. "Do you know where the flamethrower tank came from?"

Jack shook his head. "No idea."

"Britain. It was developed late in World War II. They called it the Churchill Crocodile."

"I always wanted a weapon named after me," Jack said. "Like the Sherman tank or the Pershing missile."

"Really?"

"Yeah. I thought that would be cool."

"I always wanted a university named after me," Ostin said.

"It would have happened," Jack said. "And there would be a statue of you in front of it. Ostin University."

Ostin smiled. "People would get it mixed up with the University of Texas at Austin. Maybe it would have to be Liss University."

"That's a good name," Jack said.

"I always thought you'd receive the Medal of Honor someday," Ostin said.

Jack looked at him. "You did?"

"Yeah. Maybe you still will. Posthumously."

Jack was suddenly quiet. "That may be the best thing anyone has ever said to me." He looked back toward the enemy boat. "Why is that tank not moving?"

"No idea," Ostin said. He breathed out heavily. "How do you think the girls are?"

"I try not to think about it."

"Me neither. I wish they were here with us." Ostin frowned. "No, actually, I wish they were with us but we were, like, five thousand miles away."

"Back in Meridian, Idaho. PizzaMax."

"Not there," Ostin said. "I don't think I could go there without Michael. Too many memories."

"I wouldn't even mind being at school."

Ostin smiled. "Remember Principal Dahlstrom?"

"Yeah. What a tool."

"It's hard to believe that I was actually afraid of him."

"Yeah, that's weird."

"I think if I ever see him again, I'm going to punch him. For old times' sake."

"He'd expel you."

"Ohh, I'm afraid," Ostin laughed. "Put me in his Cell 25."

"Yeah, doesn't sound that scary," Jack laughed. "Just make sure I'm there for it."

"You can punch him too," Ostin said. "For good measure."

They both laughed. Then their laughter quieted. After a few moments Ostin said, "It was a pleasure dying with you, friend. Not the dying part, per se, but being with you when it happened."

"No," Jack said. "It was a pleasure living with you."

They looked at each other; then Ostin lightly hit Jack on the shoulder. Jack reached over and hugged him.

After they parted, Jack said, "I can see why Michael liked you so much. You're much braver and stronger than you give yourself credit for."

Ostin couldn't speak. His eyes filled with tears. "Thanks."

Jack smiled at him. Then they both turned and looked back out at the ship. The first gangplank had finished lowering, and the men were lined up at the top of it, about to come out. Jack sighed again. "Here they come."

Then, out of a clear blue sky, lightning struck.

48

Uira te Atua

"**H**oly crap!" Ostin shouted. The massive blast of lightning had hit the top of the ship, dropping all of the men on board. It was so large that it shook the depository even more than the shelling had. The first strike was followed by a second, third, and fourth. The soldiers on board scattered; some jumped into the sea, others ran inside the ship, but most of them lay still on the deck. Then a blast of lightning blew apart the second gangplank, and both tanks fell into the ocean.

Enele, followed by Raphe, came running up to the fourth floor. Enele was out of breath. "Did you see that?"

"Still watching it," Jack said.

"Uira te Atua!"

Lightning struck the ship over and over until there was no movement on board. Then the lightning moved to the ship behind it, then to the third.

"It's a miracle," Raphe said.

"No, it's *Uira te Atua*," Enele said. "The lightning god."

Ostin lightly smiled. "No," he said. "It's my buddy Michael."

After all signs of life had vanished from the three ships, the lightning began striking farther out at sea, hitting the battleship with such force that after just three strikes the ship was on fire.

"If that's Michael," Jack said, "he's pissed."

"Wow," Ostin said. "That's what vengeance looks like."

Then a strike pounded down through the center of the boat. "That was huge!" Jack said.

Jack lifted his binoculars. "He sunk it!"

Ostin lifted his as well. "He did. It's sinking! Go, Michael!"

The lightning stopped. "Let me look," Enele said. Jack handed him his binoculars. "It is going down. *Uira te Atua* has saved us."

Suddenly the sky above them began to brighten, as if collecting the light from the sun itself, then forming into a ball about thirty feet above them. It grew in brightness until it was too bright to look at and they had to turn away.

"What is that?" Raphe asked.

Then the ball began to crackle and spark as it slowly lowered to the floor. No one dared speak. Then the light began to diminish and pull in tighter, taking the shape of a human form. When the light had completely gone out, Michael stood in front of them.

Ostin shouted out, "Michael!" He ran to him, but Michael held out his hand to stop him.

"Don't touch me. I'm not safe yet."

Ostin stopped. "It really is you!"

A smile crossed Michael's face. "Who were you expecting?"

"Uira te Atua?"

"You're a what?"

"Nothing," Ostin said. "It's just *so* good to see you."

"It's good to be seen," Michael said. He looked past Ostin. "Hey, Jack."

Jack looked at him in awe. "I—I . . ."

"Yeah, it's weird. I know. But it's me. That was also me on the boat."

". . . Our dream. That really was you."

"Yeah, I was still figuring out how to get back to being human. It's a little hard to explain where I've been."

"Well, you could have come a little earlier," Jack said, joking. "Maybe before we said our good-byes to each other."

"No, that was good. People say things too late. It's better this way. And you both got to apologize."

"You heard us?"

"Every word," Michael said. "But that's not why I waited. I knew you'd need the boats to get off the island, so I waited until they delivered them to you. And don't worry about the crew on board. I visited them. They're going to cooperate fully." Michael laughed. "At least once they get off their knees. They think I'm a god."

"You're not?" Enele said.

"No, Enele," Michael said. "I'm Michael. And I'm proud of you. You have risen to greatness. It's dark times like these that present us the canvas where we paint our own greatness."

"Wow. You're like a poet now," Ostin said.

"I think the electricity opened up parts of my brain," Michael said. "I might be as smart as you."

Ostin just stared at him.

"But probably not," Michael said, smiling. "Enough of this; we don't have much time. Enele, take your men and get on the boats. I will meet you in Funafuti. Hatch is about to hurt our friends, and I need to stop him."

"Michael," Ostin said.

"Yes?"

"Thanks for what you did on Hades."

Michael smiled. "That's what friends are for." He waved. "See you in a few hours."

PART SEVENTEEN

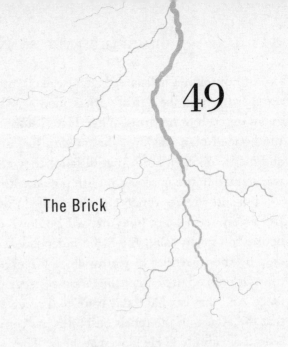

49

The Brick

Thirty-six hours after speaking with Carl Vey, Hatch ordered the Electroclan brought to him in the massive, concrete-floored storage room beneath the rim of the rat bowl. The room was cold and humid and smelled of fish and seawater, since this was where the food for the rats was brought in. This time Hatch had ordered everyone to be present, including Sharon, Coonradt, and Welch. They had no idea why they were assembled. Strangely, there was a long, horizontal pile of bricks on the ground in front of them.

Just as strangely, the Electroclan's RESATs had been turned down to the lowest level they had experienced, and the youths could even feel some of their electric power. Ian could see more than twelve feet, and Zeus could make electricity spark between his fingers. The reduction in the RESATs' power allowed them to breathe and move normally, even though their hands were still cuffed behind their backs.

An hour and a half later Hatch walked into the room with Zara, six guards, and a short man with a hood over his head, escorted by a guard on each of his arms. When Hatch stopped in front of the kids, the hooded man was brought forward just a few yards from them and made to kneel. From that distance they could see that the hood was stained in the nose and mouth region with blood.

"I'm sure you're wondering why I called this meeting," Hatch said. "It's a very special day. One that will go down in future Elgen history books. You might call it the Elgen Independence Day. A day matched only by the surrender of Cornwallis to George Washington at York-town. It marked the end of the Patriots' struggle. The end of the resistance. And that is what today is for us. I received word two hours ago that the attack on the rebels on Plutus has come to an end. Everyone is dead or captured." He looked at them. "They are presenting me with Enele Saluni's head this morning. You'll also want to know that two of your former colleagues were with them, Ostin and Jack."

Abigail and McKenna both gasped.

"Yes, they were fools to return. I'm sorry to inform you that they didn't make it. As we speak, their bodies are being brought here to be ceremoniously fed to the rats."

"No!" Abigail and McKenna both screamed. Abigail fell first to her knees, followed by McKenna.

"Ostin . . ."

Taylor knelt down too and cried with them.

"War does wreak havoc on families," Hatch said. "And speaking of families, I'd like to introduce you to someone of great significance to you. Greater significance than you possibly realize." He reached over and pulled the hood off the man's head. The prisoner's hair was wet and tangled with sweat. Even though his head was bowed, they could see that his face was swollen and bloody. He had been severely beaten. "Do you know who this man is?"

The kids looked at him but no one spoke.

"Help us out here, Sharon."

Sharon looked at the man, then said in a steely voice, "He's my husband."

"Indeed he is. This, young people, is the infamous Carl Vey. Husband to Sharon. Father to Michael. And, most of all, he's the reason you're all here. Carl Vey is the head of the resistance. He's Dr. Coonradt's boss. He's the one who gave you the insane command to come here and steal my boat. Why? Not for the reasons he told you. He wanted my boat, my *Joule*, and risked your lives for it, just so he could be unspeakably rich."

"That's not true," Vey said.

"Completely true," Hatch said loudly. "Just so we're clear, if it wasn't for Vey, you'd probably be out enjoying the life most teenagers have, instead of counting the seconds of your suffering. If it wasn't for this man, your friends Jack and Ostin would still be alive. If it wasn't for this man, Wade and Tanner and Gervaso and even Michael, his very own son, would still be alive." Hatch spit on Carl Vey with disgust. Then Zara walked up and spit on him as well. "Guards."

The guards walked through the group and uncuffed everyone except for Welch.

"What this man has done to you is unspeakable. So I'm going to give you a choice. I'm going to let you denounce this man. If you do, I will spare your lives." Hatch looked around the room. "You see in front of you a pile of bricks. All you have to do is walk up to this . . . lying, evil man, spit on him, and then hit him with a brick. And then you're free to join us. It's that simple.

"I know that sounds generous and you might wonder why, at this hour, I would offer it. This is why. I've come to the conclusion that it's not your fault you're here. It's his. And now is your chance to repent and be clean, to put your sins where they belong . . . on him. On Carl Vey." Hatch folded his arms. "Yes, this is a day for the history books. Who would like to go first?"

They all stood silently for a moment. Then Sharon Vey stepped forward and lifted a brick.

"Of course," Hatch said. "Of course you're the first. He abandoned you to a life of poverty. He took away your only son."

Carl looked up at his wife, his eyes filled with tears. Sharon stepped forward with the brick in her hand. She looked up at Hatch. "I've thought about this all night. I've wondered how he could have done this to his own family."

"Exactly," Hatch said.

"He left us alone. Destitute. Suffering."

"Yes," Hatch said. "Incredible suffering."

"And now my son is gone." Her voice cracked, and fresh tears fell down her face. She cocked the brick back in her hand.

"I'm so sorry," Carl said.

"Now he's sorry," Hatch said snidely. "It's not hard to be sorry when someone's about to hit you with a brick."

Then Sharon looked up at Hatch. "And for all our loneliness, for all our suffering, my husband was more alone. He didn't have our son with him. He didn't have me to comfort him. He came here knowing that you would humiliate and kill him, just for the chance that I might not have to suffer. He sacrificed his life for us, for the world, not for his gain but because it was the right thing to do. This man is more than my husband. He's a hero." At that, she threw the brick at Hatch. The guards, caught unprepared, barely managed to pull him down to prevent the brick from hitting him.

"Get her!" Hatch shouted.

Just then all of the teens rushed forward and grabbed bricks and started throwing them at the guards. Sharon rushed to her husband and threw her arms around him. "You shouldn't have come," she said.

"I couldn't not," he replied.

"Freeze them!" Hatch shouted at Zara. "Freeze them!"

At first, Zara looked confused; then she raised her hand. Everything stopped. The youths, Coonradt, Welch, Sharon and Carl Vey, all were frozen, unable to move.

"Thank you, Cassy," Hatch said almost to himself. "Such a useful power." He wiped his forehead. In the uprising he had been struck by the corner of a brick, and blood was trickling down his face. Only one of the guards was seriously hurt.

Hatch took a deep breath. "You have all sealed your fate. It is over." He walked over to where Sharon and Carl were kneeling together. "You got what you want. You get to die together."

Sharon just looked at Hatch defiantly.

"All right. Let's get on with this. Guards, prepare for their execution."

Six of the guards fell in line, lifting their guns. "I'd ask if you had any last words, but I think you've already said enough." He looked over at the youths. "This is the beginning of the end. For all of you."

Just then there was the sound of gunfire. Then an alarm went off. Hatch pushed the button on his sleeve to activate his radio. "What's going on?"

"Admiral-General, we are under attack."

"By whom?"

"The Tuvaluan rebels."

"The Tuvaluan rebels are dead!"

"I don't think they got the memo," the voice came back. "They've taken out the power, and they've breached the gates. The outer guards have fallen."

"All guards to posts!" Hatch shouted. "You too," he said to his guards, "after we end them all. Execute the Veys. Fire."

Before the guards could fire, lightning struck them all, blowing their guns into the air. Hatch thought it was a result of the rat bowl above them. "Turn that thing off," he shouted.

Suddenly a brilliant lightning ball floating about twenty feet in the air began to fill the room. It started as a small, basketball-size orb, then grew in size and brilliance until it was more than twelve feet across. Then, as it started to descend, the light began to dissipate, leaving a human form. The figure's head was lowered, but when he raised it, his gaze was solidly on Hatch.

"It's my Michael," Taylor said. "He's back."

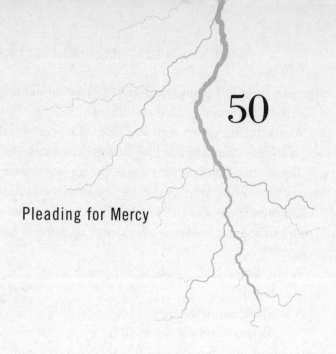

50

Pleading for Mercy

"Michael Vey," Hatch said. "What's with all you people being dead, then not being dead? Can't you just stay dead?"

Michael shook his head. "No."

"I'm not surprised. I always knew you'd be back. As the dog returns to his vomit."

"That's an appropriate metaphor," Michael said, stepping toward him. He looked at Hatch with dark, electric eyes.

"Zara, stop him!" Hatch shouted.

Zara suddenly rose into the air, her hands raised in front of her. "You're going to die, Vey," she shouted.

"I already have," Michael said. "You want my power? Take it."

Suddenly there was a massive exchange of energy between them, and Zara looked like an electric transformer hit by lightning. She screamed, then fell to the ground. Her hair and clothes were on fire, and her skin had turned black as ash.

"She probably shouldn't have done that," Michael said. He turned back to Hatch. "It's over, Hatch. It's time to pay for all you've done."

"For all I've done?" Hatch said. "For all I've done? I've advanced humanity, is what I've done. I've advanced science! Look at you. You're nothing more than a science experiment gone wrong."

Michael looked at Hatch without blinking. "You have no idea how wrong."

Hatch turned to his guards, who had all picked up their guns. "Fire! Kill all of them!"

Michael turned and looked at the guards, lifting his hand so his palm was open to them. "I'm giving you a chance to put down your weapons and surrender. I'm offering you mercy." Michael spread apart his fingers, and an oscillating blue-gold bubble surrounded him and the others.

"Now!" Hatch screamed. "Shoot them, now!"

Suddenly the room erupted with the popping of automatic weapon fire and the sound of bullets ripping through the air. But louder than the gunfire was the syncopated beat of an electrical buzz as Michael's aura disintegrated the bullets, like moths flying into a bug zapper. Or more like a comet flying into the sun. Taylor thought Michael looked almost bored with the exercise. Then the bullets began tapering off as the guns ran out of ammunition.

"Keep firing!" Hatch shouted.

Michael looked at him quizzically. "Why?" He stepped closer to Hatch. "Only a fool thinks he can keep doing the same thing and get different results." He looked at the guards and shook his head. "I offered you mercy, and you tried to kill us. So now I offer you justice." Michael slightly bowed his head and pulsed. A powerful blue wave that sizzled as it bent the air shot out from him. The guards disintegrated faster than their bullets had, leaving on the ground glowing molten puddles of metal, all that was left of their guns.

Next he held up his hand and the RESATs all blew. Everyone breathed out in relief. The Electroclan's power was back.

Michael looked at Hatch. "What am I going to do with you?"

Hatch turned and ran down one of the corridors. Michael didn't move.

"He's getting away!" Taylor shouted.

Michael looked at her with a slightly amused grin. "No, he's not." Then he rippled in an electric wave and vanished.

At the end of the dark corridor, Hatch ducked into one of the utility rooms below the bowl and locked and bolted the heavy steel door behind him. All around him were sweating pipes running from the bowl. He turned a valve, and a blast of steam shot out behind him. Then he pulled out his handgun. "Come get me, Vey."

Suddenly the room began to glow with light. Hatch turned around to see Michael, glowing brightly, standing behind him. "Okay." He looked around. "It's kind of steamy, though."

Hatch emptied his gun's clip into Michael, but nothing happened.

Michael just looked at him pitifully. "After what just happened out there, you don't really think that gun can do anything to me, do you?" Michael smiled. "I held lightning."

Hatch dropped his empty gun to the concrete floor. "What are you going to do to me?"

"What should I do to the man who killed my friends? What should I do to the man who tried to kill my parents? To the man who just tried to kill me?" Michael cocked his head. "Well?"

Hatch was too terrified to speak. Then he squeaked, "Mercy."

"Mercy? I don't think you know what that word means. Do you have any idea what it's like to be locked in Cell 25? When you stop knowing the difference between reality and pure horror? Yeah, I do." Michael's eyes narrowed. "There's an idea. I could put you in Cell 25 for the rest of your life."

Hatch turned white. "Please . . ."

"Please, yes, or please, don't do that? Because just saying 'please' is kind of confusing."

"Please don't," Hatch said.

"Okay, that makes sense." Michael took a deep breath. "Then again, the terror of being strapped down and slowly lowered into the rat bowl. Not something I like remembering. Should I do that? Feed you to your own rats? That would be kind of poetic. Kind of a Frankenstein's monster thing."

Hatch didn't speak.

"Or there's the one thing I haven't experienced personally, but I've seen the result. I could cut your tongue off and put you naked in a monkey cage. Three of your own inventions. I'll let you choose."

Hatch just looked at him fearfully. "Please, just kill me."

"Make up your mind unless you want all three. A month in Cell 25, a year in the monkey cage, then the rats."

Hatch turned and grabbed the door handle. Michael pulsed, shocking Hatch just enough to drop him to his knees. "There's no place you can hide, Dr. Hatch. I'm everywhere."

He looked up at Michael from the floor. "Mercy, please. Finish me!"

"You don't give orders anymore," Michael said. "I gave you a choice. Now, what will it be?"

Hatch closed his eyes, then said, "The rats."

"The rats," Michael repeated. "Good choice. Terrifying and painful, but the fastest of the three." Michael leaned against one of the pipes. "The problem with the whole rat thing is that I would be imitating you, and I never want to be accused of doing anything you would do. But then, if I put you in Cell 25 or in the monkey cage, that would also be an imitation, wouldn't it? And that would make me like you.

"But I can't leave you around either. You wouldn't stop trying to rule the world. You would just keep getting into trouble. So I'm going to show you what mercy is and just say good-bye."

Hatch looked up. "Good-bye?"

"Good-bye, Dr. Hatch."

Michael pulsed in full. The blast was so hot that it scorched the metal door behind Hatch a powdery white. Admiral-General Hatch, the self-proclaimed messiah, was nothing more than a pile of smoking ashes. Michael stepped on them as he walked through the door back out to the corridor. "So ends another would-be god."

51

Reunited

Michael walked back out to the bowl. He could have just rematerialized himself back, but he figured that everyone was already having enough trouble believing he was real, so he did his best to be normal. As he walked out of the dark corridor into the light of the warehouse, everyone stopped talking and looked at him.

After a moment Michael said, "It's just me." Still no one moved. "You can touch me. I figured it out."

Suddenly Taylor ran to him and threw her arms around him. "It really was you coming to me. It really was."

Michael kissed her face, then held her tightly. "Yeah, it was. I'm sorry. It took me a while to figure out how to get back."

"You came to me first," Taylor said.

"Of course I did." They kissed.

When they parted, Taylor said, "That tingles."

"Sorry."

Taylor smiled. "Don't apologize. Every girl wants to feel electricity when she kisses."

Michael turned toward his father and mother, who had stepped forward. His mother was crying and trembling. Michael walked over to her, and they hugged.

"I thought I had lost you," she said. "I never should have let you go."

"It's a good thing you did," Michael said. "Thank you." Michael kissed her on the cheek, then stepped back and looked at his father.

Carl Vey's eyes glistened as he looked at his son. "You've grown into a man," he said. "More than that, you've grown into a good man."

Michael looked at him for a moment, then fell into his father's arms. "I thought you were dead."

"I know. I did it for you and your mom."

Michael looked down for a moment and swallowed. Then he looked back up. "I know. If it wasn't for you, this world would have been owned by Hatch."

"No, Son," Carl said. "If it wasn't for *you*." Michael's father pulled him in tighter. "I'm so proud of you."

At that moment, for the first time, Michael broke down and wept. Not just for the reunion, not just because the battle was over, but for everything—for all their suffering and fear, the death of his friends, being sent into the rat bowl, even for Cell 25. Sharon stepped in and put her arms around him as well. For the first time since Michael was eight, the Vey family was reunited.

Michael was still in his parents' arms when there was a loud explosion and the doors of the warehouse flew apart. Cassy and Zeus were poised to stop them, when Enele, Jack, and Ostin came running inside the room, followed by a couple dozen of their soldiers. They stopped suddenly, surprised to find no one but their friends.

"Where's Hatch?" Jack shouted.

"He's gone," Abigail said.

"Where?"

"I mean . . . he's gone." She pointed to Michael.

"*Uira te Atua,*" Enele said, and took a knee.

"Stand," Michael said. "It's just me."

"Make way," Jack said, pushing past the others. "Coming in for the bromance." The two of them hugged.

Then the rest of the Electroclan, one by one, came up to welcome back their friend. The last in line was Ostin. The two young men looked at each other, before Michael stepped forward and put his arms around Ostin. "Still glad you came to Pasadena with me, buddy?"

"I'd follow you to hell."

"You did," Michael said. "More than once. Was it worth it?"

Ostin looked around at all his friends. Then McKenna sidled up to him and took his hand. "Yeah," he said. "Definitely. Life can't be lived on a couch." He suddenly lifted his shirt. "Besides, look. I have a six-pack."

Michael hit Ostin's stomach. "Like a rock, man. And you have a hot girlfriend."

"He does," McKenna said. "Literally."

"I'm glad you came along," Taylor said to Ostin.

Ostin smiled. "Bones?"

Taylor smiled and put out her fist. "Bones."

Ostin turned to Jack. "I've got another one. Why did the Elgen cross the road?"

Jack smiled. "Easy. To get away from Michael Vey."

PART EIGHTEEN

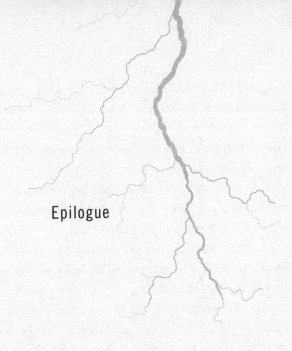

Epilogue

My name is Michael Vey. I'm finally back home in Meridian, Idaho. Home. It feels almost weird to say that. I can now honestly admit that I never thought I was going back. Part of me wondered if I even could. I once saw a movie about a soldier who was at war, getting shot at, defusing bombs—traumatic, high-stress stuff—then came home and the peace got to him. I hope that's not me. Probably not. I could stand a little peace.

A lot has happened in a very short time. Just minutes after the Elgen surrendered, Enele's grandfather was released from the monkey cage and taken to the hospital to recover. His friend, Elder Malakai, has been with him to help him through his recovery. It's been difficult for the former prime minister, but he has been given a lot of love and respect by the Tuvaluan people. He was one of the few who refused to bow to Hatch, and he suffered for it. But all heroes suffer.

Not surprisingly, his grandson, Enele, was named the new prime minister of Tuvalu. We were invited to his inauguration. We were also honored. Jack, Taylor, Ostin, and I were given the Tuvaluan Order of Merit, which is their country's highest honor. We wore ceremonial gowns and flowers wreaths on our heads. There was a lot of dancing going on. It was pretty cool.

We were also there when military honors were given posthumously to Gervaso and Tanner for the battle of Hades. I'm not embarrassed to say that there were a lot of tears shed. On the island of Niutao, the one we called Hades, there's now a monument erected to the Electroclan, who risked their lives for the Tuvaluan people. Gervaso's and Tanner's names are carved at the top.

On the homefront, we're not poor anymore. In part because my father took over the distribution of the *Joule*'s cache. That's a job in itself. He made sure the families of those hurt in the resistance were taken care of for life, college funds, the whole shebang. And he took care of us. The truth is, it's the Electroclan's gold. And when you've got a few billion sitting around, well, you can't even spend the interest.

On top of that, my father's now a big executive at the Elgen Corporation. It's weird to even think about that. The new board is thinking of changing the name of the company to VEYTRIC Inc. I don't know. It's kind of catchy. And it doesn't make me think of being eaten by rats every time I hear it.

Not everything in the reentry was smooth. There were a lot of questions asked, some that couldn't be answered. When people asked where we'd been, we just told them that Taylor, Jack, Ostin, and I had enrolled in the Elgen Academy in Pasadena and then it shut down. All true. We never tell them that we're the ones who shut it down. Or that we were almost killed in the process.

There were problems that had to be cleaned up, like with Taylor's parents and the whole kidnapping thing and the van blowing up. We kind of made a huge mess of things. But no one could really prove anything, anyway. And sometimes it's just who you know. When the president of the Philippines and the president of Taiwan called the secretary of state, who called Idaho's governor, who called the mayor, who called the police chief . . . Well, let's just say they let things slide. It happens. I'm not saying it's right. But it happens.

Fortunately, Mr. and Mrs. Liss were back in Idaho when the Elgen attacked Christmas Ranch. They had left just the day before. It was a beautiful coincidence. Maybe there are no coincidences.

Some things we lost we can never get back. Like our innocence. Or, like my father said, the time we could have had together.

Most of all, we'll never get back the friends we lost. Maybe it's being back in Idaho, but I think a lot about Wade. Especially when I walk out the back door, where he, Jack, and Mitchell tried to pants me and I shocked the daylight out of them. Strange, but if that hadn't happened, I never would have met Jack. And without Jack, well, I don't even want to think about that. It just goes to show you how good can come from bad.

It makes me sad that no one ever asks about Wade. He really had no one but Jack. Today there's a monument in the Meridian cemetery for him. It's a marble pillar with the words:

Wade West
He died a hero for his friends.
He'll live forever in our hearts.

Taylor wrote that. I thought it was really good. The pillar is six feet tall, taller than Wade was. That's good, because, in his own way, Wade was bigger than life. I once heard it said, there are no great men, just great challenges. I don't know if that's true. I know some great men and women, but maybe it was the challenges that made them great. If it hadn't been for Dr. Hatch's evil, Jack might never have found out how good or heroic he really was. Maybe that's true for all of us.

Strange, school didn't change all that much. I did. We all did. I still have Tourette's, but I'm not short anymore. Ostin's not chubby anymore. But school, well . . . same spaghetti with mystery sauce and that same sticker still stuck above my locker—the one of the skull with a lightning bolt in it. Someone said it was from an ancient rock band called the Grateful Dead. I don't know anything about them, but that sticker has me written all over it.

Of course, every school still has its bullies. My first day back I was walking down the hall with Taylor and Ostin when an overgrown, red-faced senior noticed my tics and stepped in front of me. "Hey, twitchy, you got your blinker on."

I looked up at him calmly. "Do you have a problem with that?"

"Yeah, weirdo, I've got a problem with you."

"It's Tourette's syndrome, you moron," Taylor said. "And if I were you, I'd start apologizing before you get hurt."

"Straight up," Ostin said. "Just apologize, and maybe he'll let you go."

The bully stood there, not sure what to make of us.

"Look at him," Ostin said. "What an ape. He's got the frontal lobe of a baboon."

The guy turned to Ostin. "What did you say?"

"Sorry, I'll use small words so you can keep up," Ostin said. "You're clearly not the brightest crayon in the box. In fact, I think someone left your crayons in the sun."

Taylor laughed. "That's funny."

The bully blushed at being laughed at by a cute girl. "All right, dude. I'm going to pound blinky boy. *Then* I'm going to pound you into dust."

Taylor laughed again. "Man, did you ever pick the wrong guys to bully."

"Yeah, dude," Ostin said. "You're a *stupidiot* because that was the height of *stupidiocy*. Like, inviting-Hitler-to-your-bar-mitzvah stupid."

I laughed as well. Then I said to the bully, "Look, man, I don't want to hurt you. So step aside and I'll let you walk away."

He looked at me like I was taking crazy pills. "*You're* going to let *me* walk away?" He laughed, though I could tell that, on some level, he was worried.

Just then Jack walked up. "Hey, bro." He was wearing a tank

top that showed off some wicked bullet scars and his arm muscles, which, by now, looked more like most guys' thighs than biceps. In fact, his tattoo of the jackal was so stretched by muscle that it looked pregnant. "What's going on, loser-bait," Jack said to the bully. "You picking on my friend?"

The bully stepped back. "Oh, that's why you act so tough. You get your big brother to fight your fights."

"I'm not his brother," Jack said. "And I didn't come to fight for him. I came to see him waste you. This is Michael Vey, the same guy that took out Corky *and* me."

The guy looked at me nervously. "You're . . . Michael Vey?"

"He's legacy, man," Ostin said.

"You are my brother," I said to Jack. "So, bro, what should I do with this clown?"

"Just waste him," Jack said. "That's the language bullies understand. I ought to know."

The bully looked at me fearfully.

"No, wait," Ostin said, stepping forward. "I got this." Ostin looked the bully in the eyes, then took off his glasses. "All right, brain-swamp. Wanna dance?"

The bully looked at him, then at me and Jack; then he said, "I—I gotta go." He turned and ran down the hall.

"Yeah, you better run," Ostin shouted after him.

Taylor waved. "Good-bye."

I turned to Ostin. "'Brain-swamp'? 'Wanna dance'? Where did that come from?"

"I don't know," Ostin said. "But it felt good."

Jack and I hugged. "How's reentry?" I asked.

"You know. Good seeing my sister. Still twelve credits from graduation. But Welch offered me the head security job at the Elgen Headquarters. Pays a fortune. He said I could bring my brother on too if I want."

"Are you going to take it?" Taylor asked.

"Probably," Jack said. "Abi thinks I should. It means we'll have to move to Italy. That will suck."

"Moving to Italy sucks?" I said.

"I can think of worse places to live," Taylor said.

"I'm not saying Italy sucks," he said. "It's being away from my friends. From you guys."

"We'll come see you," Ostin said. "We've got a couple of jets at our disposal."

"That would be nice. And I could definitely get fat on pizza and pasta. But it won't be PizzaMax."

"Thank goodness for that," I said.

Ostin gasped. "You didn't."

"I've seen the world, my friend," I said. "Comparing PizzaMax pizza to real Italian pizza is like comparing Richard Simmons to Arnold Schwarzenegger."

"Well said," Ostin said. "Painful, but well said."

"How is Abi?" I asked.

"She's good. She's thinking of going to nursing school. She could do that in Italy too."

"That's so cool," Taylor said. "She would be the best nurse ever."

Suddenly, down the hall, two girls in cheerleading outfits screamed. "It's Tay! Tell me it's true! Hey, Tay! Where have you been?"

We watched them bounce toward us in wonder. I looked at Taylor. "Where have you been, Tay?" I asked.

"A different world," she said.

"No," I replied. "A different universe."

The girls ran up to Taylor, practically mugging her. "Where have you been?" the first girl asked.

"Yeah," said the other. "Are you going to try out for cheerleading?"

Taylor looked at them and smiled. "No. I'm good."

"What?" the first girl said.

Her friend said to her, "She said she's good."

"We know you're good," the first girl said. "That's why you should try out."

"Thanks," Taylor said. "But I've got to go."

The girls looked stunned. "For rude . . . ," they both said.

As the four of us turned to walk away, I asked Taylor, "There's really no part of you that still wants to be a cheerleader?"

"No," she said quickly. "Isn't that weird? For so long I thought it was all I wanted. And now . . ." She shook her head. "I'm good. I've got everything I need."

"So do I," I said. I suddenly laughed. "Ostin, what did you call that kid, stupidiot?"

"Yep. *Stupidiot*. See what I did there, I combined the two words to make them—"

"Yeah, we got it," Taylor said.

"Nice," I said. "I'm going to use that." I hit Ostin on the shoulder. "You know, for a geek, you've gotten pretty cool."

"McKenna helped," he said.

"We gals are good for you guys," Taylor said. She suddenly stopped and looked at me. "And someday, Michael Vey, I'm going to marry you."

"Whoa," Jack said, laughing.

"Where did that come from?" I asked.

"My brain," she said.

"Do I have a say in this?"

"Only if you say yes."

I smiled. "You read my mind."

"No," Taylor said. "I didn't need my powers for that."

We kissed.

"Get a room," Ostin said.

After Taylor and I pulled apart, Taylor said, "So, Boyfriend, they say that before you marry someone, you should go on a trip with them. You know, to really get to know them. What do you think?"

"I think we can check that off the list."

"But if we ever get married—"

"We're way too young."

"I don't feel young," Taylor said.

"It's not the years, it's the mileage," Jack said.

Taylor laughed. "Well, you guys don't need to get all freaked out. I know we're young, and I'm not shopping for a wedding dress. I was just going to say, if we were to get married and we had a family, do you think our children would be electric?"

I thought for a moment. "Only one way to find out."

"I'm out of here," Jack said. "See you after school."

"Me too," Ostin said. "Bones."

"Bones," Taylor and I said back.

My name is Michael Vey. I told you in the beginning that my story was strange. Very strange. I also told you that I had Tourette's syndrome and I was electric. You probably didn't see where all that was going. Neither did I. And I had to live it. I almost had to die it. What a ride.

You know, through all I've been through, I've learned something important about life. Something that might mean something to you, too. It's something I had to go all around the world to learn, but it was worth it. It's simply this: It's not *all right* to be different. It's freaking *awesome*.

Shock on, my friends.

Michael Vey

Michael Vey

Join the Veyniac Nation!

For Michael Vey trivia, sneak peeks, and events in your area,

follow Michael and the rest of the Electroclan at:

MICHAELVEY.COM

Facebook.com/MichaelVeyOfficialFanPage

Twitter.com/MichaelVey

Instagram.com/MichaelVeyOfficial

RICHARD PAUL EVANS

is the #1 bestselling author of the Michael Vey series, *The Christmas Box*, and the Walk series, as well as more than twenty other books. All of his novels have appeared on the *New York Times* bestseller list; and there are more than thirty million copies of his books in print. His books have been translated into more than twenty-four languages and several have been international bestsellers. He is the winner of the American Mothers Book Award, and two first place *Storytelling World* Awards for his children's books.

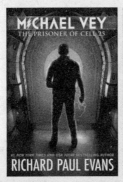

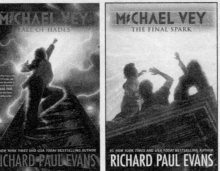